The Baby-whisperer and the Brute

The Baby-whisperer and the Brute

AN EASTPORT BAY BILLIONAIRES NOVEL

TRU TAYLOR

Contents

About

THE BABY-WHISPERER AND THE BRUTE

Angelina

Some people might call me sheltered. That doesn't *begin* to cover it. I've been practically sequestered my whole life.

Constantly warned by my eccentric and reclusive mother against the "dangers of the world," I was only allowed outside my home to attend a strict girls' school.

No parties. No sleepovers. NO boys.

Ever.

Even now in my early twenties, the extent of my social life is spending time with the adorable three and four-year-olds at the preschool where I work. I've hardly ever *spoken* to a man, except for exchanging morning greetings with the fathers of my students.

And soon, I'll obey my mother's wishes and enter religious service, training to be a nun.

But gazing out my bedroom window in the turret of my family's crumbling seaside mansion, I secretly dream of a different life, one that involves freedom, adventure, love, and children of my own.

I at least want a *kiss* before I give up and follows my mother's plan for my life.

Sullivan Reece

As a heavyweight boxing champion in prime condition, I can easily go twelve rounds with the toughest fighters on the planet—but when it comes to my two little girls… I'm a lightweight.

Now that my ex has declared herself "done" with mothering, and my spirited and mischievous daughters are living with me full-time, I'm realizing just how much I *don't* know about raising kids. My own upbringing in a tough neighborhood left a *lot* to be desired—I basically raised myself, and honestly, didn't do all that great a job of it.

And then there's my demanding training schedule and the travel required for my career. What I really need is a live-in nanny. *Yesterday.*

But as newcomer to Eastport Bay, I have no idea where or how to find the right caretaker for the two most important people in my life. So when my neighbors say they know the perfect person, I jump at the chance to hire her.

She has experience with children, she needs a place to live, and she's exactly the kind of classy role model I want for my daughters.

There's just one problem… the new nanny is everything I'm *not*—sweet, innocent, good. It goes without saying she's *completely* off-limits.

Oh, and she's a total knockout.

The Baby-whisperer and the Brute is a full-length small town rom com fairytale retelling of Rapunzel. It's a standalone single dad/forbidden love/forced proximity/slow burn romance with no cheating or cliffhangers but plenty of humor and heat and a gentle bruiser with a heart of gold.

Enjoy the story!

ONE
Window on the World

You can't appreciate all the implications of the word "conflicted" until you come face to face with the guy you've been secretly lusting after for weeks—and then learn he'll be signing your paychecks. – Angelina Rappaport

I scrubbed at the modeling clay under my nails, using a small brush to dislodge the stubborn stuff. The children had enjoyed "art day" at the preschool where I worked even more today than they usually did.

The high-spirited three, four, and five-year-olds were more excited about *everything* these days—it was the last two weeks of school before summer break.

Unfortunately, that meant the schoolroom, and their teacher—me—were also a bit messier than usual.

My shirt and skirt were splotched with acrylic paint—washable, thank God. My long, thick hair bore the evidence of the day's first project which had involved white glue. And glitter.

Lots and lots of glitter. *Ugh.*

Laughing at my disheveled appearance in the mirror, I stripped off my clothes and stepped into the shower.

Washing my hair hadn't been in my plans for the day—it was too much of an ordeal to do daily—but there was no choice in the matter now. I was expected at my next-door neighbors' house this evening.

They were literal royalty—nice people, but still, you didn't show up at the front door of a prince and princess looking like a walking, talking glitter bomb.

After my shower, I sat in front of my bedroom window, drying my long locks. It always took forever, but at least the ocean view and warm breeze were enjoyable.

My room was in the top of the stone turret that centered the rear of my family's historic Eastport Bay, Rhode Island mansion. It was a modern castle of a house, built during America's Gilded Age in 1891.

Clearly, my ancestors had harbored a fascination with Europe and its royal palaces because the waterfront home could easily have suited a monarch with more than a hundred rooms including an opulent ballroom.

Not that anyone used all those rooms anymore. For all of my twenty-three years, only my mother and I had lived here, and Mother was *not* the ball type or the cocktail party type either. We'd never had overnight guests, and even daytime visitors were rare.

As a child, I'd pretended I was a fairytale princess trapped in my lonely tower, waiting for a prince or even a willing dragon to come along and free me.

Now I loved the room for its unusual circular shape, refreshing sea breezes, and especially for its vantage point on the bay and the Bluff Walk that bordered it.

The Bluff Walk was among Eastport Bay's top tourist attractions, a busy pedestrian path that divided the back lawns of the city's famous Oceanview Avenue mansions and the rocky cliffs that dropped into the Atlantic Ocean they presided over.

More than a million visitors a year walked the path, which was in places wide and smoothly paved. Here at the southern end of Oceanview Avenue, where it curved and met Atlantic Avenue, the Bluff Walk was more rugged. Pavement gave way to the natural rocky New England shoreline, necessitating a sure foot and a bit more attention to navigate.

There was always something to see when I sat at my window.

I loved watching the seabirds soar and dive into the deep gray-blue water, fishing for their meals. In winter there were harbor seals to look for and breaching whales to observe from April to October.

Best of all were the people of all sorts and shapes and sizes.

Already today I'd seen a group of women walking together in their stretchy shorts and t-shirts, their laughter so loud it reached my tower and made me smile.

Several young families had trekked to the end of the path and made their way back, leaving their strollers behind temporarily in order to make it to the very end of the path's roughest part.

And then there were the joggers. Always plenty of those. The three-and-a half-mile length of the path paired with the cooling ocean breeze made it a perfect exercise venue.

Here was one now. Oh, I recognized him.

This one ran a little faster than the usual jogger. I assumed he always got on the path somewhere near the middle. If he'd started at its beginning point, he'd have to possess amazing stamina to still be running this hard near the end of it.

I'd noticed him for the first time about two weeks ago, his incongruous speed catching my eye along with his unusual height and his head of thick, dark hair, which gleamed in the afternoon sunlight on clear days.

He ran mornings *and* late afternoons, which might account for that unusual speed and stamina.

Today he wore a bright red t-shirt, and as I brushed and dried my hair, my eyes followed the scarlet beacon until it disappeared around the bend.

"Angelina."

A demanding voice echoed up the circular stairway that ascended to my tower room. "Where are you? I'm getting hungry."

I stood, tucking my brush and hairdryer back into the drawer of my vanity table.

"Be right there Mother."

Though my hair was fully dried now, and I knew Mother was waiting on me to come downstairs and prepare dinner, I lingered at the window a bit longer, anticipating the return of that red shirt.

It had become almost a ritual in my life to clock the tall, powerful jogger's round trips on the path.

But when he reappeared, the t-shirt was gone. Rather, it was tucked into the back of his shorts, flapping behind him like a tail as he ran with every bit as much energy as before.

He was running *shirtless*.

I fell back into my chair, instantly light-headed. All thoughts of Mother's hunger pangs and waning patience vanished.

In fact, I couldn't think at all.

Or look away.

Or move.

Or breathe.

Though I must have seen other men running without shirts, none of them had looked like *this*.

The dark-haired jogger's body was impressive—his chest wide and thickly layered with muscle. His shoulders and arms were heavily muscled as well, and he had several dark tattoos.

There was a large one on the left side of his chest, another on his left shoulder. Several more stretched down his arm, connecting as they decorated his bicep, elbow, forearm, and wrist.

His tight abdomen contracted with each footfall. A tattoo of a single word—I couldn't read it from here—covered his right ribcage.

As he ran past, I noted the back view was as remarkable as the front, revealing a wide, powerful upper back tapering to a lean waist and some *very* well-toned glutes.

My face heated from neck to scalp as his long, strong legs pumped and carried him out of my sight,

What *was* that?

Knowing I'd never be *with* a man, I'd never taken much notice of any before, certainly not in a physical way. But this one... well he was impossible *not* to notice.

He was huge—a total brute—the last thing I'd ever have expected to appeal to me.

I imagined standing next to him, looking up into his eyes, reaching up and running my fingers over those tattoos, being thoroughly outsized and overpowered...

Slowly, my senses returned to me, accompanied by a hefty dose of guilt. Surely it was wrong to look at a man with such intense interest. At least for *me* it was.

There was no place for any man in my life—and certainly none for such a thoroughly masculine creature as this one. Maybe that was why he'd fascinated me from the very first time I'd seen him run by.

Beware the evils of men.

The phrase, repeated to me throughout my life, rose to the forefront of my mind, shaming me.

Shutting the window with a decisive click, I hurriedly twisted my hair into a thick coil at the back of my head (Mother liked for me to look neat and "respectable") and practically ran down the spiral of stone steps to the mansion's first floor.

As I made my way through the long, dark-paneled hallways, a vast collection of crucifixes and oil paintings depicting Biblical scenes seemed to judge me. I lowered my head and hurried to the kitchen.

Later during dinner, Mother peppered me with questions about my day.

"Who did you speak to today? You haven't been talking to any of the fathers at the preschool, have you?"

"No, Mother. It's mostly moms who pick up their kids. And the fathers are all married anyway."

"That doesn't matter. You can't trust any of them. Don't talk to them. Don't even look at them... lecherous beasts."

"I know, Mother. I don't," I rushed to say, eager to nip the usual tirade in the bud if possible.

My mother hadn't been in favor of me taking the job as a teacher's assistant at the preschool. It had only been the intervention of the Benedictine sisters that had convinced her to allow me to work there for the past couple of years.

They encouraged discerners like me to reflect and gather information, paying periodic visits to the religious community we intended to join while still living at home and working or studying.

"At least you won't be there for much longer. Your postulancy will begin soon, and then you'll be protected from the whole lot of them forever."

"Yes, Mother."

I looked down at my plate and dragged the tines of my fork through the lasagna. Though I was an accomplished home cook and it was one of my best dishes, I was no longer hungry.

A queasy feeling unsettled my stomach as it did whenever I thought about moving into the monastery and beginning my postulancy and novitiate period, parts of the stages of formation that would culminate in my initiation into a life of religious service.

The multi-year process was meant to help an aspirant, as those who wanted to become nuns were called, gradually let go of the attitudes of the outside world and adapt to monastic life.

The problem was, I had barely *experienced* the outside world.

I hadn't really thought about it until fairly recently, but it seemed almost ridiculous that someone my age would have experienced so little in life.

I'd never left Eastport Bay, except to visit the monastery, had not gone away to college like most of the other girls from my exclusive, private, and very small girls-only high school.

Though Mother had inherited a fortune, she'd never taken me on a single trip or vacation, preferring to remain secluded in our home most of the time.

We didn't go to restaurants or movie theaters or shopping as some of my schoolmates discussed doing with their parents. I'd never been to a dance or a party or even a sleepover with girlfriends.

I *had* no girlfriends—not really.

Mother redefined the word "overprotective," forbidding me to go anywhere other than directly to school and back, and in the past two years, to the preschool down the street.

She literally timed me as I walked to and from the school building. Once when I'd stayed late to help the lead teacher decorate the classroom for the holidays, my mother had called the Eastport Bay police to report me missing.

All of it was in the name of safety—and to keep me "pure" for God's service. Which had to be a good thing, right? I couldn't argue with that.

It was only recently that I'd begun to question whether there weren't *many* ways a person could serve God.

Ones in which I didn't have to give up teaching, for instance. I loved my little students, and interacting with them was the joy of my life.

"I *will* miss the children," I finally said. "I think I would have made a good teacher."

"You won't miss them once you're sequestered with your new sisters. You'll be doing what the Lord has called you to do. When you were born, I promised God to give you into His service, and you must make good on that promise. Terrible things will happen to me if you don't. Not to mention what would happen to *you*."

It was the warning that had kept me from stepping a toe out of line my entire life. As a little girl, whenever I'd had a naughty thought or urge to disobey, the image of my mother dropping dead on the spot had terrorized me and scared me back into compliance.

"I will. Of course I will." I stood. "I'm finished. Can I get you anything before I go?"

"Go? Where do you think you're going?" Mother demanded.

My heart began to stutter. "Next door. Remember I told you one of the mothers at the school asked me to help plan the end-of-school party for the students? This is the night I'm expected at her house."

Mother's eyes narrowed. "Next door? You're not talking about that floozy Cinda Brown, are you? She had a child out of wedlock and flaunted it without an ounce of shame before she went and married that prince fellow. And don't even get me started on him, gallivanting around the globe, seducing women. Who knows how many illegitimate children he has?"

"Her name is Cinda Wessex now, and she's one of the nicest women I've ever met."

I decided not to bring up the fact that Mother had *also* borne a child out of wedlock—*me*—a fact she conveniently overlooked while passing judgment on just about everyone else of her acquaintance.

"And there were good reasons she didn't marry Prince Alexander until last year," I said. "It's a very interesting story, as a matter of fact. You'd know all about it if you actually met the neighbors and got to know them."

"I have no interest in associating with a woman of loose morals, and I don't want you around her either—or that randy prince. I forbid you to spend any time in that den of iniquity."

"Mother..."

I prayed for patience and wisdom. If I handled this wrong, I'd find myself on complete lockdown or even homeless. Mother was not above threatening to throw me out if I didn't fall into step with her wishes.

"It's part of my job," I reasoned. "The party is a school event, and the last one I'll be associated with before I move into the monastery. Sister Patrice said I should do my job to the best of my abilities. The party's only two weeks away, and the school and Mrs. Wessex are counting on me. I gave my *word* I'd help."

After a pause, I added, "Breaking it now would be a sin."

I held my breath, hoping that last point would clench it. Mother was terrified of anything that even held a whiff of sin, and she was more conscious of her daughter's spiritual status than even her own—which was saying something.

Looking around the dining room at yet another display of crosses, religious paintings, and statuary, I reflected that if the sheer number of religious artifacts one possessed could guarantee entrance into Heaven, my mother would be at the front of the line for sure.

"Well... I suppose you must keep your promise," Mother

said. "But you will not stay long. You'll go directly there and come directly home. And after that party is over, you'll spend the rest of the month in prayerful reflection, so you'll be ready for your postulancy."

"Yes, Mother."

I left the room before my mother could change her mind, carrying my plate and glass to the sink and washing them quickly before leaving the house. As I hurried down the sidewalk to my neighbor's drive, I felt lighter with every step away from my own home. Lighter and freer.

The sound of children laughing and playing in a nearby yard compounded my good mood. By the time I reached the Wessexes' front door, I felt almost giddy.

Was it pathetic to be this excited about being away from home at night?

Though I'd only be helping to plan a children's party, I would be in the company of other young women instead of reading quietly in the formal parlor with Mother until bedtime. It was honestly the social highlight of my year.

Cinda answered the doorbell herself, greeting me with a wide smile and a brief hug, which caused her hugely pregnant belly to collide with my hipbone.

"Sorry about that," Cinda said and patted her stomach. "This thing needs its own zip code. I'm positively palatial at this point."

She stepped back, inviting me into the elegant marble foyer. "Come in. I'm so glad you were able to make it. Not as glad as AJ is of course."

The Wessexes' five-year-old son AJ was one of my students. I'd helped in his class last year as well—he had a late summer birthday, and his parents had elected to have him spend another year in preschool rather than put him into kindergarten at only a few days past the age of five.

Though I never picked favorites, I'd always been incredibly fond of the sweet, intelligent boy.

"He talks about you a *lot,*" Cinda explained. Lowering her voice to a whisper, she added, "I think he's a little bit in love with you."

I laughed. "Well, if that's true, he'd be the first."

"Oh, I highly doubt that," Cinda said warmly. "Let's go to the kitchen. My friend Kristal made her famous seven-layer dip, and her sister-in-law Bonnie brought some super-yummy desserts prepared by her French chef, Monsieur Laplume."

"And I cooked worms and dirt for you!"

The exuberant announcement preceded the arrival of AJ, who ran into the foyer and slid across its shiny floor in his sock feet, dark curls flying.

"Be careful, buddy," Cinda warned, but her voice held more amusement than sternness.

"You did?" I dropped to my knees, accepting the hug AJ offered. It warmed my heart that my little student remembered the dessert we'd made at school last year on "slime day."

"Slime day was my favoritest day of the whole year," AJ informed me.

"I'm so glad."

"You're going to miss me when I'm in kindergarten next year," he announced with confidence. "But we're having a baby, and when he's big enough for preschool you can teach him to make slime, and *I'll* teach him to make worms and dirt."

"Him or *her,*" Cinda said. "We haven't announced if it's a boy or a girl yet."

"I know, but I want a brother."

"I know you do, buddy." His mother sifted a hand through her son's silky hair. "But you'll have fun teaching the baby no matter what the gender is."

Seeing AJ's frown, and sensing a change in subject was in

order, I interjected. "I *will* miss you. So much. But I know you'll love kindergarten, and I can't wait to celebrate your preschool graduation with you in a couple of weeks."

"Where is my little prince?"

Cinda's tall, handsome husband entered the foyer, sweeping his son up in his arms. "There you are. I thought we were going to play knights and dragons, but I went to the playroom and there wasn't a single knight for me to gobble up."

He pretended to bite AJ's ear, making a silly gobbling noise.

"Daddy," AJ shrieked and giggled. "You can't be the dragon until I say, 'ready, set, go.'"

"Oh, that's right. I keep forgetting that rule." Alexander Wessex gave me a smile. "Hello. Thanks for coming and pitching in. We'd really like for our first family party here to be fun for all the kids. Cinda says you're amazing with them."

I felt myself blush, my face growing warm at the compliment delivered in a cultured European accent so rich it made me feel like a peasant in comparison.

"Well, I'm happy to help if I can."

Alex grinned. "We menfolk have some serious sword-fighting to attend to now, so we'll leave you to it. Save some worms and dirt for me, would you?"

Swinging AJ up onto his shoulders, he strode up the grand staircase as AJ turned and waved goodbye to me.

I followed Cinda through the elegant mansion, which was modeled after a European manor home. Reaching the bright, airy kitchen—so different from the dark, outdated one in my own historic house—I spotted the other women at the massive center island.

A vivacious woman with long, curling caramel hair and a slight New York accent turned and came toward me, extending both hands. "Angelina. Wow—you really *do* look like an angel. I'm Bonnie."

I shook my head in confusion. "An angel?"

Bonnie laughed. "AJ and I are big pals. He's told me *all* about you, about your golden hair and your face that's 'pretty as an angel'—not to mention your amazing skills with glue, scissors, and glitter."

Now I joined in the laughter. "Those are high compliments. I feel like I should slip him some gummy bears or something."

The other woman made her way over to say hello. A dark-haired beauty with a flawless fair complexion, Kristal Bianco—now Kristal Bestia—was as lovely as I had ever seen her. We'd met several times before when she'd come to pick up AJ at the school.

"Hi Angelina, it's good to see you again."

"Good to see you, too. It's so nice of you and Bonnie to help with the party."

"I'm not sure how much help we'll be—neither of us knows the first thing about kids. I'm here to learn—and to *eat*. Check out those pastries Bonnie brought."

"I can't take any credit. Monsieur Laplume is better than any chef I ever came across in New York." To me, she explained, "I moved here from Manhattan when Jack and I got married—he and Kristal's husband Hunter are brothers."

"I've always wanted to see New York. I'll bet living there was amazing," I said.

"It was interesting, that's for sure. You've never been, even for the day? It's so close to here."

My cheeks heated. "I know. I know it's weird, but I've hardly ever left Rhode Island—only to go to the monastery in New Jersey."

At the shocked stares, I hastened to add, "I'd love to travel. I just haven't had the chance."

"Well, you've *got* to see New York City. Take the train down," Bonnie said. "We have an apartment there we hardly ever use. You're welcome to stay there. Feel free to bring some friends along or your family if you want to."

"Why don't we all fill our plates here at the counter and take them to the table so we can talk?" Cinda suggested, sparing me from having to explain I didn't really have friends and that Mother was my only family.

"I've started a few lists for the party—food, games, decorations," she said. "But I haven't gotten very far. I really want to hear your suggestions, Angelina."

Turning to the others, Cinda said, "She's an absolute genius when it comes to preschool kids."

Kristal rested a hand on her lower abdomen. "I'll keep that in mind in about three or four years."

Looking down, I detected a small bump below the waistband of her pretty red shift dress.

My eyes met Kristal's again. "Oh... are you..."

The question died on my lips. It was rude to ask someone if they were pregnant, especially when it was anything less than completely obvious.

Kristal didn't seem the least bit offended. In fact, she confirmed my suspicion with a wide grin. "Yes. We're expecting. I'm due in November."

"Congratulations. That's wonderful. And your baby and Cinda's will be so close in age."

Cinda sidled up to her friend, sliding an arm around her shoulders and squeezing. "We couldn't be more excited. They'll be almost like cousins. Kristal's the closest thing I've got to a real sister."

She smiled over at Bonnie. "That one, too. Tell Jack to apply himself a little more diligently in the baby-making department so we can add another little 'cousin' to the mix."

Bonnie barked a laugh. "I'm not sure he could *be* any more diligent. I'm not ready yet though. I want to focus on my work a bit longer."

"What do you do?" I asked.

"I work remotely for the book section of the New York Daily Report, and I own a bookstore on Main Street. I also write fiction. My first novel is coming out this year."

"Wow, that's amazing. Congratulations."

Over the course of the evening, between planning food and entertainment for the party, I learned Kristal was also quite accomplished.

A renowned landscape photographer, she specialized in winter scenes, especially those in and around Eastport Bay. She also ran the Art Preservation Guild, which her late mother had created to maintain and preserve public works of art.

Cinda had founded a home-cleaning agency, the Fairy Godmother Home Cleaning Service, and until recently, when she'd stepped away to spend more time with her son and prepare for the arrival of the new baby, she'd run its day-to-day operations and even pitched in doing the physical work of cleaning when needed.

Next to these accomplished women, who weren't that many years older than me, I felt positively infantile.

However, they treated me with kindness and included me fully in the conversation all night long, seeming interested in everything I had to say and making me feel like part of the tight-knit group.

Was this what it would be like with my new "sisters" at the monastery? If so, maybe it wouldn't be all bad.

If only I wasn't leaving to begin my postulancy so *soon*. If only I had more time to see and experience some of the things these bright, funny, smart women talked about in their rambling, high-spirited conversation.

"So... my parents knew your mother in high school," Kristal said, grabbing my attention.

"They did?" I knew very little about my mother's life

before I was born, when Caroline Rappaport was a pretty young socialite, mixing in Eastport Bay's high society circles.

Old pictures displayed around our home told me that had once been the case, but as long as I could remember, Mother had been a recluse, rarely leaving the grounds of our mansion, with only me and a handyman/groundskeeper for human companionship.

Year after year, she wore the same dated and increasingly threadbare clothing she'd worn all of my life and *never* spoke of any past relationships, not even friendships.

"Oh yes," Kristal said. "And she and my mother lived on the same hall when they were both students at Salve Regina freshman year. They lost touch after that though."

"What was she like? Did they say?" I asked, eager to fill in at least a few of the missing puzzle pieces of my mother's bizarre transformation from party girl to hermit.

Kristal didn't answer immediately, seeming to weigh her words first. "They said she was very fun-loving... a bit wild. A great dancer." She smiled. "She was the life of many an Eastport Bay mansion party. Everyone liked her."

It was impossible to imagine Mother even attending a party, much less laughing and dancing. The wildest thing I'd ever seen her do was venture out in the rain to get one of her cats when it escaped.

"Speaking of parties," Bonnie began. "Do you think Sullivan Reece will come to yours? Jack is *dying* to meet him."

"Who's Sullivan Reece?" I asked.

Cinda answered. "He's the reigning heavyweight boxing champion of the world. He bought the house on the other side of us about a year and a half ago, but he hasn't spent much time in Newport until just recently. I'm hoping he'll come and bring his two little girls."

"*I'm* hoping he'll come and bring his two big biceps," Kristal said with a humorous smirk. "Not that Hunter isn't stacked and jacked—I love his physique—but have you ever seen Sullivan Reece shirtless in the boxing ring?"

She made her mouth into an O and fanned herself. "I bet that man could bench press my three-ton Mercedes G Wagon. With all of us in it."

"And those tattoos... oh mama," Bonnie added. "I know a lot of women who'd love to read between *those* lines."

All the women laughed.

Everyone but me.

I was too disconcerted by a sudden flashback to this afternoon when the massive dark-haired jogger had removed his shirt... and stolen my breath.

I hadn't seen *him* on the Bluff Walk until just recently.

Was it possible there were *two* recent arrivals to the neighborhood, both of them possessing enormous muscles and tattoos and a powerful allure to women of all ages and backgrounds?

I developed a new and urgent hope that Mr. Sullivan Reece and his daughters would *not* be attending the party in two weeks.

Because I suspected the wild streak Mother had apparently once possessed had not actually disappeared... but had been passed on to me.

And that it would be, as it had been for my mother, my downfall.

TWO
Hide and Seek

Sully-- Two weeks later

I stood in front of the full-length mirror in my bathroom, tugging at the collar and sleeves of my pressed dress shirt.

Inside me a struggle raged—on one side, the desire to look respectable and make a good impression on my neighbors, the Wessexes, who'd been kind enough to invite me and my two daughters to their lawn party today. On the other, the need to rip off the confining garment, which seemed to have shrunk considerably since the last time I'd been forced to wear it, and rip it into very expensive confetti.

To be fair, it wasn't the shirt that was the true source of my frustration but my ex-wife, Anouk.

She hadn't returned my calls over the last several days, though I'd left increasingly impatient messages.

Her "long girls' weekend" had now stretched into more than a week.

I'd stopped caring long ago where she went and what she was doing or with whom, but our two young daughters missed their mother.

She hadn't bothered to call them once since I'd picked up the girls at her Manhattan penthouse on short notice—at which point she'd informed me I would be keeping them for the *entire summer*.

Anouk had handed me a temporary change of custody filing from her attorney along with all their clothes and belongings packed into several suitcases.

Since then life had been nothing short of chaos. Skyla and Claire were undisciplined, rebellious little hellions who refused to eat anything but junk food, popped out of bed all throughout the night, and ignored almost every request I made.

They were also very clearly starved for affection, so instead of cracking down on them, I'd gone the other way, offering them as much love, support, and time as I possibly could.

But I was tired. More tired every day. And nothing I did for them could ever replace the presence of a mother.

Having spent large chunks of their lives traveling and training for my boxing career, my parenting skills weren't much better than Anouk's.

At least *I* cared. Somehow, despite my best efforts to do the exact opposite, I'd fallen for a woman without a drop of motherly instinct.

The sound of my phone ringing sent me running into the connected master bedroom. I grabbed the device from my bed, bringing it to my ear.

"Anouk. Where are you? Are you back in New York?"

The connection was weak, but I could hear her reply well enough. "I'm still in St. Croix. How are Skyla and Claire?"

"How *are* they?" I worked to moderate my angry tone. "They miss you. They need to see their mother. When will you be back?"

She laughed. "Now you know how it feels to be tied down

all the time. I can't tell you how many amazing parties I missed because I couldn't get a sitter—not to mention what it did to my summers."

It was getting harder for me to control the fury burning in my veins. How could she not miss her own children?

They looked just like her—exquisite little beauties who displayed their mother's Swedish-Filipino ancestry and fashion model bone structure along with a hint of my own Scotch-Irish heritage.

And when they weren't misbehaving, they were the sweetest creatures God had ever put on earth.

It had killed me to be away for work. I'd literally counted the days each time until I could come home and see my little family again—that was, until I no longer had a home to return to.

Now apparently, Anouk had grown tired of the reality of parenting, just as she had bored of the more mundane aspects of day-to-day, year after year marriage.

In the same way she'd preferred the travel, celebrity-studded parties, and material trappings associated with being married to a sports star, she seemed to prefer the "Hollywood" version of motherhood, one where her children were more like set decoration than actual people.

While her apartment and social media pages were filled with gorgeous professional photos of our pretty daughters, she spent as little actual time with them as possible. They were mere accessories in her glamorous life.

"I've always wondered... why did you want to have kids?" I asked.

I could almost hear her answering shrug through the line. "It's what you do. And you wanted children so much—I wanted to make you happy."

Happy. I huffed a humorless laugh. Had we ever been

happy? Not since the first few weeks, when it was all wild passion and extravagant dates and gifts.

"I looked over the papers you sent. I'll sign them... if you're sure it's what you really want."

"I'm sure. I'm fine with visitation for the summer," she said blandly. "They're better off with you, anyway. You're a good father."

"Yeah, well..." I stopped there. What was there to say?

No matter what kind of father I was—and I suspected it wasn't all that great—I was all Skyla and Claire had for the next three months. I had to find a way to be good *enough*.

I needed to get off the phone anyway. Things had gone far too quiet in the other room where the girls were supposed to be watching a video.

"Let me know when you get back in the country. We'll set up a time for you to come visit them," I said.

On the other end of the line, Anouk made a non-committal noise. "I may pick up a job or two while I'm here. They're casting for an Italian swimsuit campaign next week."

"Okay well..." I sighed. "Take care."

Picking up a small brush and a handful of tiny hairclips and elastic bands from the top of my dresser, I headed to the girls' playroom to attempt, once again, the task I'd been trying futilely to perform all day—wrangling my children's unruly thick hair into some sort of style presentable for the party.

Not only would they be meeting the Prince and Princess of Aubernesse, otherwise known as Alexander and Cinda Wessex, they'd be meeting the Wessexes' son AJ and all the other neighborhood children.

If my daughters were going to be living here all summer, I wanted them to be liked by the local kids and have some friends.

I entered the playroom, and sure enough, the squeaky

animated video was playing on the flat screen TV, but the girls were nowhere in sight.

"Sky? Claire baby? Where are you two?"

From beneath a pile of stuffed animals in one corner of the room came a delicious double trill of giggles. I smiled.

"Hmmm... I wonder where they could be?" I asked in an exaggerated tone. "They don't seem to be in here. Claire? Skyla? Where are you?"

I didn't move toward their hiding spot but took a seat on the red leather sofa that sat in front of the television. If I took them up on their favorite game—hide and seek—they'd dart away, and I'd never get them to the party on time.

Small though they were, my kids were fast as jackrabbits and somehow able to spring away from my grasp like little grasshoppers.

As a professional athlete, I had to admire their quickness and lightness on their feet. As a father whose disciplinary skills were on the *underdeveloped* side... I was dismayed by it.

I didn't want to threaten them into obedience. That was Anouk's sole parenting strategy, and I'd never seen it be all that effective. I wanted their *willing* cooperation.

Dropping my face into my hands, I faked loud, cartoony sobs. "I've lost my little girls. What am I going to do now? Who am I going to give piggyback rides to? Or throw into the swimming pool? Who's going to eat all that ice cream in the freezer?"

Through the cracks between my fingers, I saw two tiny pairs of bare feet—one with purple painted toenails, the other with pink ones—creeping toward me.

And then they were all over me, one climbing onto my back while the other jumped at me and hugged me from the front.

"Here we are Daddy," Claire, the four-year-old squealed in my face, clearly thrilled to have "fooled" me.

"You didn't know where we were," my older daughter, Skyla, announced. "But we were right here."

I looked up and around, making a comical dumb-guy face. "What? Where? I looked *everywhere.*"

The girls giggled again, and I pulled them both onto the couch where I tickled them just to hear more of the addictive sound.

They shrieked with delight, and when I paused for a moment, Claire shouted, "More Daddy, more." I obliged with another round of tickles.

It had been obvious in my call with Anouk she thought *she'd* gotten the better end of this deal, but I was thrilled with the development.

I wanted my daughters with me every day—not just this summer but year-round.

Thankfully I wasn't training for a fight at the moment. If I had been, the unexpected change in our custody arrangement would have meant finding some daytime babysitting pronto. For now though it was just the three of us, and I loved it.

After a minute I stopped tickling and pulled Claire onto my lap.

"Okay now, let's settle down. The party is about to start, and we don't want to be late, so I'm going to need you to let me fix your hair with these thingamabobs and then you two need to get dressed in something nice."

Spotting the brush I'd picked up from the sofa cushion, Skyla skittered away from me. "You can't catch us," she taunted. "Come on Claire, let's hide."

Claire contorted her spine and slipped from my lap like she was an eel coated in cooking oil. And then they were off, flying out of the playroom with their matching pink cartoon-character-covered nightgowns flapping around their skinny legs.

I stood and followed them, throwing my hands up in frustration. "Girls... no. Come on now. We have to get ready."

All I heard in response was the slap of their little feet on the marble floors, the sound growing fainter and fainter as they sought out one of the mansion's limitless hiding spots.

THREE
Thing One and Thing Two

Angelina

I couldn't have been any happier.

The party was a smashing success by anyone's estimation. No fewer than fifty children, all dressed in miniature versions of "Eastport Bay casual," cavorted on the grounds of the Wessex estate.

The weather had cooperated fully, offering clear blue afternoon skies and a light, crisp sea breeze. Beyond the expanse of manicured green lawn and the Bluff Walk that bordered it, the Atlantic sparkled and provided that ever-present "ocean smell" that made you feel like you were on vacation, even when you were in your own back yard.

All of the preschool's graduating class along with many of my former students were there.

I'd received more friendly gap-toothed smiles and sticky-fingered hugs than I could ever remember having in one day, and Cinda was thrilled with the response to the food, decorations, and especially the games and entertainment.

"I have to say it again—no one understands little kids like you do," she said as we stood together on the patio, surveying the nearby pony ride attraction. "I still can't believe you're leaving the school. You're such a natural teacher, and you have such a strong mothering instinct."

The remark stung. Not because it was delivered cruelly or because Cinda was seeking to make me regret my decision to go into religious service—it wasn't, and she wasn't.

It was just that hearing the word "mother" associated with myself pinged one of the deepest-seated most secret desires of my heart.

While Mother had bought me tiny nun's habits and a miniature kneeling bench for my bedroom, I had longed for baby dolls and tiny versions of bassinets, and feeding chairs, and those magical little bottles that seemed to empty or fill with milk, depending on which way you tipped them.

When I'd looked at the numerous paintings of Madonna and child that adorned the walls of our home, rather than feeling the proper amount of reverence or any sort of inspiration to full-time religious service, my first thought had been how adorable the baby was and how lovely it would be to have one of my very own one day.

Mother had been quick to quash any such talk, informing me that babies weren't all they were cracked up to be and reminding me of the binding vow she'd made to God regarding my future vocation.

"Thank you," I said to Cinda. "But my course in life is set. Maybe after my postulancy and novitiate period are complete, and I'm initiated, I'll be assigned to a parochial school somewhere. I *am* sad I won't get to meet the next crop of little ones coming into the preschool in the fall."

"I just hope you get to meet *this* little bundle before you go away." Cinda patted her rounded belly. "I may look as big as a house on Oceanview, but I've still got almost two months to go."

"Maybe it's twins?" I said.

Cinda gave me a mischievous smile. "You never know. Be sure you're around in about an hour when we make the big announcement."

I covered my open mouth with one hand and gasped.

Before I could say more, my attention was diverted by a flash of pink in a very unexpected place.

There was a narrow gap in the continuous green line of the twenty-foot-tall boxwood hedge separating the Wessex estate from the neighboring one, and through it slipped a little girl. Followed by another, smaller one.

Both of them wore long pink nightgowns and had bare feet. Their identical curly dark hair was wild, as if they'd just gotten out of bed.

Maybe their mother had put them down for afternoon naps, and they'd slipped out of the house without anyone realizing they'd awakened?

They reminded me a bit of Dr. Seuss's Thing One and Thing Two as they charged up to the refreshment table, both grabbing a cupcake in each hand.

My instinct was to move toward them, find out if their parents were right behind them or if they perhaps needed to be returned to their home, but beside me, Cinda laughed, clearly delighted to see them there.

"Well hello little neighbors. Looks like Mr. Reece's daughters have decided to skip the front door in favor of a more Alice in Wonderland style of entry."

I turned to her. "Sullivan Reece? The boxer? Those are his girls?"

"I believe so. They look like the pictures he showed us, and that *is* his yard from which they emerged in such a creative way."

My nervous system went on high alert. I turned to look at the back doors of the Wessex mansion, anticipating the arrival of Sullivan Reece, who'd no doubt come through them at any moment.

Could I possibly excuse myself? Say I needed to go home and check on my mother?

If my suspicions were correct, and my jogger—as I'd come to think of the tall, wide-chested man—and Sullivan Reece the boxer were one and the same person, I did *not* want to make his acquaintance.

My reaction to the man from a distance was bad enough. I hated to think what might happen if I were to encounter him up close.

I hadn't seen him on the Bluff Walk at all this week and had wondered what had happened to him. Apparently his daughters had happened.

"Oh, there he is," Cinda said, shading her eyes as she gazed toward the far end of the lawn.

Appearing from around the end of the tall privacy hedge, a man jogged in our direction. The serene backdrop of blue ocean and bluer skies behind him was a sharp contrast to the stormy expression he wore.

His face was red, and his head moved as if on a swivel as he scanned the large property.

The man was wearing a nice pair of pants and a dress shirt, which was coming untucked as he ran. But I most definitely recognized him.

It *was* my jogger. And he was headed directly toward us.

He'd spotted the girls, who were now standing just outside the pony ride ring, trying to interest the animal inside in some frosted baked goods.

"He looks like a brute, but he's so nice," Cinda said. "Seems a bit overwhelmed by the girls though." She chuckled before adding, "They look like they could keep anyone on their toes."

"Alex," Cinda called to her husband who stood nearby

talking with two other fathers from the preschool. "Sullivan is here."

The prince began to stroll toward his wife, and I saw my chance to take my leave. "I'm going to head over to the bounce house. Some of the bigger kids have gotten in, and I want to make sure they're not overwhelming the little ones."

"Oh, good idea. Thank you so much, Angelina. You are a superstar."

Walking as quickly as I could manage without running, I moved toward the bright inflatable and out of Sullivan Reece's trajectory.

When I reached the bounce house, I turned to see he was now talking with the Wessexes. His body language was apologetic, and he used his hands a lot as he spoke.

I looked away. But after I warned a pair of eight-year-old boys about watching out for the younger children while bouncing, my attention strayed back to Sullivan.

He stood near his daughters now, bending low to speak to them. The girls didn't appear to be listening at first. Then they began arguing with him.

As he spoke, he pointed behind him in the direction of his own estate. Apparently, he was trying to convince them to return home and get dressed.

Instead of complying, the taller girl took off running, followed closely by the little one. Sullivan straightened and pushed both his hands through his hair, his lean cheeks puffing outward as he blew out a long breath.

The poor man looked frazzled. And exhausted.

Maybe the girls had been down for a nap because they hadn't been sleeping well at night. I wondered about their mother. Where was she today? Why was she not at the party as well? Perhaps she was out of town or ill.

A spark of sympathy landed on my heart.

Small children thrived on routine. And during my two

years working at the preschool, I'd seen lots of fathers completely undone by the particular challenges of wrangling small children.

One had even referred to himself as the "backup quarterback" when his children had arrived for the school day in their pajamas with unbrushed hair and teeth.

"I'm just trying not to lose the game until the lead quarterback gets off the DL list," he'd said with a self-deprecating smile.

Of course, there were fathers who were the primary caregivers in their households. I suspected Sullivan Reece was not one of them.

After veering precariously close to a small table where brightly wrapped graduation gifts for the children had been stacked in a pyramid, the two little Reece girls changed direction and headed for the bounce house. They were surprisingly fast.

Their father changed direction as well, his long, powerful stride carrying him directly toward me with alarming speed.

The girls reached the inflatable bouncer and scrambled inside. One of them squealed, "Let's hide from Daddy in here. He's too big to fit."

With Sullivan only steps away now, I also had the impulse to hide.

Stepping to the opposite side of the bounce house, I watched the children inside through its mesh window. I could also make out Sullivan's large form as he stood and looked in from the other side.

He shifted back and forth with impatience, appearing barely contained and a little bit dangerous.

Though I knew he was wealthy, he looked slightly rough around the edges, like maybe he'd started life somewhere very different from an opulent Eastport Bay mansion. And while he was dressed nicely, I had the impression he'd be more comfortable in a pair of worn jeans or maybe gym shorts and a t-shirt

Inside the bounce house, Sullivan's daughters ignored his watchful presence, springing around like popcorn kernels, their wild hair flying with each jump.

He called out to them. "We'll go home, change real quick, and come back. But only if you get out of there right now and come with me."

In spite of his deep voice and intimidating size, I was surprised to hear no sternness in the man's tone. Rather, he sounded like he was begging these infinitely smaller humans to cooperate.

Suddenly I understood what was going on.

He was the one who was intimidated. And his daughters knew it.

Like any children, who would gladly accept any and all power you would give them, the adorable little girls were playing him.

Sullivan Reece might look like a bruiser, but inside he was a marshmallow, at least when it came to these two girls.

The spark of sympathy grew into something larger, something warmer. The man needed help. And if I'd learned anything during my time as a preschool teaching assistant, it was how to get unruly children to cooperate.

"I. Want. To. Keep. On. Bounce. Ing," one of the Reece girls said in an obstinate tone as she jumped even harder and higher.

"I mean it now," her father said, sounding increasingly frustrated. "If you two don't listen to me, I'll..."

His threat trailed off into nothingness, and he looked heavenward as if seeking wisdom from a higher power. That was when I started moving, walking around to the side of the bouncer where he stood.

When I reached his side, he still stood with his head

dropped back on his shoulders, his hands low on his hips as he breathed in and out with audible gusts, perhaps struggling to remain calm.

His sleeves were rolled up to expose his forearms and one of those tattoos I'd noticed from afar. I also noticed he wore no jewelry.

No wedding ring. My heart gave an extra thump.

He was even larger up close than I'd anticipated. Being next to him was something like standing near a high stone wall, though this particular stone wall smelled *amazing*. Some sort of cologne or manly soap, I guessed.

And the texture of his hair was anything but rough. The shiny, dark locks looked so soft and touchable I felt a literal ache in my fingertips from resisting the impulse to reach out.

What was *wrong* with me? I'd never felt an inappropriate urge to touch a stranger before.

And this man was clearly in distress. The last thing he needed was a ridiculous girl ogling his various physical attributes.

Swallowing down the large lump that had mysteriously formed in my throat, I managed to find my voice.

"Kids that age can be a handful, huh?"

Sullivan dropped his arms to his side and swiveled abruptly in my direction, looking down to locate me. His mouth opened slightly, though he didn't immediately respond, and his eyelids flared wide, revealing the lightest blue eyes I'd ever seen. They were like faded sea glass, transparent and soft and incredibly beautiful.

"Uh... yeah."

That was all he said, and for the life of me, I couldn't think of anything more to say either.

Those spectacular blue eyes studied me as if they'd never beheld a creature like me before. I became abruptly conscious of my lack of makeup, my easy ponytail, the simple yellow sheath dress I wore with no jewelry other than a pair of tiny diamond studs my grandmother had given me shortly before passing away.

Compared to the other women at the party, I looked plain. That hadn't bothered me in the least—until this moment.

No doubt the heavyweight boxing champion of the world was used to moving in a glamorous crowd.

The women he knew were probably movie stars and bikini models and beauty pageant winners. He probably thought I was one of the servants, or maybe the big sister of one of the children. People were always assuming my age to be younger than my actual twenty-three years.

"Are you... is one of these kids yours?" he finally asked.

Oh. He thought I was a mom. For some reason the thought tickled me.

"They all are," I said. "I'm their teacher—or I was their teacher at some point during the past few years. At the preschool, you know?"

"Oh. Fantastic. You're a preschool teacher. My youngest is starting preschool in the fall. Where do you teach?"

The question made me a little sad. Rather, it was the answer that made me sad. "I'm just an assistant actually—and only for a short while longer. I won't be going back after the summer break."

"Get a new job?"

I looked away, unable to tolerate the penetrating blue gaze without a break and strangely reluctant to tell him *why* I wouldn't be returning to the preschool in the fall.

"Something like that," I said.

The guy stuck out a hand—a massive one. I didn't know hands could even *be* that muscular. "I'm Sullivan. Reece. Sullivan Reece. I live next door."

Interesting that he didn't seem to expect me to know who he was—and that he didn't tell me. He'd identified himself as a next-door neighbor rather than a boxing champion.

He was humble. I liked that.

When I offered my own hand in return, it was completely swallowed in the guy's steady, but not overly hard, grip.

Before I could give him my name, one of his daughters yelled to get his attention. "Daddy, watch me."

The younger of the two girls was jumping with all her might, gaining some pretty impressive height with each bounce. When her nightgown flew up over her head, Sullivan turned back to me, his face flushing with color.

"I've been trying to get them to go home and put on some clothes and shoes, but I'm striking out. You must think I'm a terrible father."

A swell of compassion supplanted any feelings of discomfort I had with him.

"Not at all. You wouldn't believe how many kids I've seen show up for school in footy pajamas. PJ's are comfy. Comfy is good."

That was when I decided to move beyond sympathy and help him. "Not listening to Daddy is *not* good."

I'd planned a treasure hunt game for after the gender reveal, but there were still at least forty-five minutes until then, and that was plenty of time.

Earlier today I'd hidden a treasure chest filled with small cardboard swords, eyepatches, and costume jewelry and had prepared colorful picture clue cards for the pre-reader party guests to guide them from one spot to the next until they found the treasure's hiding place.

Ducking my head into the bounce house through its mesh and canvas flap, I said, "Who wants to play a super-fun game?"

Children scrambled from the bouncer with cries of, "me!" and "I do!."

When they quieted, I explained the treasure hunt to them,

adding a line to the instructions specifically for the two Reece girls.

"Is everyone ready? Okay, get your shoes on and let's go."

Both their little faces fell in dramatic despair. The younger one wailed, "Wait. I got no shoes."

"You have no shoes," I corrected gently then asked a question to which I already knew the answer. "Did you take them off here at the party?"

"No, they're at our house," the older girl said.

"Oh dear." I feigned grave concern. "That's a problem."

After a moment I held up a finger and pretended I'd just had a great idea. "Maybe we could delay the treasure hunt for just a few minutes... if you think you can go and get them on very quickly. And treasure hunting will be difficult in your nightgowns, so some regular clothes would be good too."

"We can be fast," the big sister said.

"Fast," the little one echoed, bouncing in eagerness.

"Okay then. I'll time you and see how fast you are. Ready, set... go!"

The girls spun around and raced across the yard toward the opening in the hedge leading to their own back yard.

Next to me, Sullivan gasped. "You're a miracle worker."

He started after his daughters but turned back to face me as he jogged backward. "Hey. I never got your name."

I hesitated before answering. For some reason it felt like a big deal to give him my name. People met and exchanged names every day all day long in every part of the world, and it meant precisely nothing.

But with this man, it felt... significant. It felt like the beginning of something. And I had no business beginning *anything* with Sullivan Reece.

I should just ignore his request, wave and yell, "Nice to meet you," or maybe, "Good luck," and pretend the wind had carried his question away.

Sometimes *should* just wasn't happening.

My heart thundered in my chest. I swallowed hard and moistened my lips. "It's Angelina."

Sullivan Reece smiled widely, turned around, and ran to the far edge of the lawn, disappearing around the end of the tall hedge and leaving me breathless.

* * *

By the time he and the girls returned for the treasure hunt, I'd managed to compose myself. I made sure to avoid any more private conversations with him. There was no point to it.

I couldn't avoid my awareness of him though. As he chased his daughters around the Wessex estate, my eyes followed involuntarily. The three of them were back near the bounce house when Cinda announced it was time for the gender reveal.

Standing at the edge of the patio with all the other adults, I watched as Alexander Wessex walked around and offered each of them a gold-foil-wrapped party popper from a basket.

Cinda handed out poppers to the children who were interested in participating.

On the count of three, everyone pulled their poppers, releasing their contents. There were shouts of delight and then a few moments of silence as confusion reigned.

The adults' poppers had expelled bright pink confetti. But the confetti projected from the children's poppers was distinctly blue.

Had someone made a mistake with the party favors? As Cinda and Alex hugged and nodded their heads, I and the rest of the party guests understood—there were *two* babies. Fraternal twins.

A boy *and* a girl.

While I clapped along with the rest of the assembly, inside

I was rocked by a wave of longing so powerful it nearly knocked me off my feet.

Oh, this is not good.

It was not good at all. I was mere weeks away from beginning my postulancy and sequestration from the outside world. At this point I should be more certain about my decision than I'd ever been.

Instead I was filled with turmoil and a sense of doubt that was growing faster than Cinda's waistline.

Beware the evils of men… evils of men… beware.

Shutting my eyes, I repeated the familiar mantra to myself over and over. But instead of settling me, today it only caused the agitation inside me to grow.

And behind my closed eyelids danced a vision of icy blue eyes… and a pair of large, warm hands reaching out to capture me.

FOUR

Top Contender

Sully- the next morning

The front doorbell chimed, and I walked across the wide entry hall to answer it, still thinking of the preschool teacher.

Angelina.

I hadn't been able to get her off my mind for more than a few minutes at a time since the party, had even woken up this morning thinking of her.

It was a strange thing. I'd never had such a strong initial reaction to a woman in my life—not even Anouk, who was stunning—I mean, she was a fucking supermodel.

Angelina was different in every way—shy rather than bold, sweet rather than aggressively sexy. Anyway, whatever the reason behind it, she'd seized my attention like no one ever had before.

And the way she'd managed the girls… maybe she really *did* have a divine gift. Speaking of my daughters, those little stinkers were about to go on lockdown.

I reached the door and opened it to the head of Viridian Security who'd agreed to come out personally and assess my house for weak spots. There would be no more sneaking out and running away to the neighbor's yard or anywhere else.

"Mr. Reece, I'm Wilder Lowe."

The man on my threshold was larger than I'd expected, though I probably should have. I'd read on the company's website that its founder had played college football and been a Navy SEAL before starting his own security firm.

The guy looked like he could still play ball. Six-four or six-five, he had a powerful, athletic build that probably gave his clients an extra feeling of comfort about putting their property —and personal security—in his hands. I'd also read that Wilder occasionally still worked as a bodyguard for very select celebrity clients.

"Hey Wilder. Come on in. Call me Sully." I shook Wilder's hand and motioned for him to come inside.

"Good to meet you in person, Sully. I've seen all your fights. I'm a big fan."

"Oh yeah? That's cool. Thanks for watching. I guess that makes you one of the reasons I've got this place."

I gestured to the soaring two-story foyer and the grand staircase curving up to the second floor. "Now I just need to make it four-and-five-year-old proof."

The security expert chuckled. "I think we can handle that. What did you have in mind?"

"Come on into the kitchen. We'll talk in there." I turned and started leading Wilder through the house. "I was just making a protein shake. Want something? You have breakfast yet?"

"Hours ago," Wilder said. "I get up early. What are you drinking?"

"Whey protein with almond milk, almond butter, and a mix of berries."

"Sounds good. Maybe I will have one."

We continued talking as I added ingredients to the blender and ran it.

"I definitely want cameras in all the rooms, so I can keep an eye on my girls even if I'm somewhere else in the house. I need to get back to training," I said. "I have a full gym here on the lower floor, but they're not gonna want to stay in there with me all the time. And I need some sort of system that'll let me know when a door or window opens—from the *inside* as well as outside."

My new greatest fear was that the girls would slip out of the house while I was asleep at night and get snatched up by some lowlife. They'd gotten up several times last night, which was probably why they were still sleeping this morning.

Wilder nodded, making a note in the phone he'd pulled from his pocket. "Surprised the house didn't have that already."

"Well, the people who owned it before me were old. They'd lived here forever, and they had a whole houseful of servants to watch over things."

"You don't have any help?" Wilder looked around, evaluating the massive space. "Pretty big place for one guy to take care of."

"Tell me about it. I've got a cleaning service coming a couple times a week now—my next-door neighbor runs it."

"Cinda Wessex? Yeah, I've heard her company does a great job. She and I went to school together here in Eastport Bay."

"Cool. Yeah, it's been great so far. To tell you the truth, I haven't had a chance to hire anyone else yet or even figure out what I need. I bought the place a year or so ago, but I've been on the road so much, I haven't spent much time here."

"I remember. You were going pretty steadily there for a good number of years. You taking some time off now? I've been seeing that kid Travis Diggs trash-talking on TV, trying to get you to give him a shot at the title."

I cringed. Diggs and his constant goading to take him on were my least favorite topics of conversation. But it couldn't be avoided for much longer.

"I'm gonna see how long I can put him off. I'm trying to give my girls some stability, you know? I've got them full-time for the next three months, and I don't want to drag them around from hotel room to hotel room. I'm still not even sure how all this is gonna work."

"Have you looked into getting a live-in nanny or an au pair? You've got plenty of room to put someone up," Wilder said.

"I could definitely use some help. You know of someone?"

Though I didn't know Wilder Lowe well, I had an instant liking for him. He inspired a sense of trust.

I also liked what I'd read about his background—we could relate on the levels of athletics and the rigors of grueling training routines.

In fact, what he'd been through as a Navy SEAL probably surpassed even what I had to put my body through in preparation for every prize fight.

"Do you have a sister or something?" I asked.

"Me? No. I've got three brothers—none of them are 'nanny material.'" He laughed.

"That's right. A couple of them play in the NFL, right?"

"Yep. And the youngest is playing college ball."

"How come you never went pro?" I asked. "Your college record was outstanding."

"Thanks, man. I don't know. That life just wasn't for me, you know? I loved the game, but I always dreamed of being a Frogman. I wanted to serve my country."

"That's awesome. Well, I'm glad you decided to get into security after that. How soon do you think your guys could start installing the systems?"

Just then my phone rang. I looked at the screen and held

up a finger to Wilder. "Excuse me. Gotta take this. I'll be right back."

Taking a few steps away, I answered. "Hey Frank. What's up?"

As if I even needed to ask. There was only one thing fight promoter Frank Balletto would be calling about—the same thing he'd been calling about for months now.

"Hey Sul. Listen, buddy, I can't put the Diggs camp off any longer. We gotta set a date. They're making noise about talking to the boxing commission, asking them to vacate your title and take back your belt."

"What?" I practically yelled. "They can't do that."

"I'm afraid they can. With his nineteen knockouts and undefeated record, he's earned the right to demand a title fight."

"That pipsqueak is only twenty years old."

"That 'pipsqueak' is six-foot-three and two-hundred-sixty pounds of solid muscle. And he's the *same age* you were when you took the boxing world by storm. He's the new 'you.' You gotta fight him, Sully. Come on, give me the green light and let me get this thing in motion. Couldn't you use a few hundred million more in your pocket? I know I could."

My take from each pay-per-view fight was eighty percent. At a hundred dollars a head and with a viewing audience of about twenty million people, it was a hefty fee.

I thought about it. There was no denying the money I'd earned boxing had changed my life completely, elevating me from the worst neighborhood in Worcester, Massachusetts to the ritziest street in Eastport Bay, Rhode Island, America's very first playground of the rich and famous.

It had taken me from hungry and dressed in thrift store clothing that never fit quite right to eating in the finest restaurants and wearing designer clothes that cost more than a year's rent on my mom's shitty old apartment.

It had meant going from walking everywhere I went to driving a fleet of expensive sports cars.

Most importantly, if I'd never become rich, Anouk would never have married me, and I wouldn't have my two girls.

But those girls *needed* me right now.

Preparing for a title fight would be no joke. Normally, I trained for at least three months—hard—before each fight. This one might need more. It was an all-day thing, requiring my full concentration and effort.

With this new custody situation taking place at the beginning of summer break, my daughters needed care and supervision all day long.

How could I be there for them and train at the same time?

"I don't know, Frank. You know it's not really about the money anymore."

"What about your legacy? What about going forty and O?" the promoter asked, knowing exactly where to jab me. "You once told me that was what you wanted most in life. You're only a few fights away. The Sullivan Reece I know is no quitter."

"Yeah, you're right. I still want it. More than anything. It's just such a bad time for me. Listen, I've gotta get off the phone but I'll think about it, okay?"

"Don't think about it too long. The boxing commission is eager for a title bout, and every day you wait, Diggs' position grows stronger... and his taunts that you're scared of him gain more credibility."

"Okay, okay, I hear you. I'll give you a call tomorrow."

When I hung up, Wilder gave me an alert glance. "Everything okay?"

I blew out a breath. "Yeah. I don't know. Travis Diggs is making some noise about getting my title vacated if I don't give him his shot—and soon."

"You going to fight him?"

"I don't really have a choice. He's the top contender. He's earned the shot."

"You're undefeated right? How many wins—thirty-five?" Wilder asked.

"Thirty-six. My goal was always forty."

"Well, goals are good for sure, but there's always a choice. You could do the same thing I did—walk away—just let it go, you know, for the sake of something more important."

Staring out the kitchen window at the waves rolling on the Atlantic, I shook my head. "I made this promise to myself when I was a kid, living in one grubby apartment after the other, just praying I didn't get shot or knifed on my way home from school every day, that I wasn't going to quit till I got out of there and changed my lot in life, till I was on top of the world instead of under its bootheel. I'd never have made it through even that first fight if I'd been a quitter. I sure as hell wouldn't be the defending heavyweight champ of the world. Besides... this is what I do. It's my job. It's my passion. It's who I *am*."

"Right. I get it," Wilder said. "It's just... well, I learned when I was over in Somalia, you only get so many days here on this earth. You never know when you wake up each morning if it'll be your last. Just make sure you're spending each one the way you want to."

I nodded. I wasn't sure *what* I wanted. My vision for my life used to be crystal clear.

Fight. Win. Claim the prizes—all of them.

Now... everything felt topsy-turvy. My thinking wasn't clear. All I knew was that my daughters had to be okay.

And that I had to take the fight.

When Wilder left, I picked up the phone again and called Anouk. It was the only solution to my dilemma.

The phone rang so many times I thought it would go to voicemail—again—but then she finally answered.

"Sullivan. What do you want?"

"Hey. Listen, I know you're probably still out of the country but there's something I need to talk to you about. I'm gonna have to take another fight pretty soon."

"And?" She didn't sound all that interested.

"Well, you know what training is like. It's gonna take up all my time. And I thought... well, I had an idea. What if you were to come to Eastport Bay? The house here has a lot of space. You could move in—just for the summer—just until the fight. You and the girls could explore the mansions and go to Boston and New Hampshire for daytrips. The beaches here are great, and you've got plenty of good restaurants and spas and stuff, a bunch of cute little shops I bet you'd love."

There was a long pause. When she responded, her tone was filled with exaggerated patience. "Sully... there's a *reason* I gave you full custody for the next three months."

"Whoa—wait—are you getting remarried?"

"What? No." She laughed. "I like my freedom too much. Even if I wanted to play 'happy family' again, I couldn't. I'm in Italy now. I'm working."

"I thought you were in St. Croix."

"I was, but I *told* you about the swimsuit campaign. We're shooting for the next week. And it looks like it's going to lead to some runway work in Milan. I'll have to go straight there from here. I haven't been there in ages."

"When exactly were you planning to come back and visit your children?" I asked.

"Don't try to guilt-trip me. It won't work. I *did* my time with them. Now it's your turn."

"You make it sound like being in prison or something," I snorted in disgust. "They're not a life sentence—they're our *children.* They need someone to take care of them while I train."

"You're a smart guy. You'll figure it out. Hey, I've gotta go. I'm on the set, and Lorenzo is getting impatient. Ciao."

And she hung up.

If I didn't know what a pain in the ass it would be to replace it, I would have crushed the phone in my bare hand. The woman didn't have a maternal bone in her body.

But I'd have to find someone who did. Fast.

FIVE
Dreams

Angelina

A question burned on my tongue, spinning through my mind on a constant loop since the Wessex party yesterday.

But I hadn't dared ask it of Mother. She didn't like questions.

I'd reached the point though, where I couldn't hold it in any longer.

We were seated at the dinner table, fine china and silver at the ready. Mother had just completed saying grace, a nightly ritual that lasted at least ten minutes and seemed born more of desperation than true faith.

As soon as my mother uttered the word, "Amen," I blurted it out.

"When did I decide I wanted to enter religious service?"

Mother didn't look at me but lifted her fork and took a dainty bite from her plate, chewing thoroughly and swallowing before responding.

"What do you mean?"

"I mean, do you *remember* how old I was when I told you

I wanted to be a nun when I grew up? Was I really young or something, because *I* don't remember it."

"I don't know exactly—it's just something you've always wanted." Now Mother lifted her eyes. Her tone dripped with displeasure. "What's brought all this on? Did something happen at the party?"

"No," I said quickly. "The party was lovely. The children were all adorable, and the parents were very nice."

Mother studied me, assessing eyes narrowing in concentration. "It's a man, isn't it? You met a man. I knew I shouldn't have let you go."

Now it was my turn to look away. I stared down at my plate, trying to hide the blush I could feel overtaking my face. "I barely spoke to any of the adults. I was with the kids the whole time. All the men there were fathers."

Mother's hand came down hard on the tabletop, making the fork on my plate jump and land with a clank.

"Don't *lie* to me. If I know anything in life, it's having your head turned around by a man. You've been corrupted."

I met my mother's accusatory stare with a wide-eyed one of my own. "I haven't. I promise. I didn't do anything wrong. I *never* do anything wrong. I only ever do what you tell me to."

My own words echoed back to me and left a stinging sensation that felt something like being slapped.

How odd. It had never occurred to me before there might be something *wrong* with that. But the resentful sound of my own voice made me wonder.

"*Did* I ever tell you I wanted to be a nun?" I asked my mother bluntly. "Or was it your idea?"

"How dare you take that insolent tone with me," Mother spat, instantly enraged. "After all I've done for you. I sacrificed *everything* to have you—my reputation, my friendships, any hope of marriage. I've been here for you every day of your life.

All I've ever wanted for you is to be fulfilled and protected. Serving God is the best way to do that."

Chastened, I stood and lifted my plate, no longer hungry. "I know that. You're right. I'm sorry."

"Where are you going?" Mother demanded.

"To get a head start on the dishes. I made a mess of the kitchen tonight, and I don't want the food to sit on the pots and pans for too long."

"You didn't finish eating."

"I wasn't very hungry. I'll come back for your dishes in a little while."

Once behind the closed kitchen door, I placed both hands on the countertop and dropped my head, breathing in and out rapidly.

Was Mother right? Maybe I *had* been corrupted.

Truth be told, the question of whether my choice of vocation had actually been my choice wasn't the *only* thing that had occupied my mind since the party.

Shaking my head, I tried to dislodge the disconcerting images of Sullivan Reece's wide smile and powerful hands and square jaw and unnerving blue eyes.

I didn't know him at all really, but I suspected if any man was capable of corrupting a woman, it was him.

Dropping to my knees right there in the kitchen, I began to pray for strength and that all these newly formed doubts about my life's path would be erased.

My prayer was cut short by the doorbell.

Knowing Mother wouldn't answer it, I got to my feet and hurried to the front door, expecting to find a package left there by a delivery driver. Instead, I saw Cinda's face through the door's leaded glass windows.

I opened it quickly. "Hi. I'm surprised to see you here. Did you walk over?"

"Waddled is more like it," Cinda said with good humor.

"The doctor said walking is good for me. Running is definitely out, but I never was a big runner anyway."

At the words "big runner," images of Sullivan Reece snapped right back into my mind as if they'd been at the end of an elastic band, and my prayers had only stretched them temporarily out of frame instead of removing them.

"Oh. Right. Me too—I mean, me either," I said.

Cinda smiled and lifted her hand, offering me a beautifully wrapped box. "This is for you, to thank you for all your help. I meant to give it to you yesterday, but you slipped away a little before the party ended."

"I'm sorry about that. I really needed to get home to my mother." The truth was I'd seen Sullivan heading my way and had fled the scene.

"Oh please. Don't apologize," Cinda said. "It went a lot longer than I expected. Everyone seemed to have a good time though. The games and entertainment were a huge hit, and the kids loved those little gifts you picked out for them. All the parents were very impressed... especially my neighbor, Mr. Reece."

My pulse took off like a rocket, racing through my veins and stealing my breath. Stepping outside, I shut the door behind me and spoke quietly, though there was no chance of Mother overhearing through the solid oak.

"He mentioned me?"

"He sure did. He was amazed at how you were able to manage his daughters. Apparently the girls are quite a handful, and he's a bit overwhelmed."

"Oh." I felt a sinking sensation. Which was weird. Why should I feel disappointed?

"And..." Cinda added a bit more slyly, "he mentioned how attractive he found you."

The churning excitement returned, exponentially more powerful. "Really?"

"Why do you sound so surprised? Everyone thinks so. I don't think you have any idea how stunning you are. It may be the first time in history a girl has had to choose between the runway at Fashion Week and becoming a nun," she teased.

"Yeah right," I said. Trying to keep my voice casual, I asked, "Did you tell Sullivan I might be going into religious service?"

Cinda shrugged. "It didn't come up. I didn't realize you hadn't made up your mind yet. When we spoke about it before you sounded like it was a done deal."

"Oh it is," I said quickly. "Even if... someone was interested, I wouldn't do anything about it." My face flared with incriminating heat.

The reaction seemed to interest Cinda. "Have you ever been in a serious relationship?"

"You mean with a man?"

"Yes. Or a boy, back in high school or college."

"I didn't go away to college. I took some classes at Salve Regina while living at home. Before that, I went to all girls' schools. I didn't even really know any boys."

Cinda's small jaw dropped. "You've *never* had a boyfriend?"

"I've never been on a date," I admitted then wondered why I'd ever said such an embarrassing thing out loud.

Hastening to explain, I added, "I just figured... what was the point, you know? I knew I was going to be a nun, so why bother with dating?"

I chose not to mention my mother's prohibition against any and all socializing with members of the male species.

Cinda looked thoughtful. "I didn't date much myself. There were group outings in high school and a couple guys I went out with a few times after that. Then I met Alex one summer and fell head over heels in love. After that AJ came along, and there was no time for dating. You know Alex and I didn't speak or see each other for five years, right? He didn't know about AJ, and I had no idea how to reach him. I didn't even know his real name."

"What a story you two have," I said. "It's like a movie or something."

"Why don't we go out to lunch this week, and I'll give you all the juicy details? We'll spend most of the year in Aubernesse because of Alex's responsibilities, but we're here for the whole summer. I want to have the babies here in the U.S.."

From inside the house, a sharp voice cracked, "Angelina. Where are you?"

I glanced over my shoulder, anxiety cramping my belly. "That's very nice of you, but my period of postulancy begins in a month, and until then, my days will be very busy caring for Mother."

"Is she sick?" Cinda asked with obvious concern.

"No. Not exactly. But she's... she needs me. Thank you so much for the gift—I've got to go in now."

Cinda still looked concerned. "Okay, but my invitation for lunch stands. Or just come on over for coffee or tea, anytime you want to chat. I like you, Angelina, and you might be surprised how much we have in common."

That made me pause. "Really?"

Cinda nodded. "I spent a long time going about life, doing my duty, *not* following my heart. It wasn't until I looked inside myself to see what I really wanted that things started to change for me. I almost missed out on one of the best things in life by deciding to play it safe and preserve the status quo. Thankfully Alex—and a conveniently timed hurricane—changed my mind."

Placing a gentle hand on my arm, she said, "Being there for your family is important. But there's nothing wrong with having your own dreams as well. As Walt Disney said, 'All our dreams can come true if we have the courage to pursue them.'"

I simply nodded and thanked Cinda once again for the gift and the invitation to get together, eager to open the former and knowing I'd never accept the latter.

And as I shut the door and walked through the house to find out what Mother needed, I reflected.

I'm not sure I even know how *to dream.*

SIX

Serious Doubts

Angelina

For the next week I tried to regain my equilibrium.

Any time an image of Sullivan Reece's face invaded my mind or a snatch of our brief conversation came back to me, I dug deep into my store of willpower and re-focused on the things that *were* possible in my life.

When willpower failed me, I unearthed the little leather-bound book of prayers my mother had given me in childhood, reading the childish rhymes aloud over and over again, hoping their rhythm would impart a bit of peace.

That lasted for a week, at which point I began scheming to find a way to visit Cinda. I didn't expect my new friend to have all the answers, but speaking to Cinda did seem to make things clearer, as if talking to her shined a light on some things I'd kept locked away in a dark corner of my own mind.

Now that I'd had a little taste of it, I wanted *more* light.

I wanted to examine those hidden artifacts a bit more closely. Things like a long-forgotten dream of becoming a dancer. Once I remembered it, I also had a snatch of another memory—mentioning it to Mother, who'd told me, "Good girls don't dance."

I'd put the aspiration out of my mind immediately. Now, for whatever reason, the memory was back, along with a new curiosity about *why* it would be so unacceptable for a good girl to dance.

And then there was my new dream of becoming a full-time teacher. I wanted to bounce these ideas off someone else —someone who would listen instead of covering my ideas with blanket condemnation the instant they were out of my mouth.

"I need to get out of the house," I told Mother. "It's a beautiful, sunny day. Let's go for a walk on the Bluff Walk."

"I don't like walking. I certainly don't want to be out with all those people," my mother sneered, just as I'd known she would.

"Well, if you don't mind, I'll just go alone. I need some exercise and fresh air."

"I do mind. It's not safe."

"Mother." I fought to keep my eyes from rolling up. "Look out the window. There's a steady stream of people up and down the path. It's broad daylight. Nothing will happen."

Secretly I hoped that was not true. I was desperate for something to happen, though I wasn't sure quite what.

"How long will you be gone?" Mother asked suspiciously.

"It takes about an hour to walk to the other end of the path, then another hour to return."

"Be back in an hour," she barked.

"Yes, Mother. I will. I promise."

Kissing her cheek first, I walked directly to the back door, not bothering to stop and change my shoes but grabbing my sneakers and bringing them outside with me. I sat on a rusted patio chair to tie them then literally ran to the Bluff Walk and opened the gate that separated my family's property from the public path.

Instead of going to the path's midpoint, I walked only a short distance before turning and heading into the Wessexes' back yard.

I was grateful for the tall, thick privacy hedge that shielded it from the view of the neighboring properties on both sides. As I walked to the back doors of the Wessex mansion, I glanced at the hedge on the other side, the one that bordered the Reece estate.

Was he home? He might be just on the other side of that green wall.

I was shocked by the strength of the urge I felt to tiptoe over and find out. Instead, I went to Cinda's back door and knocked.

A servant with a posh European accent answered and invited me to come inside and wait in a gleaming formal parlor. Feeling every bit the outsider I was, I followed the woman and took a seat in one of two upholstered damask wingback chairs flanking the elegant cast-stone fireplace.

Within minutes Cinda joined me. She rushed into the parlor. "Angelina! I'm so happy to see you."

"I hope I'm not bothering you. You're probably busy, but I was able to get away for a few minutes, and I thought I'd take the chance and see—"

Cinda cut me off, coming to me and taking both my hands with a friendly squeeze. "I'm thrilled. Really. And not busy at all. Alex has taken AJ out to the beach, and I was just about to sit down for a cup of tea. Can you stay and join me?"

The tightness in my chest loosened at the warm welcome. "Yes, thank you. I'd love one."

"Wonderful." Cinda settled into the chair next to mine. "So what's going on? How has your week been?"

"Honestly? It's been awful."

"Oh no. What happened?"

"Nothing happened. It's just... I feel all... upended."

"I see. Do you know why?"

Shaking my head, I searched for words to express the upheaval that had filled my mind in recent days.

"My life has always been very... predictable. There were no surprises, no real questions to wrestle with. I was on a certain path, and I was at least fairly sure it was where I should be. But ever since your party, I've felt like a sail that's torn loose from its mast, like I'm swinging free and flapping back and forth in the wind. It's kind of scary."

"Change *can* be frightening," Cinda said. "It can also be a good thing."

I nodded, fervently hoping she was right. "I thought about what you said the other day—about having a dream and following your heart. I'm not really used to looking at my heart too closely, but I've been trying lately. And the thing is... when I look at mine... it's not a very happy picture."

"I thought maybe that was the case, but you never really know about someone else. I think you're very brave to admit it."

Cinda's sympathetic gaze was too much to bear. I tore my eyes away from it and looked down at my own lap. "I'm not sure if it's bravery or if I'm really chicken. Maybe I'm just scared of making a lifelong commitment."

"You *should* be cautious. From what I understand, going into religious service is like taking wedding vows, right? That's not something you enter into lightly."

"That's true," I nodded. "The sisters said it would be a mistake to make the choice without deep, prayerful consideration. Becoming a nun isn't meant to be an escape from the outside world, but something to be joyfully entered into because you just can't imagine doing anything else with your life—because you want it more than anything. They said a candidate should be very, very sure before entering the monastic enclosure for the postulancy period. That's why the stages of formation last so long in the first place, so we can make certain it's what we really want before taking the vows."

"And you're *not* certain." It was a statement, not a question. And Cinda was right.

"I'm having serious doubts... for many reasons," I admitted. "But I don't know how *not* to do it at this point."

Cinda leaned closer and cocked her head. "What do you mean?"

"My mother is very... invested in this. She believes with all her heart it's my life's calling. I can't even talk to her about any other possibilities. And somehow..."

I stopped talking and dropped my face into my open palms, hiding it. "...it's too embarrassing. I'm sorry I'm even bothering you with this."

"I'm not bothered in the least, and you shouldn't be embarrassed. I'm very interested, and I promise you, questioning your life choices—especially a commitment like this one—is a good thing. Thinking for yourself is a good thing. So what were you saying? Somehow..."

Following her prompt, I continued. "Somehow I've let her have total control of my life. I'm twenty-three, and I can count on one hand the number of decisions I've made for myself. I don't have a phone because she didn't want me to have one. I have no friends because she's never allowed me to go out and socialize. I don't even pick out my own clothes. I've just worn whatever she ordered for me, whatever she said was 'appropriate.'"

I picked at my outfit, examining it as if seeing the garments for the first time. "I don't think I even *like* this stuff. You must think I'm very strange."

"I don't. I do think you're very sheltered," Cinda said. "And I think perhaps your mom could use some therapy. It's not healthy to lean on your child so heavily, to make your only child your only friend. I *know* it's not healthy for the child. You're remarkably well-adjusted considering all the things you've just told me. In fact, I never would have guessed—except for maybe the clothes."

She smiled in a way that made me feel understood rather than insulted.

Cinda went on. "It sounds to me like you're well on your way to making up your own mind—even if you haven't had much practice. I bet you'll be really good at it once you get going. It's the first step toward achieving your dreams and having the life you *want*."

"That's the thing—I don't even *know* what I want," I said, embarrassed. "I've always just known what I was going to do because it was what my mom wanted."

"Well what do you like, what do you enjoy? What's your passion?"

"I'm not even sure what that means. I mean, I know what the word 'passion' means, but I don't think I've ever been 'passionate' about anything."

"What gets you excited?" Cinda asked. "What gives you butterflies when you think of it?"

A vision of Sullivan Reece's face popped into my mind, but I was pretty sure *that* wasn't what Cinda was talking about.

"I love working with the kids at the school."

Cinda nodded. "That's what I see, too. Not all teachers have it, you know? That enthusiasm and obvious joy about working with children. You're good at it—really good. I'd go so far as to say you have a gift. I think you'd be an incredible teacher and someday, an incredible mom too."

There were the butterflies. Motherhood and Sullivan Reece—those were the only two things I could ever remember triggering them. Both seemed like sheer folly to even consider.

"I don't think it's possible," I told Cinda. "My mother will oppose it with everything she's got—and she has *everything*. I may live in a mansion, but I have no money of my own except for what I earned at the preschool, and it didn't pay much. I was a part-time assistant. Besides, I've already quit my job there, and they've hired a replacement. Becoming a real teacher would mean going to college. There's no way I could afford the tuition—or the room and board. Mother will kick me out of the house and probably disown me if I go against her wishes."

"Oh, I'm sure it's not as bad as all that. If you explained to her—"

"I'm not exaggerating in the least," I assured her. "She'll absolutely do it. She's told me as much whenever I've dared to question her."

Cinda sat quietly for a few moments as a servant brought in a tray with a selection of teas and several small plates of cookies. When we'd both thanked the woman and she'd left the room again, Cinda stirred sweetener and cream into her cup of tea.

"You know... I'm sure Alex wouldn't mind if you were to move in here with us for a while until you got on your feet."

"No," I blurted. "I mean, thank you but I couldn't. You're still newlyweds. You're about to have two new babies, and you have a full household of staff already, so it's not like I would even be helping you out by being here. I could never impose on you like that."

"It wouldn't be an imposition, and I'm sure it would make AJ's whole year. In fact, we'd probably have a hard time dragging him away to Aubernesse in September if he knew he was leaving you behind."

I shook my head vigorously, battling the threat of tears. "You are so sweet. I can't even believe how nice you're being to me. But I absolutely cannot do that. I have to find my own way out of this."

Cinda actually looked disappointed, but then her face brightened. "I think I *might* have a solution for you."

"What?" I couldn't fathom any way out of my predicament, but I was eager to hear Cinda's idea.

"Well, I took AJ to the playground at Harbor Park yesterday, and Sullivan Reece was there with his daughters."

My breath caught, and my pulse rate sprang.

"He looked horrible, frankly, like he hadn't slept in a week." Cinda continued. "He told me it's been more like two weeks. He's having a hard time keeping up with the girls, and he's been having to stay up throughout the night, doing his workouts and training while they're asleep. They're running him ragged. He said he's desperate to hire a nanny but doesn't know who he can trust to watch his daughters. He's tried going through an agency, but apparently the people they've sent him so far aren't what he's looking for."

I nodded, paying rapt attention and struggling to continue breathing normally.

"I mentioned the possibility of an au pair—you know, girls who come here from another country and live in your home, take care of the kids in exchange for room and board?"

Cinda made a funny face and laughed. "He didn't like that idea—at all. He said he was concerned they'd be too young and inexperienced to deal with his two rambunctious girls. Besides, he's single, and he's afraid the press might have a heyday if they got wind of a teenage girl living in his house."

There was a pause. "What do you think?"

"About what? Do *I* think they'd be too young? Or do I think he should be leery of having a teenage girl live with him?"

It wasn't clear to me whether Cinda wanted my professional opinion on childcare qualifications or a moral judgment. I felt qualified to give neither.

"No silly." Cinda laughed. "What about *you* taking the position as the Reece girls' full-time nanny? At least while you're trying to figure out what to do next. Sully needs help immediately since the kids are out of school for the summer, and he has a title fight coming up in a few months. He needs to train for it. He didn't mention how much he'd be willing to pay, but I'm sure the salary would be generous. He said money is no object. Those little girls are the most important thing in the world to him."

"I don't know... I'd still have to find a place to live."

"No, you wouldn't. A lot of Eastport Bay families have live-in nannies. I've been in his house—it's gorgeous, and there's more than enough room. I bet you'd have your own suite."

"I've never been a nanny before."

Cinda waved her hand in a dismissive gesture.

"You're a natural fit for it, and he's already seen how you interact with them. You'd be helping those little girls in addition to Sullivan. You could work there this summer, gather a little nest egg for yourself, and then you'd really be able to make a sound decision about what to do with your life. If your mom does pull a Mrs. Havisham act and cut you off from the family fortune, you'd at least have first and last month's rent saved and maybe even tuition for your first year at community college."

She lifted her phone from the small table between our chairs. "I could give him a call right now. I know he'd be thrilled."

It all sounded so sensible. And yet, I couldn't imagine actually taking the leap, telling my mother I'd changed my mind, moving in with a family of strangers—with Sullivan Reece of all people. It would never work.

"No. Don't do that. I'm sorry. You're so kind to try to think of a solution for me, but this just isn't it. Maybe it's not as big or permanent a decision as committing to a religious vocation, but it's still... big. It's too much. I'm not the right person for the job."

Cinda's exuberant posture sagged. "Well, all right, if you're positive. I don't want to be another person coercing you into doing what they think is right for you. I've made a lot of mistakes in my life and caused myself some undue hardship and pain. And if I've learned anything, it's that someone else's dream will never be a good fit for you. I believe you *will* figure yours out though."

"Thank you. I appreciate that. And I appreciate you letting me talk through this more than you'll ever know." I stood. "I'm afraid I have to go now. I feel like I could talk to you for hours and hours."

Cinda stood as well, surprising me by embracing me in a warm hug.

"I feel the same about you. You have such a sweet heart. And I want you to keep something in mind, especially as you go back home and deal with your mom—no matter how dark and murky things may look, there's always a way through. Just trust that, and a solution will present itself. And remember I'm here if you need me."

Dark and murky were the perfect descriptors for my thoughts as I left the Wessex mansion and walked through the back yard toward the Bluff Walk.

It had been one thing when my doubts were knocking quietly at the edges of my mind. Now they'd burst to the forefront, demanding to be dealt with.

How was I ever going to talk to Mother about this? But

how could I hold my tongue and go through with the plans to enter full-time religious service when I felt so uncertain?

A high-pitched squeal pierced my troubled thoughts. A shrieking laugh followed it. The sounds were coming from the next yard over.

Sullivan Reece's yard.

As if pulled by a giant super magnet, I moved toward the happy sounds. Finding a spot in the hedge that was thinner than the rest, I drew near and peeked through it.

On the other side, the two Reece girls danced around the edge of a large swimming pool, jumping in and out of the water like a pair of penguins.

"Be careful," a deep voice warned. "I don't want you to slip."

Sullivan.

I shifted so I could see the rest of the pool. He was treading water in the deep end. In spite of the idyllic setting, he looked and sounded stressed out.

As Cinda had mentioned, dark circles underscored the airy-blue eyes. His voice was rough with exhaustion.

"Don't run!" he yelled then moderated his volume. "Please. The stone is wet. You could really hurt your heads if you fall."

As usual, his daughters did not listen to him. The smaller one darted in one direction while the older girl ran off in the other.

"No running," he pleaded.

The frazzled tone of his voice plucked at my heart. His daughters were completely adorable but so naughty, and the poor guy had no idea how to handle them.

He really *did* need help.

Thanks to my experience at the preschool, I knew exactly what to do to get the girls to listen. For a moment I was insanely tempted to squeeze through the hedge and go offer some guidance.

But of course I didn't.

For one thing, it would be bizarre to appear out of nowhere like a garden fairy on a moonlit night. Sullivan would *know* I'd been spying.

For another, he had just climbed out of the pool himself, and there was no way I could act like a normal, rational person if I were to get any closer to *that.*

He was wet and shirtless, his powerful form on full display and literally glistening in the sunlight like a golden statue atop a sports trophy.

He was the most intensely masculine being I'd ever seen in my life. He made me feel nervous and restless and elated. Unfamiliar feelings I didn't necessarily like.

I could never handle working for him, much less living under the same roof with him.

Turning away, I walked home, willing myself to forget the magnificent sight of Sullivan Reece in a pair of swim trunks—to forget about him and his daughters completely.

There was simply no place for them in my life—or in my rapidly beating heart.

SEVEN

Lock In

Angelina

Whether it was the contrast between the dark wood walls and heavy draperies to the bright summer sunshine or my mother's glowering expression and sharp voice, I felt positively suffocated for the rest of the day.

Lunch and dinner both tasted like sawdust. My room, which I'd always considered to be cozy and familiar, now seemed too small, its décor far too young for me.

My clothes, which had been serviceable and comfortable before, itched and chafed at my skin.

I felt like tearing them off and diving naked into the Atlantic, swimming as far and fast as possible until my skin—and everything contained within it—was chilled and numb.

But I couldn't seem to sink back into the numbness that had characterized my life up to this point.

I felt unstrung and alive, like the end of a powerline ripped from its anchoring pole during a storm. It was a wonder sparks didn't jump from my fingertips as I suffered through the interminable pre-dinner prayer that night.

Evidently, Mother noticed a difference in me because she remarked on it. "What's gotten into you today?"

A guilty drumbeat pounded in my ears, muting my own voice as I responded. "What do you mean?"

"You're antsy. You *said* the exercise outside would do you good, but you seem more restless now than you did before your walk. And you've hardly said two words to me since."

"I'm sorry, I'm just..."

This was it. I had to say something. If I didn't, I'd combust. Maybe I would anyway—I felt hot all over, and my palms were sweating. I wiped them on the napkin in my lap.

"I've been thinking."

Mother's expression soured. "About what?"

"Things. Life. The future."

Though Mother's expression was forbidding, I forced myself to go on.

"I think I'd like to delay my postulancy... just for a little while. I think it might be good to gain more life experience. Maybe I could take a summer job and begin my discernment in the fall instead. For instance... there's a local family that needs a nanny for the summer."

"What family?" Mother snarled, her eyes glittering and dark like a snake about to strike.

"One of our neighbors on the street. I met them at the party. They're new to town—two little girls. Their father works a lot and has to travel a good bit. It would just be for the summer."

"What about their mother? Why doesn't she take care of them?"

"I'm not sure. She doesn't live here."

"So they're divorced." Mother's tone held an *aha* note, as if she'd caught me in a lie. "I *knew* it. He wants to lure you, to ruin you for the Lord, to spoil your purity."

I bristled at the way my mother characterized Sullivan

Reece as some sort of demonic beast. She'd never even met him. She hadn't seen the way he loved and worried about his little girls.

"You're wrong. He's not like that," I said, defending him though I didn't know him well enough to know *what* his reputation with women was.

"They're *all* like that. You don't know. You're still innocent. But he'll change that. Oh, believe me... he'll ruin you."

"He doesn't even know I'm interested in the position. I heard about it through a friend. She says the money is very good."

"What do you need money for? You're going to be a holy sister. See? He's already ruining you by making you crave the material things of the world."

Mother stood in such a rush her chair fell over backward, striking the thick dining room rug with a loud thud. "I won't allow it. In fact, pack your things. I'm going to take you to the monastery in New Jersey tomorrow. I'm sure they'll be fine with you arriving early."

Now it was my turn to stand abruptly. "Tomorrow? I'm supposed to have another month before I go."

"What good will an extra month do you? You're going *now*—no talking back."

Throughout my life, that phrase would have signaled the end of all conversation. But something had broken free inside me. I couldn't have stopped now even if I wanted to.

"But it's my last chance to experience the world before I shut myself away from it."

"Experience the world? I'll *tell* you about the world."

Mother's mottled skin tone and deep inhale warned me to prepare for a rant.

"The world tells you to take risks and follow your heart then cheers as you fall in disgrace. The world turns its back on you and kicks you when you're down. The world makes promises it has no intention of keeping."

She lifted a bony arm and pointed toward the hallway. "Now go upstairs and pack."

The fury of injustice made me braver—stronger than I'd ever felt in my mother's presence before.

"What if I don't?"

Mother's hand trembled, as if she was fighting the impulse to slap me. She didn't, but her words inflicted just as much pain.

"If you don't, you can just move out—without your things. And I will no longer consider you my daughter."

I felt like I'd been kicked in the chest. It was hard to gather enough breath to respond. "You'd really throw me out of my own house? You'd disown me?"

"Don't doubt it little girl. And don't think you're going to just hang on until I die and leave you the family fortune. I'll call my lawyer tonight and have you taken out of the will. Is that what you want? Now go on upstairs and think about it."

Running up the winding staircase, I went to my tower room and flopped into the chair in front of the window. I stared out at the dark night sky, listening to the toss and roll of the ocean, filled with disbelief and a growing sense of despair.

Now that the timeline had shrunk and my future was immediately at hand, my doubts about dedicating my life to religious service were even more pronounced.

The sisters had said I should feel peace as I entered the postulant phase. All I felt at the moment was anger and betrayal and an increasing suspicion that Mother had planned my entire life not to protect me but rather in an attempt to soothe her own conscience over her wild youth and reckless life decisions.

I *hated* feeling like a pawn in someone else's game. But did I have the guts to wipe the board clean and start over?

Cinda had been kind—she might even become a good friend. But she had her own life and family. I couldn't hang everything on her advice and offer of help.

Sullivan Reece wasn't the answer either. I didn't *know* that he'd hire me to watch over his children—I hadn't even interviewed for the job for heaven's sake.

Oh, why couldn't I have just kept my mouth shut? Why had I talked back to my mother and set this whole horrible ball in motion?

Maybe there was a way to turn things around again. Yes, there had to be. I'd pack my suitcase, carry it downstairs to show Mother how cooperative I was being, and then I'd apologize.

Maybe Mother could still be convinced to cancel the driver for tomorrow morning.

A month wasn't much time, but to me each day felt precious right now. Maybe I could at least preserve that short window of time to experience a bit of the world before being confined once again to a tiny corner of it.

Kneeling to peer under the bed, I pulled out the large suitcase stored there and unzippered it.

Because I hadn't planned to leave so soon, I hadn't yet made a packing list, but at the very least, I knew I'd need underwear. I crossed the room to my dresser, opening the top drawer and lifting a stack of undergarments to transfer into the suitcase.

A loud *click* sound made me whirl around.

What?

Was that the door lock? I couldn't remember when, if ever, the door to my room had been locked.

It could be done from the inside or the outside, but only with an ancient iron key, and there had never been a need with only Mother and I living here and never any overnight guests.

Running to the door, I twisted the knob. There was a noise on the other side.

"Mother! What are you doing?"

The voice from the other side of the heavy wooden door was muffled, but the words were clear enough.

"Protecting you from yourself. I was young once, and I know what a wild hair looks like. You had that look in your eye —the one that leads to heartache. Believe me darling, I'm doing you a favor. I'm saving you."

I rattled the doorknob again, turning it back and forth in frustration as it refused to budge. "You don't have to save me. I'm doing what you asked. I'm packing. There's no need to lock me in."

"That's good sweetheart. I knew you'd come to see reason. We'll get on the road to New Jersey bright and early tomorrow. I've already called a car service. The driver will be here at eight a.m. to pick us up. Sleep well."

Sleep well? Really? After being locked in my tower room like some sort of mythical princess at the mercy of a wicked witch?

"No," I yelled.

There was no answer. I banged on the solid surface with the side of my fist. "Come back and unlock this door, Mother. I'm not a child. I'm not a *prisoner.*"

Or was I? The door would open tomorrow morning, but if I went along with my mother's plan against my own will, wouldn't I be just as trapped as I felt at this moment?

Everything inside of me rebelled at the thought.

I can't believe this is my life.

Cinda had been right. Each of us only got one life, and mine should be *mine.* I was the one who had to live it day by day after all.

Whirling away from the door, I went to the window, threw it open, and let out a scream of impotent frustration.

Not that I expected anyone to hear it. The sound was carried away harmlessly by the night wind and absorbed into the dark, rolling ocean.

Though it provided a temporary release, crying for help wasn't the answer. There *wasn't* one as far as I could see. Cinda had promised a solution would present itself, but I had run out of time.

The distant sound of pounding footfalls drew my eyes down to the Bluff Walk. A lone jogger ran in the moonlight. I couldn't see him clearly, but I could make out the shape and size of him.

It was unmistakably Sullivan Reece. Had to be—no one else looked like him.

He must have gotten a babysitter or something because he was alone, running hard, as if trying to dispel an entire week's worth of frustration and energy.

I could relate.

Sinking into my chair again, I turned off the lamp in my room so I couldn't be seen from outside. I folded my arms on the windowsill and rested my chin on the flattened knuckles of one hand, waiting for him to reach the end of the path, turn around, and come back again.

And as I watched him pass by then disappear into the darkness toward his own house down the path, I realized a solution *had* presented itself already.

All I had to do was reach out and take it.

* * *

When the bedroom door opened the next morning, I was awake, dressed, and sitting on the edge of my neatly made bed.

Mother peeked inside, her expression reticent until she spotted me ready and waiting to go. Opening the door fully, she actually smiled.

"Good morning. Are you ready?"

I stood and lifted my suitcase and toiletries bag. "I am."

The two of us went downstairs where I discovered Mother had breakfast ready and waiting on the table.

I glanced at her in surprise. "You cooked."

"Yes. I'll have to get used to doing it for myself again, and I wanted to give you a nice sendoff."

Mother looked younger and healthier than I'd seen her in years. There was a glow about her, an energy that almost made her seem like a different person.

"I'm so proud of you, Angelina," she said as we ate. "I'm sorry about last night. You're a good daughter. I know you're going to be happy in your chosen life."

The life you *chose for me.*

Aloud I said, "I hope so."

When the driver rang the doorbell forty minutes later, Mother and I walked out to the crushed shell driveway. Beyond it, Oceanview Avenue was quieter than usual, much less busy than it would be later today when the summer tourists descended, filling the roadway as well as the sidewalks that lined each side of it.

A black sedan waited in the drive. The driver opened a back door and held it as Mother climbed inside. I walked around the open trunk to the other side of the car, my heart pounding so hard I worried it might actually be audible in the quiet of the early morning.

After closing the door on my mother's side, the driver, whose name tag identified him as Michael, opened my door and reached for my bags.

But when he grasped the handle of my suitcase, I didn't let it go.

On the sidewalk just outside the estate grounds, a young family walked by hand-in-hand, loudly singing the theme song to "Sesame Street" together. The song seemed to be coming from very far away as the sound of my own breathing and pounding pulse filled my ears.

The driver laughed uncomfortably. "I'll get that for you ma'am."

My fingers loosened, and he took the heavy bag, swinging it up and placing it into the trunk.

Leaning around it to see me, he asked, "You want to keep that smaller one with you in the backseat?"

I didn't answer. I couldn't. All I seemed to be able to do was stand frozen in place beside the open back door of the car, staring at my black flats and clenching the handle of my overnight bag with one hand and the strap of my purse with the other.

"Ma'am?" the driver asked, sounding concerned. "Everything okay? Did you forget something?"

Inside the back seat, Mother leaned down so her face was visible. "Angelina? What's going on? Get in the car, darling."

My eyes met hers, which were filling with alarm as the seconds ticked by. "I can't," I said in a strangled whisper. A little louder, I said, "I'm sorry. I just can't."

"You're turning your back on your promise to me? Your promise to *God*?"

"No. I can still become a nun. I'll just go to the monastery at the end of the summer—when I'm ready."

"You're ready now," Mother insisted.

I didn't respond, knowing nothing I said would convince my mother. Instead, I turned and walked away toward the estate's tall iron gates.

Behind me, the sounds of a car door opening and closing preceded a shriek. "If you leave now, don't bother coming back."

When I didn't stop or even turn around, Mother turned up the volume and intensity of her vitriol. "How can you do this to me after all I've done for you? You're not my daughter anymore. I don't even know you anymore. You are no longer welcome in this place."

Tears streaming down my cheeks, I kept walking. When I'd passed through the gates to the sidewalk beyond them, I turned right and proceeded, nearly blind, to the entrance of the Wessex estate next door.

The guard at the entrance asked my name, relayed it to someone inside the house, and then let me pass.

Before I'd even reached the front door, Cinda stepped out, first walking toward me then increasing her pace to a run.

"Oh my goodness—honey, are you okay? What happened?"

She looked me over, taking in the tear-stained cheeks, stricken expression, and the small overnight bag at my side.

"Oh wow. I guess you did it, huh?"

I nodded, swallowing back a sob. "I did it."

My tone indicated I could hardly believe it myself. "Do you think Mr. Reece would still be interested in hiring me?"

EIGHT

Iron Will

Sully

I had never been so happy to hear a doorbell in my life.

When Cinda Wessex had told me the preschool teacher, Angelina Rappaport, was available and interested in taking the nanny opening, I couldn't believe my luck.

She was exactly the kind of person I'd been looking for. Capable, mature, experienced with children, and from what I'd seen, quite possibly a miracle-worker as well.

It might *take* a miracle to bring my two adorable little hellions under control.

From what I'd seen at the party, Angelina had a better shot at succeeding than anyone. And Cinda said Angelina needed a job and a place to live for the summer. This was going to work out perfectly.

My optimism died the second I opened the door.

There she stood, a small overnight bag in one hand, her light brown eyes round as saucers. She looked like she might be hyperventilating.

My breathing was no better, but my struggle wasn't due to nerves.

No, it was the sight of Angelina that robbed me of the necessary air to inflate my well-conditioned lungs and made me question my sanity for agreeing to hire her.

I'd remembered very well from that day at the party what a pretty girl she was. "Pretty" didn't cover it today. She was stunning. She wore a pair of cream-colored pants with heels and a sleeveless black and cream top.

Her cheeks were pink with either embarrassment or excitement, and her hair was pulled back in a thick ponytail like it had been the first time I saw her.

It was longer even than I'd realized—really, really long, falling down her back all the way to her hips. Its color was like spun gold, threads of it catching the sunshine and shimmering as she moved.

She looked almost otherworldly, angelic. Untouchable.

"Hi. I'm Angelina Rappaport. We met at the party? Cinda said you'd be expecting me."

Oh. Right. I hadn't invited her in yet, just stood staring stupidly at her waiting on my doorstep.

Snap the fuck out of it man.

"Yes. Of course. Please come in."

Forcing a little cough to clear the gravel from my throat, I stepped back and gestured her forward. I shut the door when she was fully inside.

"Of course I remember you. You were amazing with all the kids. Thanks so much for coming. I'm so glad you wanted the job. When you told me you were leaving the preschool, I thought you had another offer."

She looked away toward the right then down at her foot then back at me with a shy smile. "I had a change of plans. I'm grateful for this chance."

I inhaled, feeling shaky. Her voice was soft, a bit breathy, and it seemed to reach inside my chest like a wisp of smoke, curling down and around my spinal column and causing a shiver.

This might have been a mistake. I forced myself to smile and behave normally, but inside I felt stricken. I wasn't sure I'd be able to handle having this celestial being living in my house.

Angelina was *too* beautiful—at least as far as my own personal brand of beautiful went. Everything about her appealed to me in a major way.

Yes, I desperately needed a nanny, and yes, she was by far the best candidate for the job, but was it smart to hire a woman I had such an instantaneous, lightning-bolt attraction to?

"Is that all the luggage you brought?" I asked. "Or is someone delivering it later?"

She swallowed hard, and the pink cheeks darkened a shade. "This is all I have. I had to leave home... r-rather quickly. Cinda let me borrow the clothes I'm wearing now. I'll have to go shopping for some more things when I get a chance."

"I see." But I didn't.

Cinda had said Angelina lived right down the street. She was a rich girl from an old money Eastport Bay family. How could she have nothing but the clothes on her back?

It troubled me. Maybe this job for her was more than just something to keep her busy over the summer. Maybe she *needed* it.

Suddenly curiosity was eating me alive.

Skyla and Claire ran into the foyer, dark curls flying as they bounded across the shiny floor in their sock feet—something I'd warned them against repeatedly—and skidded to a stop right in front of Angelina.

"Are you going to live here and take care of us?" Skyla asked, her voice echoing off the walls and high ceiling.

She didn't sound exactly thrilled at the prospect. Claire as well had her little arms folded across her chest and surveyed Angelina with suspicion but also a healthy dose of wonder.

Angelina sat on the floor so she was at eye level with the girls. "I'd like to. But only if it's okay with you. And only on a trial basis. We have to make sure we all like living together, and that you two like the breakfasts and lunches and dinners I'm going to cook for you, and going to the zoo and the children's museum in Providence and the other places I'm going to take you, and that you like all the art projects I have planned and the games I've thought of to play with you."

"We like games," Claire enthused, clearly won over already. "And the zoo!"

Skyla tapped her small chin, gazing up at the chandelier and dramatizing deep thought. "I did like the treasure hunt you made up at AJ's party."

"Speaking of that," Angelina said, "we're also going to have lots of playdates—with AJ and with some of the other kids I know who also have nannies watching them for the summer."

"Do you know a lot of kids?" asked Skyla, warming to the prospect. She loved her little sister, but I knew she'd been longing for some children her own age to play with as well.

"I do. I've been a teacher for the past few years, and I know lots and lots of kids—many of them live on this street or very close by. A lot of them like to go to a certain beach nearby in the summer, and we can go there too. Do you like the beach?"

As my daughters chatted happily with her, I was amazed at how easy it was for Angelina to engage them, and how she knew the exact topics girls their age would like to talk about.

She was still down on their level, seeming oblivious to the cold hardness of the marble floor, focused only on the bright, interested faces of my little girls. My heart swelled at their clear fascination with her.

At one point, Claire reached out and stroked a long lock of hair that had fallen over Angelina's shoulder.

"You're pretty," she said.

Angelina smiled. "Thank you. I think you're pretty, too. Both of you. I love your curls. We'll have to play beauty shop one day soon and find all kinds of ways to put your hair up with ribbons and jewels and things."

Claire clapped in excitement, but Skyla scowled. "I don't like having my hair brushed. It hurts."

I felt a twinge of shame. I'd never known how to manage my daughters' natural curls, though I'd tried.

They'd come from my side for sure—my Irish mother and my father, whoever he might have been.

Their mother Anouk's hair was as dark as theirs but shiny and board-straight like everyone's on both sides of her family tree. She'd declared their hair "impossible" and basically stopped trying, pulling it back into ponytails whenever they were with her.

"Oh, I would never brush your hair," Angelina assured the girl. "Beautiful curls like yours need to be handled differently. But it just so happens I've had several little curly-heads in my classrooms."

She reached out and gently tugged one long coil of Claire's hair, causing it to spring back into place. "And I know *all* the secrets to fixing curly hair without any pain at all."

"Yay," Skyla said and did a little spin move, which Claire copied.

That was when I knew without a doubt, I'd done the right thing. The woman sitting cross-legged on my entry hall floor not only looked like an angel, she was as gentle and patient as one. I could tell my daughters were already falling in love with her.

The trick would be avoiding it myself.

I shook off the surprising thought the way I shook off a

jarring hard left hook. I would *not* screw this up. I'd keep my dealings with my new nanny friendly and polite and above all, professional.

Inside the boxing world, I was famous for my discipline and self-control. You didn't get to my level of the sport without an iron will. And I would do anything for my girls.

Their needs were far more important than my own feelings and desires.

Yep, this was all going to work out perfectly.

NINE
Family Fun Day

Angelina-- One month later

Sunlight streamed into the kitchen, bathing the room in warm, yellow light as I prepared breakfast.

Classical music played at a low volume through the surround speaker system. Not only was it my personal favorite, I'd read that listening to symphony music was a great way for children to start the day, soothing their emotions and preparing their minds for optimal learning.

Sullivan and his daughters sat nearby at the round table in the breakfast nook where they chatted happily together. I smiled over at them, touched and amused by their sweet conversation.

"Daddy, did you know that when I close my eyes sometimes I see things?" Claire said. "At night when I'm sleeping, I watch TV."

"You were dreaming. What did you see on your dream TV last night Claire-bear?" Sullivan asked.

"I saw a bagel dog."

Big sister Skyla rolled her eyes. "It's called a *Beagle* dog."

"Not the one I saw," Claire insisted. "Mine was a bagel dog. And he had a drowsy mouth."

From the stove where I stirred eggs in a skillet, I explained for their father's sake. "We went on a long walk yesterday, and we saw a Bassett Hound. He was very friendly, and the girls got to pet him."

"We had a *really* big walk, Daddy," Skyla said. "My feet were so tired, and they both got tired at the same time."

Sullivan chuckled, then his gaze turned to me, inviting me to share in his appreciation of the cuteness. When our eyes met, his rugged face broke out in the biggest smile, as if to say, *isn't this great*?

And it was. The conversation, the laughter, the smell of good food, and the coziness of the kitchen. It all felt so... family-ish—like nothing I'd ever experienced before.

Unexpected tears sprang to my eyes as I returned Sullivan's smile.

"You have duck balls, Daddy," Claire exclaimed. She reached over and rubbed his forearm with her tiny hand.

He turned to her with a perplexed expression. "What did you say? I have *duck balls*?"

"I mean goosebumps," she clarified. "Sometimes I have ideas, but I can't find my ideas."

"Oh. Right." He chuckled again.

Familiar now with where everything was, I grabbed a plate from an upper cabinet and slid an enormous six-egg omelet onto it from the skillet then carried it to the table.

The girls were eating "fruity-nutty" oatmeal as they'd named their favorite new breakfast concoction. Sullivan had already finished his second bowl of the stuff.

He smiled in anticipation as I set the heaping plate of protein in front of him so his daily monster breakfast could continue.

The man ate more than I would have thought humanly

possible—and he never gained a pound, unless perhaps it was all converted to muscle.

"You don't have to cook for me, you know," he said, digging into the food. "But I can't lie—I'm glad you do."

"I've told you… it's no trouble. I'm already making an egg for myself every morning."

"One egg." He chuckled. "I don't know how you manage to stay alive on so little food."

"I don't know how *your* cholesterol isn't through the roof."

"My doctor says I'm as healthy as a horse." Then to amuse his girls, he made a comical neighing sound.

They laughed, of course.

"Daddy… you sound like a donkey," Skyla said.

"Yes, a *silly* donkey," Claire added with a giggle. Sullivan reached over and tweaked her nose, pretending to remove it and showing her the tip of his thumb poking through the fingers of his fist.

She swiped at it, pretending to take her nose back and put it on again.

"Seriously, though…" Sullivan's tone changed, becoming more earnest as he returned his attention to me. "I'm not sure how we got so lucky."

My cheeks grew warm. "It's only eggs."

Stepping back to the kitchen counter, I picked up my own plate and carried it to the table, busying myself with the salt and pepper shakers as I felt him staring at me.

No one had ever looked at me the way Sullivan Reece did. His gaze held appreciation, appraisal, and I could swear at times… interest. The guy and girl kind.

At least I *thought* so. I couldn't be sure—I had no experience in that area. But there was definitely… something. And it made me all kinds of nervous.

Risking a glance up at him, I experienced a little tingly

shock when I found him still watching me. A brew of heat and delight bubbled up inside me, and I dropped my gaze back to my plate.

"Why do you wear the same three or four outfits all the time?" he asked.

"What?"

That was unexpected. I tried not to be insulted. There was no trace of meanness in his tone, just genuine curiosity.

"Are you afraid you'll mess them up with, like the art projects and stuff—or cooking?"

"No."

Sullivan held up his hands in a defensive gesture. "I mean, no offense, you look great. It's just, well, you said you were going shopping. The girls came home with bags of stuff they picked out. Are you saving your new clothes for a special occasion or something?"

Looking down at my outfit, I tried to come up with an answer that would satisfy him without embarrassing myself too deeply.

"I only bought a few things. I didn't think it really mattered what I wore. I don't need much anyway."

The truth was, when we'd gone shopping, I hadn't gotten my first paycheck yet. All I'd had to my name was a few hundred dollars I'd kept stashed in my room after cashing my final paycheck from the preschool.

Besides, if I was going into postulancy at the end of the summer, it would be foolish to spend a lot of money on clothing I'd never wear again.

My mind still wasn't made up concerning my future plans. In the case I *didn't* move into the monastery, I would need a place to live and tuition money for college, so either way, it made sense to be minimalistic when it came to possessions.

I didn't expect Sullivan to understand. His lifestyle and taste were extravagant to say the least. His favorite saying was, "if some is good, more is better," and it showed in everything from the contents of the fully stocked oversized refrigerator, to the home décor, to the toys in his daughters' rooms and playroom.

Their closets, too, were brimming with the largest collection of children's clothing I had ever seen.

It was like Sullivan had gone through a catalog, trying to decide what to order and had given up and purchased one of everything in each of their sizes. In fact, he probably had.

It was obvious he enjoyed owning nice things and *lots* of them, and he enjoyed buying things for his daughters, encouraging me to take them shopping whenever they wanted to go.

He was, in a word, a spoiler. It was kind of sweet, really.

He didn't look very sweet at the moment. His prominent forehead was creased with frown lines, and the corners of his usually smiling mouth were pinched.

Apparently, my answer had *not* pleased him.

"I gave you a credit card. I expected you to use it."

Why was he so perturbed? "I did. I used it to buy the things Skyla and Claire wanted."

"I meant for you to get some stuff for yourself too," he said as if it was the most obvious thing in the world. "You shouldn't have to wear the same things all the time. I want you to go shopping again and this time get some clothes for yourself—good clothes—things you really like. And *this time*, put it on my card."

"You don't need to buy me clothes," I protested. "If you don't like what I've been wearing, I'll go get a few new things on my own, and—"

Sully's fork clanked against his plate as he dropped it in order to gesture with his hands.

"It's not that I don't like what you're wearing. I just want you to have everything you need. I want you to be happy here.

You do so much for all of us. I want you to feel like you're being well-treated."

I blinked in surprise. "I do. Of course I do. You bought me a phone. You gave me room and board, and you pay me very well."

"But you don't *spend* anything."

"Well... I'm not used to spending a lot on myself. And I'm saving my money."

"For what?"

"For when the summer ends," I said quietly.

The frown lines deepened. "What *are* your plans by the way? You've never said."

My breath caught. I hadn't mentioned the monastery to him. Apart from discussing the girls, our conversations had been limited to the topics of his career and travels.

As far as my own life, I hadn't spoken much about it—mostly because there was so little to tell but also because I didn't want to *think* about it.

I was enjoying my reprieve even more than I'd expected to. Thinking about what came next made me anxious.

Thinking about how my mother was getting along without me made me feel guilty.

Even when Sully had specifically asked about my personal life, I had turned the focus to stories about my work with the kids at the preschool, leaving out my strange upbringing and my mother's grand plan.

All I'd told him about my family was that I had precious little of it and that my mother was extremely religious and overprotective. He knew we'd had a falling out over me taking the job, but I hadn't gone into detail.

"I'm... not entirely sure," I said in answer to his question. "Most likely I'll move to New Jersey."

He blinked in surprise. "New Jersey? What's there?"

"The St. Wallaburga Monastery. It's a community of Benedictine Sisters."

For a moment, Sully's expression went blank. Then his eyebrows shot up practically to his hairline. "You mean like nuns?"

"Yes."

"Why would you go *there*?" He seemed truly baffled.

"To join them."

"What's nuns?" asked Skyla, who'd stopped eating and tuned into our conversation.

Her father answered. "Nuns are ladies who don't get married and spend their lives praying and going to church and stuff."

I would have laughed at the over-simplified explanation if I hadn't been on the verge of cardiac arrest. Discussing this topic with Sully had *not* been on the breakfast menu this morning.

Now Skyla turned her inquisitive gaze on me. "Don't you want to get married and have babies?"

Yes. My brain practically shouted the word, shocking me to my core. Aloud I said, "I'm not sure. I haven't made up my mind yet."

"I think you should have babies," Claire said. "You would be a nice mommy."

A large hand reached into my chest and squished my heart. Blinking back tears, I reached over and stroked the little girl's hair. "Thank you, sweetheart. That's a very kind thing to say."

Sully looked like a 100-watt lightbulb had switched on in his brain. "So that's why your mom kicked you out. And why you won't buy any nice clothes for yourself."

Casting a meaningful glance toward the girls, I used a measured tone to answer him. "I don't really feel like talking about this anymore. What are your plans for the day?"

Sully didn't answer. He just stared at me, his jaw shifting

slowly from side to side as if he were using all his concentration to work out a challenging puzzle.

"Daddy," Claire interrupted the silence, climbing onto her father's lap. "Daddy, Daddy, Daddy." She put her tiny hands on either side of his jaw and turned his face to hers.

"Yes, Claire-bear?" he said, wrapped thoroughly around his youngest daughter's little finger.

"Can you play with us today?"

"Oh, baby, I'd love to. But you know Daddy has to train. And Angelina is here to play with you."

"But you train *every* day," the child whined. "You can come and do stuff *with* Angelina and Skyla and me—all of us. Just for one day? Pleeeeeeeease?"

Sullivan's expression went through a succession of emotions from longing to regret to ultimately defeat.

I knew he was worried about not being ready for his upcoming fight. He'd been training long hours seven days a week since I'd moved in and started working for his family. But it was clear his youngest daughter's plea for his company would win the internal battle.

Finally, he said, "Okay. Just for one day. What do you girls want to do?"

Both Skyla and Claire answered at once.

"Get ice cream!"

"Swim!"

I laughed, relieved at the change in topic and tickled to see them so excited at the prospect of spending a whole day with their father instead of only seeing him at breakfast and dinner and for a few minutes at bedtime.

"That sounds good, but don't forget you two have your Maker Club at the Children's Museum at eleven," I reminded the girls. "Today it's balloon-powered rockets."

"Oh yeah!" Skyla said.

"Yay! Rockets," said Claire. "Can we still get ice cream?"

"And swim?" asked Skyla.

Sullivan answered. "Sure. We can do it all. We'll go get ice cream after your rocket class. Then we'll come home and swim. Okay, go get dressed so we can start our family fun day."

The term gave me a warm feeling inside as well as a pang of concern that perhaps I would be out of place on this outing.

As the girls scooted back from the table and darted away, I called after them, "I put out two choices of clothes for each of you on your beds. Pick the one you like best, put it on—*with* shoes—and be back down here in ten minutes please."

Sullivan shook his head at me, his eyes sparkling. "I still don't know how you did it. It used to take me *hours* to get them dressed."

"I didn't do all that much, really," I said. "Everyone likes having choices, but little kids can be overwhelmed by too much choice. They do better with just a few options. It's a lot easier to pick between option A and option B than it is to follow a vague request to pick 'something' from a closet full of a hundred things."

"Well, I still say you're brilliant."

He dipped his chin and looked at me from beneath his raised brows. "You were *born* to raise kids."

There was another pang—not of concern but of something else, something like hunger but emotional instead of physical. I was getting them more often lately.

Seeing Sullivan with his daughters, the way he treasured them, the way he thought every little thing they did was adorable, simply melted me.

And then there was the way I felt in his presence *after* the girls went to bed.

In spite of my best efforts to control it, I'd begun to look forward to those moments when it was just the two of us, discussing how his training had gone during the day, what the girls had seen and learned and enjoyed, laughing over something cute one of them had said.

It was in these moments of innocent, casual conversation that I was getting to know him, to learn bits and pieces of his past and about his life in the present.

It was in these moments I was growing to like him.

No, I should definitely *not* go along today.

"Um... Sullivan..."

"When are you gonna start calling me Sully?" he asked, interrupting. "All my friends call me Sully."

"But we're not friends. You're my employer."

"Can't I be both?"

"I guess so." I hesitated. "Sully... wouldn't you like for it to be just the three of you today? I can stay home and do some cleaning while you take them to the children's museum and out for ice cream."

He gave me an *Are you crazy?* look. "What? Hell no."

Realizing he'd cursed—which I never did—he mumbled a quick "Sorry," then went on. "The girls will want you there. *I* want you there. It wouldn't be family fun day without you. And cleaning is definitely *not* part of your job."

"I don't mind."

"I *do*. Let Cinda's employees earn their money. I'm paying you to spend time with the girls, not be a maid. All right, well, I'm gonna go up and change too. Do I get a prize if I'm back in ten minutes?"

He gave me a wicked grin, those blue eyes twinkling.

You get whatever you want.

I banished the dangerous, unexpected thought. "I'll put a gold star on your chart," I said in a light, carefree tone then fled to the pantry to pack snacks for our outing.

TEN

Pretty Woman

Angelina

The balloon inventions class was a huge hit. Afterward we had snacks and juice in the museum's garden before heading for the car to continue our adventure.

On the way to the parking lot, Sully stepped off the sidewalk and plucked a few of the tiny purple flowers growing wild in the lawn.

He presented one to each of his daughters. "Girls, these are called Toadflax.'"

"Toadflax?" Skyla repeated then giggled with her sister.

Then Sully turned to me. With a shy smile, he handed me a delicate bloom.

Something in his eyes struck me, and I experienced a flash of intuition—had he been looking for an excuse to give me flowers? Was that why he'd stopped for the impromptu botany lesson for the girls?

"How did you know what this was called," I asked.

He shrugged and looked away, training his eyes on the girls though the parking lot wasn't busy.

"Wildflowers were the only kind of flowers that ever grew

in our yard. I used to look them up online to see what they were."

"It's very pretty," I said. "I love wildflowers, too."

His gaze slid to me again, the corners of his mouth tipping upward.

That mouth. I thought about it *far* too often, noticing the soft-looking lips and contemplating their varied expressions whenever we were together—and even when we weren't. Sometimes, like right now for instance, I even thought about what it might be like to feel them on mine, to taste them, to—*no*. This time I was the one to look away because my cheeks and neck and chest were blazing hot and no doubt fire-red.

Thankfully the ice cream shop was our next stop.

True to form, Sully bought the girls sundaes far too large for them to eat and ordered a double cone for me in spite of my insistence I only wanted a small single scoop. After a valiant but futile protest, I laughed and ate every bite.

How was I supposed to return to a normal existence at the end of the summer—or begin an even *more* austere one at the monastery?

It shocked me how quickly I'd grown accustomed to Sully's world of excess and indulgence.

Having never lived with anyone other than Mother, the bright, energetic, opulent Reece household had been a shock at first. It was so different from the dark, solemn, puritanical home where I'd grown up.

Life now was so busy, so… full. The past couple of months had been like a whirlwind as the girls and I traveled all over the small state and up to Boston, too, exploring and learning, taking in everything the beautiful New England summer had to offer.

We met other kids with their nannies at the beach, went on nature walks, and paid regular visits to the town's resident lovebirds, Romeo and Juliet the swans, at the Harbor Park pond.

I had honestly never had a better time in my life. It was strange to think it would all end in a few weeks.

Perhaps it had been a horrible mistake to take the job and expose myself to all of this.

Now I'd know what I was missing.

But then, that was the point of this, wasn't it? To *change* my life, explore new paths, try new things, and find out what I liked and what I really wanted.

Mistake or not, I was here now. I might as well embrace all the opportunities and freedom this temporary new life had to offer.

Might as well enjoy the ride—and the ice cream.

When we arrived back in Eastport Bay, instead of driving straight to the mansion, Sully parked the Bentley Bentayga SUV in a parallel spot near one of the town's swankiest shopping areas.

"What are we doing?" I asked.

"We want to go swimming," Skyla reminded him.

"We'll go swimming in just a little while," Sully told his daughter as he adjusted the rearview mirror to see her. "But first we're going to do a little shopping."

Something in his tone sparked my suspicion. "For what?"

"I need a gift for my mother, and I heard these shops have really nice stuff."

"You could drop me and the girls off at home first," I suggested. "I'll be happy to watch them in the pool until you get back."

Sully turned off the car and opened his door. "No. I need your opinion. I'm no good at picking out women's clothes. Come on girls. I'll buy you something too."

That was all it took to send Skyla and Claire scrambling from their seats to comply.

As Sully and I walked together on the aged brick sidewalk, the girls skipped a bit ahead of us, stopping to press their noses against the glass windows of the shops that interested them.

They oohed and ahhed over the Cake Gallery, peeked into a divine-smelling soap shop called Beauty and the Bath, and barely glanced at Grooves on Main, a retro record store that actually looked really interesting to me.

The front window of Bonny Books, which was owned by Cinda's friend Bonnie Bestia, featured a fun beach-themed display and had the girls begging to go inside.

"We will—after we get Nana's gift. I promise. I'll buy you all the books you want."

"Yay," Skyla cheered and pulled Claire along with her to the next store window.

"You really do spoil them, you know," I said quietly.

"You say that like it's a bad thing," he teased.

I laughed at his lack of repentance. "Well, it's not generally considered to be a *good* thing."

Sully was quiet for a long moment before responding. "I just want them to be happy. I want their childhood to be the exact opposite of mine, with plenty of everything, no worries, no fears—only good things."

It was the first time he'd mentioned anything negative about his past. I wondered what had caused him worry and fear as a child—and why he hadn't had all he needed.

My heart surged toward him, or rather toward that long-ago little boy.

That was all it was—empathy for whatever had made his childhood the opposite of happy and secure. I had the most powerful urge to reach for his hand, to offer comfort and understanding, but I resisted.

"Did you grow up without much money?" I asked casually.

He huffed a laugh that was devoid of humor. "That's an

understatement. We were dirt poor. We lived in a series of run-down month-to-month rentals, each one worse than the last. I swear if I never see another rat again it'll be too soon."

He shook his head as if trying to dislodge a particularly sticky bad memory.

"Your parents didn't work?" I asked, trying to understand the source of the abject poverty that had made his early life so difficult.

"It was just me and my mom. There were some substance abuse issues. Her own home life wasn't so hot when she was young. She had me when she was in high school and dropped out. She did odd jobs here and there, and she had boyfriends who'd give her money from time to time."

"Where was your dad?"

"Who knows? I never even knew who he was."

I nodded, unable to relate to his experience of living in poverty and squalor but completely understanding the experience of growing up missing a father you'd never met.

"I never knew my dad either," I confessed. "All Mother would say was that he was in her life until he found out she was pregnant with me. Then he was gone. She wouldn't even speak his name."

Sully turned to look at me, his blue eyes intense with compassion. "I'm sorry. I know that was hard. I guess we're both kind of experts on damaged moms and absentee dads."

An electric thread of connection hummed between us as we walked the next few steps in silence. I wondered if Sully felt it too.

If he did, he gave no indication. His eyes were on his daughters, making sure they were not getting too far ahead. Making sure they were safe. Being that protector he never had.

"You don't have to buy them things to make them happy, you know," I finally said. "After being with them day in and day out, I can tell you what gives them the most joy is being with *you*. They crave your time and attention."

So do I.

God help me, it was true. It shouldn't be, but I couldn't seem to prevent the spike in my pulse rate every evening when Sully came up from his basement gym, drenched with sweat and declaring himself "disgusting" before he trotted upstairs to shower.

I couldn't stop myself from looking forward to the nights when the four of us would gather in front of the giant TV to eat popcorn and watch family-friendly movies or the times we'd play Candyland and Connect Four, sitting on the floor around the wide, low coffee table, laughing as the girls "defeated" Daddy round after round.

Today's mutual revelations weren't going to help matters. At all.

"Well, that's nice," Sully said, sounding not quite convinced. "But I figure, what's all this money for if not to spend it on the people I love, right?"

I nodded, unable to find fault with his reasoning. After all, there were worse things than a man who was *too* generous.

"True. Hopefully we can find something your mother will love."

He nodded noncommittally. When we reached a particularly posh-looking boutique called Saltwater Style, he opened the door for me and his daughters.

"Will you two behave yourselves in the store? I'll take you to the toy shop next if you're real good."

As usual, Sully sounded like he was pleading with them, giving them all the power—giving them a choice. I had found in situations that required compliance, that wasn't the best technique.

It still amazed me a man as large and powerful as Sullivan Reece could be so easily cowed by two small girls.

Without answering him, the children ran into the store as Skyla shouted, "I want that."

Sully threw up his hands in frustration, and I decided to demonstrate for him a more effective approach.

"Skyla. Claire," I said in a low but authoritative voice. The girls stopped and looked back at me. "Come here please."

Gathering them close, I looked them directly in the eye. "You have shown me lately what mature, well-behaved young ladies you're growing into. I've been very impressed. Now, I'd like to see excellent behavior from you while we're in the store today—calm, quiet, and keeping your hands to yourself—and I'm sure your daddy and the shop ladies will be very impressed as well at how grown up you are."

The girls nodded and turned to walk slowly back into the shop, each holding her hands clasped together in front of her.

Sully gave me a look that expressed wonder and maybe even a little awe. "What would I do without you?"

Pleasure rushed through me, mixed with a degree of discomfort. I didn't know what to say. Because lately I'd started asking myself the same question. What was I going to do when I had to do without *him*?

Luckily, we were interrupted when a classy blonde woman approached us. She was impeccably dressed and looked like she *belonged* in a place like this—unlike me.

"Hi, I'm Chelle. Welcome to my shop. Looking for anything in particular?"

Sully answered. "I'm not quite sure what we're looking for yet, but she's gonna pick out some stuff she likes and try it on."

My head whipped around to face him. "What? Me?"

"I told you I need your opinion. I don't know what to get. I want you to pick out whatever you like. I'm sure... Mom will like it too. And you're about the same size, so if you wouldn't mind trying them on, I'd appreciate it. You'd really be doing me a favor."

I studied his face. His expression was straightforward, and his tone was so sweet, so filled with hope.

Also, after the things he'd just confessed, my heart was feeling rather soft toward him. He could have asked me to stand on my head in the middle of Brady's Wharf, and I'd probably have done it.

"Okay. What should I look for? What's her style?"

"I don't think she really has one," he said. "Just whatever you think looks good. Don't look at the price tags."

I walked through the store, having difficulty at first. As I'd explained to Sully earlier, it wasn't easy to make a decision with so many options.

Obviously, I wasn't a small child, but I wasn't used to shopping with an unlimited budget—or at all, really.

My mother hadn't encouraged me to wear pretty things, teaching me that clothes were meant to cover the body for decency and warmth, not to impress people or attract attention. And Mother had done *all* the shopping.

Sully's gravelly low voice came from over my shoulder, countering the inner one that told me I had no idea what I was doing. "Pick a bunch of things and try them. Whatever catches your eye. You can't make a mistake—just go with your gut reaction. I'll make the final choices."

I began moving faster, relaxing a bit and trying not to think too hard about it, reaching for the colors and patterns that attracted me and pulling them from the racks before I could question myself.

Chelle periodically took items from me and carried them to a changing room. Finally, having made my way around the whole shop, I followed her toward the changing area with the last batch of garments.

"I'm going to take the girls next door to the toy shop while you try those things on, okay?" Sully said. "No hurry. Take your time. Hang on to the things that fit and look good on you, and I'll take a look at them when we get back."

When I got to my dressing room, I was surprised at the number of items hanging on the hooks inside.

"Wow. This is going to take a while."

Chelle grinned at me, her eyes sparkling. "I added a few things I thought would suit you."

"Oh, these aren't for me," I corrected her wrong assumption.

"Have fun. Call me if you need any help."

She pulled the curtain closed, and I got started. I'd promised Sully to help him with this, and I was determined to do a good job at it. I tried on every item.

Some of them were *really* cute, fitting me like they were made just for me and making me wish they weren't destined for another woman's closet. Hopefully Sully's mom would be thrilled to own one of them. I certainly would be.

Admiring the fit of one particularly cute pair of cropped pants, I checked the price tag. If my eyeballs hadn't been securely attached, they would have popped out of my head.

Five *hundred* dollars? For a pair of pants? I stripped them off and hurriedly tried on the other items, trying not to look too long at any one of them.

When I was about to take off the last one, I heard Chelle's friendly voice outside the changing room door.

"Mr. Reece is back, and he's asking to see whatever you have on at the moment."

I looked at myself in the mirror, at the wrap dress I wore.

The color was so bold—a dramatic red—I wasn't sure what I'd been thinking picking it up. In all likelihood, it wasn't something Sully's mother would even wear.

It was a "notice me" dress—the exact opposite of what *my* mother would have approved of—with fanciful ruffles drawing the eye to a neckline that wasn't exactly plunging but definitely emphasized the attributes of a feminine figure.

The thought of Sully seeing me in it caused a swarm of combat butterflies to ambush my stomach.

"I... was just about to change back into my clothes," I called through the door.

"Do you want me to tell him that? He seemed pretty insistent."

As Chelle waited for my answer, I considered hastily changing into another, more modest outfit.

Beware the evils of men.

The much-repeated mantra, spoken in my mother's hate-filled voice, rang through my brain like a jarring alarm clock shattering a beautiful dream.

But Sully's not evil. He was nice.

He was good to his daughters—and to me. He was even kind and generous to strangers. Based on the outgoing mail I'd seen on the counter, he made frequent donations to charities around the country.

And he'd admitted (unlike so many other people) that he *didn't* know everything, that he needed help. My help.

Besides, was it *really* such a terrible thing to be noticed?

Straightening my shoulders, I turned and opened the fitting room door. The boutique owner gave me a wink and a thumbs up as I walked past her and onto the shop floor.

Sully was facing the other way, speaking to his daughters and pointing at something out the window.

I cleared my throat, which seemed to be inhabited by a large boulder all of a sudden.

Sully turned around. When his eyes landed on me, his strong jaw literally dropped, going slack as his eyes widened involuntarily.

"You..." He stopped, swallowed, started again. "That, uh... looks great. Nice... choice."

Looking down at myself, I let out a nervous giggle and smoothed the already-smooth fabric over my hips and thighs. "Do you think your mom would like it?"

He chuckled. "I don't know about her, but I sure do."

The girls had joined him. "You look so pretty, Angelina," Skyla said, her eyes alight with appreciation. "Like my Holiday Barbie."

Claire ran forward, wrapping her arms around my legs and rubbing her little face against the exquisite fabric. "I *love* this dress. I love you so fancy like this."

I smiled at the little girl's misunderstanding, stroking her hair. "It's not for me. It's for your grandmother."

Skyla laughed out loud. "That red dress can't fit Nana. Nana is *way* too big for that dress."

Sully shushed her, stepping forward and addressing the shop owner. "We'll take that one, if you could wrap it up. And whatever else fit her."

"All of it, sir?" Chelle asked, clearly shocked but hopeful.

"Everything."

"Well, I'll just—I'll get that wrapped up for you." She scurried away toward the dressing room, leaving me standing with Sully and blinking in confusion.

"Don't you want to see them first and make some selections? There were a *lot* of things that fit."

"Did you like them all?" he asked.

"Yes, but it's way too many. You need to pick the ones you want for your mother."

Sully brushed off the suggestion. "Are you putting a limit on how many things I can buy for a gift? I told you, there's no point in killing myself to make all this money if I'm not free to spend it however I want. And what I *want* is to spend it on the people I care about."

That was hard to argue with. The man was a billionaire.

Though I had gasped at the price tags, I knew he could

easily afford to buy the entire contents of the pricey store if he wanted to. He'd probably never even notice the relatively infinitesimal subtraction from his account.

"Fine. I'll just... go change. Be back in a minute."

He gave me a satisfied nod, and I turned to go, leaving him standing by a rack of swimsuits. Before entering the changing area, I glanced back over my shoulder.

He was still watching me, making me wonder... what did this red dress look like from behind?

ELEVEN

Surprise Present

Sully

When we got home, Angelina went to the kitchen to prepare a snack for the girls.

I handed the shopping bags to my newly hired butler Julian along with some quiet instructions for what to do with them then went upstairs to change.

When I came back down dressed for the pool, I saw Skyla and Claire had finished eating and had put on their suits as well. Angelina still wore what she'd been wearing earlier, a pair of long shorts and a loose button-down short-sleeved shirt.

"Hey," I said as I entered the room.

Angelina looked up, flicked her gaze over me, then glanced away quickly, wiping invisible crumbs from the countertop and returning a bottle of juice to the refrigerator.

"Hi. We're just about ready." Her voice sounded different, kind of thin and breathy.

Was it what I was wearing? She'd seen me in shorts and a t-shirt practically every day for the past month.

The only difference today was that my protective sun-shirt was form-fitting. It had to be if I was going to swim in it.

Nothing worse than some floppy thing floating around me and chafing my skin.

Wait... did she *like* the way I looked in it?

I guessed the spandex blend left little to the imagination—the cut of my chest, abdominal muscles, and arms would be pretty obvious through the thin, clingy material.

The idea that Angelina would notice it pleased me, sending spirals of heat through my midsection and lower. I stepped closer to the counter to hide the growing bulge in the front of my swim trunks.

I wanted to see *her* figure as well. The red wrap dress at the shop had been such a contrast to her usual drab, shapeless clothing, and it had looked so good on her I'd almost had to gather up my tongue like a dropped roll of bathroom tissue.

I'd never seen her in a swimsuit—but I desperately wanted to.

"Aren't you gonna change?" I asked. "The girls want you to go to the pool with us."

Angelina gave me an overly bright smile. "I know. I'm going. I'm fine like this. Anyway, I don't have a suit. We didn't use the pool at our house—it was never filled."

And now I was confused. "What do you wear when you take the girls swimming?"

She gestured to her clothing.

"This. I just sit on the edge and dangle my feet in while they play in the shallow end. Don't worry, it's safe. I never take my eyes off them, and I'm ready to jump in at a moment's notice. They're always begging to go in the deep end, but I told them they'd have to wait until Daddy was with them. Today, you are."

She smiled.

"Yeah, and I'm gonna need your help to supervise both of them in the pool at the same time," I said. "I'd like for you to go up and put on a suit as well. Please."

"I told you—I don't have one."

I smiled, feeling rather pleased with myself. "That's not exactly true. I picked one up for you at the shop. The sales lady told me it was the right size."

Angelina's eyes rounded. "You did? You shouldn't have done that. I told you, you don't need to buy anything for me."

"Sorry," I said, knowing I didn't sound the least bit regretful. "But you do need a suit to swim with Skyla and Claire. So really, I did it for them. We'll just wait for you here while you change."

"Hurry Angelina," Skyla pleaded.

"Hurry," her little *me-too* Claire echoed.

Sighing and shaking her head, Angelina headed for the stairs. "I hope it wasn't an expensive one."

I chuckled. There wasn't an item in that store that *wasn't* expensive, which was exactly why I'd chosen it.

Hopefully the saleswoman had removed all the prices as I'd asked her to because when Angelina got to her room, she'd find a hell of a lot more than just the pretty swimsuit waiting for her.

She would discover my surprise.

I'd instructed Julian to deliver all her new clothing to her suite. *Her* clothing—not my mother's.

I was looking forward to seeing her wear each and every garment—especially that red dress, maybe with a pair of strappy high-heeled sandals.

Speaking of that, I'd need to get her shoe size and pick some up. I'd already started trying to manufacture an occasion appropriate for it.

More than that, I was looking forward to seeing the look on Angelina's face when she told me how excited she was about her new wardrobe.

Within minutes she returned to the kitchen, still wearing

the same clothing she'd had on before. She did not look excited.

The complete opposite in fact. She wore an angry scowl.

"*Why* are all your mom's new clothes in my room?"

I gave her a sheepish grin. "Skyla was right. Those would never have fit my mother. I figured you'd be able to wear them though, since you tried them on and all, and they fit you."

"How much does your mother weigh?" she demanded.

A shrug. "I don't know. I'm not good at that."

Angelina's brows lowered menacingly. "Guess."

I wrinkled my nose. "A couple bills maybe? A little more, like two-twenty, two-thirty?"

"I *knew* it." She threw up her hands and blew out a loud breath. "I knew it when you wanted me to try them on. Why did you do that? I told you I didn't want you buying me clothes."

"No... you said I didn't *need* to."

Angelina shot me a death glare worthy of my toughest opponents. Luckily I was a master at deflecting blows.

"I can't have you taking my kids all over the place without nice clothes. They're part of your job."

In actuality, I loved the way Angelina looked just as she was. I just wanted her to have nice things, and it was obvious she wasn't going to buy them for herself, even with the generous salary I was paying her.

Besides, if there was anything I could do to influence her decision *not* to move into the monastery, I was going to do it.

Her eyes rolled so hard I worried they'd detach. "That's ridiculous. None of the other nannies wear designer clothes."

"You're not just another nanny. You're..."

Special. You're much more *than that. You're important to me. You're* mine.

"You're *my* nanny. And I don't want my nanny dressing like some frumpy old lady."

"Old lady?" She gasped. "Is *that* what you think of my appearance?"

She was mad now. And I was well on my way to getting there myself. There was nothing wrong with buying a gift for someone, and she needed to work on her gift-receiving attitude, especially if she was going to continue living in my house.

I'd never met a woman who didn't like getting presents—it was the only thing that had seemed to make Anouk happy.

And I *liked* giving gifts. So what? It wasn't like I was hurting anyone.

Unlike Anouk and I, Angelina and I had never argued before—a fact I hadn't realized until this moment.

But her refusal of my goodwill gesture felt like a slap in the face. The ding to my pride ignited my temper and loosened my tongue.

"You wanna know what I think? I think you hide." I gestured to the blousy outdated shirt she wore. "Behind all that cheap fabric and your pinned-back hair."

"What's wrong with my hair?" Her hand flew up to her head, and her face was all offended tension.

But I didn't stop. "Nothing. If you want to look like my great-grandma Olive, God rest her soul. You scrape it back off your face and ball it up in that little bun thingy like it's something to be ashamed of. *I* think you're afraid for anyone to see the real you. Because then you might have to admit you *do* want things. You might have to go for what you want instead of acting like the pious little church-lady your mom wants you to be. You'd have to step off your holier-than-thou pedestal and face the fact you have needs and desires just like the rest of us mere humans."

"You... you..." Her face was white with fury. "You insufferable brute."

Nearby, my daughters sucked in audible breaths and then

giggled. Like me, they'd never heard Angelina raise her voice before or even speak harshly. She certainly didn't spit out insults, but apparently her temper was just as hot as mine was.

"You don't know *anything* about how I was raised," she said. "You couldn't possibly understand the kind of childhood I had or how much I struggled just to be normal instead of some kind of freak, how I had to learn to put away any notions of what I might want for myself or my future because I knew it was *never* going to happen."

"You might be surprised," I interjected. "I understand better than you think I do. I basically raised myself from the age of thirteen."

"I'm sorry to hear that, but we are *nothing* alike. You bully everyone and pull out your big fat wallet and use your money and your big muscles to *force* things to go your way. No wonder your wife left you. And for your information—I wouldn't wear that tiny little bikini if my life depended on it."

Angelina whirled from the room and practically ran up the stairs, apparently unable to endure my company a minute longer.

Following, I stopped at the bottom of the staircase and watched her go in helpless astonishment.

What had I been thinking?

Where had that even come from? I hadn't planned to provoke her. The last thing I wanted was for sweet Angelina to be mad at me.

I craved her smiles, her approving glances whenever I happened to stumble upon a rare moment of competent parenting, her laughter when one of my dumb jokes managed to tickle her funny bone.

But her rejection of my gift had hurt my feelings, and like a little kid, I'd lashed out without thinking.

I was ashamed of myself and more than a little afraid I'd alienated her for good.

My gut roiled with an intense nausea I'd only felt after being on the wrong end of a kidney shot, an illegal boxing move fighters sometimes tried and occasionally got away with.

I heard the padding of tiny bare feet, and little fingers wrapped themselves around mine. I looked down to see Claire's big hazel eyes trained on the top of the staircase.

"Is Angelina still going to swim with us, Daddy?"

And now my stomach hurt for another reason. What if I'd offended Angelina so much she no longer wanted to work as my children's nanny? What if my stupid mouth had ruined the best thing that had ever happened to my girls?

"I don't know, baby," I said. "I wouldn't count on it. Angelina might need a little time to... rest. Come on, Daddy will take you swimming."

Lifting her, I walked back toward the kitchen to collect Skyla and all our towels and pool toys. We stepped out the back door, and oblivious—thankfully—to the grave mistake their father had made, the girls whooped and cartwheeled all the way across the yard.

It was a perfect day for swimming, with clear skies and bright sunshine that made the pool's glossy surface sparkle like glass. But a cloud hung over my heart, blotting out my enjoyment of family fun day.

All I could think of was the coming storm, the possibility Angelina might walk out of our lives forever.

I made a vow to myself then and there that if she'd stay and give me another chance, I wouldn't put a single toe out of line.

I'd stop trying to impress Angelina, cease my pathetic attempts to woo her.

I'd be the perfect employer—respectful, professional, and above all, self-controlled.

TWELVE
Frumpy Old Lady

Angelina

What a horse's ass.

I stared at the array of fine clothing spread out across the king-sized bed in my room. It must have cost a fortune.

Well, Sully was going to get his money back. I wasn't going to wear a stitch of it. I'd insist he return the whole lot, and if he refused, I'd give the unworn items to charity.

Grabbing one of the empty shopping bags, I began filling it with the beautiful clothes.

When I reached for the red dress, I felt a prick of regret. It was so pretty, and it had felt so good on. I remembered how Sully had reacted to seeing me in it, the way his eyes had widened and traveled over my figure, and a tingly heat spread through my abdomen.

I knew he was only trying to be nice, buying me all this stuff. I'd witnessed many examples of his extreme generosity in the past month. It was part of his nature.

But I couldn't keep the dress. I couldn't keep any of it. It was too personal, too intimate to allow him to buy clothing for me.

The lines were already too blurry with my attraction to him growing stronger every day.

Besides, I was still furious at him for the things he'd said. A "frumpy old lady?" I had half a mind to open the second-floor window and dump the whole collection of haute couture out on the front drive.

And the thing he'd said about my hair?

The fury intensified, blended with a heaping measure of hurt. The more I thought about the sneering tone of his voice and the challenging look on his stubborn face, the more my blood boiled.

Instead of stuffing more garments into the bag, I dropped it and picked up one of them to examine more closely. The orange bikini.

It was tiny. *Really* tiny.

I'd told Sully I wouldn't wear it if my life depended on it, and I'd meant it.

But now it felt like something else depended on it. My pride. My self-respect. I wanted to show Mr. Sullivan Reece that he couldn't bully me, that I wasn't cowed by him. I wanted to show him how *wrong* he was.

I wanted to shut that beautiful, infuriating mouth of his.

I'd show *him* what a "frumpy, old lady" I was. I'd make him sorry he'd ever dared to say such things to me. I was going to make his head spin around.

Hurriedly stripping off the shapeless blouse and shorts ensemble, I yanked the tag off the swimsuit—before I could change my mind—and put it on.

Then I turned to look at the full-length mirror on the closet door.

Oh my.

The woman in the reflection looked like someone else. I wasn't sure who exactly, but not me. This woman looked bold. She looked fun. She looked young and vibrant, not to mention shapely in the way a man like Sullivan Reece might appreciate.

But that wasn't the point of this exercise, was it?

No. Not at all. I only wanted to make him eat his words and maybe a side of crow to go along with them.

Something was still wrong with this picture though. With sharp, nearly frenzied motions, I yanked the pins and elastic from my hair, freeing it to fall to my bottom and stream over my shoulders.

There. I nodded, stunned at my own actions but filled with a strange new sense of satisfaction.

There's your "great-grandma Olive," Mr. Smartypants.

They were in the middle of a game of Marco Polo when I reached the pool. Sully was the finder, yelling out "Marco," every few seconds while his elated daughters scrambled and splashed to a new location before yelling, "Polo" back at him.

One of his large hands was over his eyes, but I knew he was peeking because there was no way he'd take his eyes off his kids in the water.

Also, he spotted me coming.

How did I know? As soon as I came into view, his hand dropped to his side and he stared.

"Can I play?" I asked in a happy-go-lucky tone.

"Angelina!" Skyla and Claire reacted with screams of delight, not even noticing my attire.

Sully noticed.

His eyes roamed over me, taking in the sight of my long hair hanging loose and all the newly exposed skin. It tingled everywhere his gaze landed. I forced myself not to look away or wrap my towel around myself.

When he spoke, Sully's voice sounded rough. "You..." He cleared his throat and began again. "You changed your mind."

"Yes," I said, purposely missing his meaning. "I decided not to let you three have all the fun when *I'm* the best Marco Polo player around."

With that, I ran and leapt into the pool, splashing him. The girls laughed like it was the funniest thing they'd ever seen.

"Look at your face, Daddy," Claire said. "You're all red."

He swiped at it. "Yeah. I guess I'm... sunburned."

For the rest of the afternoon, we swam and played in the pool. Though Sully was attentive to his daughters, I noticed him casting side glances at me throughout the day, especially when I was in shallower water that didn't cover me to the neck.

Apparently I'd succeeded in disproving his "frumpy" diagnosis. That pleased me probably more than it should have.

When I announced it was time for me to go inside and get started on making dinner, the girls asked to play one final game, a chicken fight.

Ever the softy, Sully said, "Okay, just one more."

Skyla climbed onto her father's shoulders while I supported Claire, who was lighter, on mine. Shrieking with laughter, the two little "chickens" grabbed each other's hands and wrestled, each trying to topple the other into the water.

At one point their hand wrestling became a sort of clench, with the two girls hugging each other tightly. That meant Sully and I were dragged toward each other and obligated to stand close.

Very close.

We weren't exactly face-to-face since he was so much taller than me, but my nose was at his chest level, and the fronts of our bodies were forced together.

Wow did he feel good—hard muscle on a large, solid frame my fingers ached to reach out and hold onto. I wondered if the closeness affected him as much as it did me.

A heavy weight pressed against my belly. For a few seconds, I was baffled. I had no idea what it was—did we get a pool toy caught between us? And then I realized what the hard-but-pliable shape was.

Oh. I guessed I had my answer. In spite of the cool water, I was suddenly boiling, and every hair on my body stood on end.

Abruptly, Sully moved back and announced in a terse voice, "Okay, game over. Time to go in."

"Daaaaddeeee," Skyla complained until he plucked her off his shoulders and tossed her into the water the way she loved.

She popped up, giggling wildly. "Again. Throw me again."

"First I gotta throw back *this* guppy." He reached for Claire, lifting her from my shoulders as if she weighed nothing and tossing her as well.

"You can go if you want to," he whispered to me.

I swam to the shallow end, taking the stairs out of the pool. Maybe I should have run for the house, considering what had just happened. But I decided to stay and dry off a bit instead.

Actually, it had nothing to do with drying off. I wanted to watch Sully get out of the pool—to *see* with my eyes what I'd just felt pressing against my abdomen.

Unfortunately, he stayed in the pool for several more rounds of toss-the-daughter.

Oh well. I stretched out on one of the loungers, waiting for them to finish so I could help the girls dry off when they got out.

The late afternoon sun and light breeze were so heavenly, I closed my eyes for a minute to enjoy the sensations. I could easily have taken a cat nap right here.

When my eyes opened again, Sully was standing over my lounge chair, his half-lidded gaze sweeping down to my toes then slowly up again. I'd never seen him wear quite that expression before. He looked… absorbed. Sort of far away and yet *very* present at the same time.

Excitement danced in my belly and stole my breath. Though his shadow blocked the late-day rays of sun, a warmth pulsed between my legs and spread to my upper thighs.

"Hi," I managed to say. "Are you hungry?"

Sully's head jerked back, and he blinked several times. "What?"

"For dinner. Are you hungry for dinner?"

"Oh." He shook his head in a series of rapid jerks. "I'm uh… going out—meeting my friend Wilder."

"Wilder Lowe, the security expert?"

Sully frowned. "You know him?"

"Not really, but I remember him from the Wessexes' party."

"Of course you do," he said in a surly tone. What was all *that* about?

"Did you meet him there?" I asked.

"No, but they suggested him. I had him come to the house and put in the security system the next day. We got to talking and struck up a friendship. He's a big sports fan, too. We're gonna watch the Red Sox at Padraig's Pub and grab some food."

"Sounds like fun. You're going to miss my cooking though," I teased. "I'm making lasagna tonight."

A look of genuine regret passed over Sully's face. He glanced down at my bikini again and the look intensified.

"Yeah… well… save me some."

Then he turned and walked to the house in long, digging strides that made me raise a hand to my mouth to cover the wide smile developing there. I didn't have any experience with men, but there were some things a woman understood instinctively.

I'd wanted to prove something to Sully—and to myself, too. Judging by the look I'd just seen on his face it was a mission accomplished.

The only question now was… where did we go from here?

THIRTEEN

Angelina

After that day at the pool there was a subtle change in our relationship.

Nothing I could point my finger at definitively and accuse him of pursuing me or even call inappropriate for a work relationship. Sully never said or did anything overtly flirty. In fact, he seemed to choose his words more carefully than before, being polite and respectful and solicitous.

It was more a *feeling* I got when we were together, a new sort of awareness between us and a heightened quality of attention he showed to my preferences and interests.

There were always vases of wildflowers in the house now. Whenever he brought home ice cream for the girls, he made sure to pick up a pint of my favorite flavor, chocolate chip, as well. He left notes on the counter almost daily thanking me for doing even the simplest things that frankly were just part of my job.

It was almost embarrassing, but I felt more appreciated—and more capable—than I ever had in my life.

And I felt needed.

For instance, the following weekend as Sully was dressing to attend the annual Charity Relief Foundation Ball, he texted me from upstairs and asked if I'd come to his room for a minute.

-I need help.

My response had been as bland as unbuttered toast. **Sure. Be right there.** On the inside, though, my nerves were crackling. I'd never been past the door of his room.

"Girls, let's go upstairs and help Daddy, okay?"

My eager little chaperones and I went up the stairs and down the long corridor to Sully's private wing of the mansion.

Claire and Skyla skipped ahead of me, calling out, "Daddy, we're coming to save you."

Reaching the double doors to his suite, they burst through them and ran to him, dancing around his legs in excitement.

"I like your pretty suit Daddy!" Skyla said.

"You look like a restaurant man," Claire added, with obvious admiration.

"Thanks girls." Sully turned to me wearing a sleek black tuxedo and an exasperated expression. Each of his hands gripped the loose ends of a bow tie.

"I don't know what the fu—" His eyes darted to his daughters. "...fudge I'm doing with this thing. I wish they'd just sent a clip-on. Do you know how to tie a bow tie?"

"No. I've never had occasion to tie one. But I'll figure it out the way I do everything else I've never done before."

Pulling out my phone, I scanned through You Tube, finding and watching a short instructional video.

"I tried that, too," Sully said. "I can't seem to tie it on myself, though. Either I'm tie-dyslexic or my hands are too big."

"Here let me try."

I stepped up in front of him, and he dropped his hands to his sides, staying very still. After a minute of straining my neck upward while fumbling with the slippery fabric, I said, “You’re too tall.”

Then I pressed my fingers to his chest and gave him a little shove to make him sit on the edge of the bed.

Sully obediently sat, raising one eyebrow and quirking his lips in a little smile. “You can be tough when you want to be. I’m a little scared.”

Now *that* was a flirty tone. I should have ignored it, but I couldn’t help but laugh.

“Don’t be. I won’t hurt you… much.” I gave the ends of the tie a little jerk and wrinkled my nose at him in an expression of mock-threat.

Sully bit his lower lip, but his grin grew wider, and those gorgeous blue eyes sparkled.

“Don’t worry Daddy. Angelina is sweet, and she has very soft hands,” Claire assured him.

Sully didn’t say anything to that, but the spark in his eyes turned into a smolder. They stayed locked on me as I tried, failed, and tried again to replicate the tie-knot from the video.

It didn’t help that my hands were shaking now. Or that he smelled absolutely delicious.

Or that I realized—belatedly—this position required me to stand between his spread legs.

The whole thing probably lasted only a few minutes, but it seemed like time had slowed to a crawl. I was aware of the sound of his breaths, the heat of his skin, the scents of minty mouthwash and freshly-showered male, the way his hands clenched and unclenched on top of his thighs.

“I think I’ve almost got it,” I said then giggled nervously because I’d sounded so out of breath.

Sully’s response was a velvety murmur. “Take your time.”

By the time I finally managed to complete the process, I was light-headed and sweating. Sully looked a little dazed as well, and his breathing sounded like he'd just come in from a run.

"There." I gave his shoulder an awkward pat. "All set."

He didn't immediately stand but stayed in place, holding contact with my eyes. "Thank you, Angelina," he said softly.

I nodded and stepped back, wiping my hands on the sides of my shorts. He stood up and turned to face the girls, who'd been rolling around on the enormous bed.

"How do I look?"

Claire ran up to him and flung herself into his arms. Of course he caught her, and she planted a kiss on his cheek. "You'll be the cutest daddy at the ball."

"Thank you, baby."

Skyla smirked at her younger sister. "Daddies aren't *cute*—they're hanson. And you're the hansonest one, Daddy." She turned to me. "Right Angelina?"

My nerves stood on end as Sully turned around as well, waiting for my answer. I glanced away and straightened the bedspread they'd rumpled.

"I think the word you're looking for is 'handsome.' And yes... your father looks very nice."

When I looked up, he was grinning ear to ear and actually gave me a wink.

Heart thumping, I herded the girls from the room. "It's time to start the unicorn movie. I'll make the popcorn. You two get your pj's on please and meet me in the theater in five minutes."

FOURTEEN
Secret Stash

Angelina

Putting the girls to bed was always an adventure.

Usually Sully and I divided and conquered, but since he was still out at the charity ball, I let Skyla and Claire share a bath then read them a story at the same time before tucking them each in individually.

Claire, who seemed pretty tired, protested only minimally before dropping off to sleep with one thumb in her mouth and the other hand clutching mine.

Skyla was more challenging. She never wanted to miss anything and begged me to let her stay up until her daddy returned.

"Now that I'm five, I can stay awake later."

"Yes, but it will be *very* late when he comes home tonight. Way past your bedtime. If I let you stay up, you'll be cranky tomorrow and too tired to jump around with your friends at the trampoline park."

"I'm never tired," she argued before her mouth stretched wide in a yawn.

"Still, it's time for bed. No more stalling."

I kissed her forehead then walked to the door, pausing with my hand on the light switch.

"Angelina?"

"Yes Skyla?"

"How do you spell 'stalling?'"

A snort of laughter escaped me. "We'll spell it out tomorrow if you still want to know. Goodnight little skylark."

I flicked off the light but before I shut the door, I heard her voice again.

"Angelina?"

Expecting another stalling tactic, I took a deep breath then said, "Yes?"

"I love you."

My heart contracted in a sweetly painful squeeze. These kids—how could I *not* fall utterly in love with them?

"I love you, too, skylark," I said honestly. "Sweet dreams."

Feeling a little melancholy, I wandered around the house, picking up stray toys, little shoes, and a glass Sully had inadvertently left out. He was usually pretty good at cleaning up after himself. He must have been in a rush tonight to get to the party.

I wondered if he was enjoying himself. He wouldn't be partaking of the open bar, but there was bound to be really good food there, which he'd love. Probably music and dancing.

Would he ask someone to dance? Hold her close and chat intimately as they moved around the floor? Maybe that was why he'd worn cologne tonight and styled his hair so nicely and wanted his tie to be perfect.

A burst of sizzling heat lit me up from head to toe. And just what was *that* about?

Don't be an idiot, Angelina.

He'd dressed up because he'd been asked to come and take fan photos with the party guests. He was doing his part to help the charity fund. The images would no doubt be posted and reposted all over social media—of course he wanted to look nice.

As far as spending time with women, he was a single man. He had every right to.

He hadn't been, though, at least that I was aware of. Other than the occasional night out at a sports bar with Wilder Lowe, Sully spent his evenings at home.

At his *home, not yours.* It seemed important to make that distinction.

No matter how cozy it felt at times, I needed to remember I was a guest here, an outsider. An employee. And he was my boss.

Nothing more.

Strolling through the dining room, I came across several belts and ties strewn across the tabletop and floor. The girls had played pirate earlier. They must have borrowed these from their dad's closet thinking they'd make good costumes.

I gathered the masculine accessories and walked upstairs to return them to his room.

In the past whenever I'd returned his "borrowed" possessions, I'd left them just outside the doors of his suite on a console table in the hallway. But this was such a large, unwieldy pile, some of it was bound to slip off the narrow table and end up on the floor.

Besides, I'd been in Sully's room just a couple hours earlier, and the floor hadn't opened up and swallowed me.

It was no big deal if I just went in and put these things away in his closet for him. He'd told me before that housecleaning wasn't my job, but a little tidying up certainly was, and after all the thoughtful things he'd done for me, I didn't mind doing him this small favor.

Opening the door, I crossed the large room to the attached

bathroom where I assumed his closet was located. Ah, I was right.

There it was—a huge walk-in closet with upper and lower rods on three sides and a center-island sort of shoe rack. Only a few pairs occupied the slots. The rest of the openings were filled with... books.

Wow. I had no idea he was such a reader.

There were dozens of paperbacks, stacked neatly in the cubbies. Unable to help myself, I picked one up. And did a double-take.

It was a romance novel.

I hadn't read any myself, of course. That sort of reading material was frowned upon at Mother's house—but I recognized it instantly. A beautiful couple embraced on the cover looking happily-in-love. I even recognized the author's name—I'd heard some of the other nannies discussing her books.

Intrigued, I reached for another book from the stack, then another, then another. They were *all* romance novels.

Could these really be Sully's? Maybe they belonged to his ex-wife. But no, he said she'd never lived here, so unless he got them in the divorce, these were all his.

My question was answered when I left the closet and was about to leave Sully's room.

Off to one side near an ocean-facing window sat a comfortable chair and a small table. On the table was a lamp—and a book.

With a bookmark in it.

I stood with my hand on the doorknob waging a battle with myself.

I shouldn't invade his privacy.

But it is *right there in the open—on a table.*

A table in his *room. Not the living room, not the kitchen. His private space.*

Right. Privacy. That was important. How would I feel if he was snooping around my room?

Ultimately, to my shame, my better nature lost out to my curiosity. I tiptoed across the room and picked up the book, feeling like a cat burglar. It was definitely a romance—this one had an even sexier cover than the others I'd found in the closet.

Opening the book to the bookmark, I began to read. My jaw dropped as I reached a paragraph in the middle of the page.

The chapter was told from a man's point of view. He'd apparently been trying to find a way to get the main female character close. I didn't know the whole backstory, but it seemed she was a skittish sort, and nothing had been working out for the guy.

So he asked the woman for help with his tie.

My heart began pounding so hard I could hear it in my eardrums. Was *that* why Sully had asked for help with his tie tonight? I couldn't have stopped reading if my life literally depended on it.

Breathing like I'd just climbed several flights of stairs, I read further, my eyes racing over the words on the page. Several times I had to go back and read a passage again—particularly the one where the man was so turned on by the woman's nearness, he'd had to drag a pillow over his lap to hide his... I swallowed hard... erection.

I should not—should *not*—have read what came next.

As the book's heroine stood between the hero's thighs, tying his tie, he placed his hands on her hips then ran them down and around to grip her bottom, caressing it.

When she responded... *favorably*, gasping his name, he began unbuttoning her shirt, pushing it open and touching her over her bra, then pulling that aside and kissing her on the *—oh my God.*

I dropped the book and staggered backward, my heart

thundering and heat blooming between my legs. Like the woman in the book, my nipples hardened and yearned to be touched.

Had Sully been thinking of *this* while I worked on his tie tonight?

Is this what he imagined happening? Had *wanted* to happen—had his daughters not been there, of course.

I blinked a few times and looked around, searching for a clock. Red numbers glowed from a small device on Sully's bedside table. I let out a sigh of relief.

It was still early—he wouldn't be home for a while now. I'd completely lost track of time while reading. It was like I'd been transported somewhere else into someone else's life.

As for my life, I felt like everything had changed in the past few minutes. What did it all mean?

On one hand, my nanny friends said the romances they read were escapism, fantasies they didn't necessarily want to live out in real life but enjoyed visiting whenever they felt like it.

Maybe that's all it was for Sully. An escape. A fantasy. A safe outlet for thoughts a single-dad training for a boxing match had no time to live out in real life.

On the other hand, he'd basically recreated the scene I'd just read.

With *me*.

FIFTEEN
Twister

Angelina

I bent to pick up Sully's book, planning to return it to the reading nook table and—if necessary—wipe it for fingerprints.

Oh no. The novel was closed—and the bookmark wasn't in it.

Snatching the cardboard marker from the floor, I thumbed through the pages, trying desperately to relocate the place where Sully had marked his reading progress.

It was somewhere near the middle? Maybe. I wasn't sure.

Unable to find the correct spot, I just stuck the bookmark, which bore the logo of Bonnie's Bonny Books, between two random pages and set the book back down on the tabletop in the approximate location where I'd found it.

Before I went to my room to hide (and pray Sully had also forgotten where exactly he'd left off reading) I returned to his closet and took one of the other novels from the closet island dresser, from one of the lower cubbies on the back side.

If Sully was reading these books and imagining me in the scenarios they contained, I wanted to see exactly what I was dealing with.

* * *

Bad idea. Very bad.

I read the entire book in one sitting. The next day, I could barely meet Sully's eyes. I managed to evade him nicely for most of the day, but unfortunately, that night was our weekly Game Night.

Sully had promised the girls we'd play anything they wanted. After several rounds of Go Fish and a game of Trouble, they begged for Twister.

"Please Angelina?" Skyla begged. "You never play this one with us, and it's not as fun with only three people."

"I'm not very good at it," I said, scrambling for an excuse. "I fall down."

The very *last* thing I needed after reading that novel of Sully's was to be in any twisty positions with him.

"Maybe you won't fall this time. I want yooooouuuu," Claire begged, dragging out the last word.

"Me too," Sully said, then quickly corrected himself. "I mean, I'd love for you to play. With us. It would make the girls happy."

"Please?" Skyla chimed in and blinked at me with her best puppy dog eyes.

I sighed in defeat. "Okay, well I can't play in a dress. Let me go up and change. I'll be right back."

A few minutes later, I returned to the living room in a t-shirt and yoga pants. Sully and the girls stood barefoot on the colorful plastic mat waiting for me. I took my position opposite him with Skyla to my left and Claire to my right.

Sully, who was the referee for this round, reached over and flicked the plastic spinner. When it stopped spinning, he called out the first move. "Right foot on red."

Each of us followed the instruction—or tried to—placing a foot on the nearest red circle. For Sully that meant stepping all the way across the mat to my side. Skyla and Claire had only to move a foot a few inches to reach a red circle, but Claire was confused as to which foot was her right.

"I said to my mind to write it down, but I forgot," she said.

Skyla laughed. "You don't even know how to write."

"Yes, I do," Claire replied, the indignation clear in her tone. "I can write a "O" and a "T."

The game was going to be hard if the girls were unsure of which was their left and right. I had an idea. "Claire, which letter does 'right' start with?"

"R?"

"Yes! Very good. I think I know something that will help. Hold on a second."

Leaving my spot on the mat for a minute, I went to the girls' craft area and selected a pink washable marker from one of the bins. I returned to the mat, knelt down in front of Claire, and drew a large letter R on the top of her tiny right foot.

She giggled. "That tickles." I smiled up at her and asked for her hand, drawing an R on the back of the right one as well.

"Now you'll be able to remember which is which."

In my peripheral vision I noticed Skyla hovering. Turning to her, I asked, "Would you like me to write on your hand and foot as well?"

She shifted from one foot to the other. "I don't need it. I know which one is which... mostly. But I do like that pink marker."

"How about this? Want me to draw a pink flower on your right hand and foot?"

Skyla lifted her little chin and made an obstinate face. "No. A heart."

I smiled. "Okay, give me your foot."

After I decorated her right foot and hand with pink hearts, the game resumed. Another spin. Another call.

"It says left hand on green," Sully said, sounding a bit worried.

Once again, the instructions didn't require much of a stretch for the girls. Sully on the other hand had to practically do a backbend to put a hand on a green circle behind him while maintaining a foothold on the red circle across the mat.

The call required me to bend forward, stretching as far as I could to reach a green circle with the fingertips of my left hand.

Which put my face inches from Sully's uplifted crotch.

I turned my head as far as it would go to the opposite side, averting my eyes and trying *very* hard not to think of the scene I'd read about seventy percent into the book. While reading it hadn't taken me all night, I'd barely slept, imagining that scene—and others—happening with Sully in real life.

"Skyla baby, can you spin it this time?" he said through gritted teeth. "Daddy can't reach it."

"Okay Daddy," the little girl responded, oblivious to our awkward positioning.

"Great. Hurry please."

She twirled the spinner. "Left foot on yellow."

The call required me to execute a move that wasn't impossible but was certainly embarrassing. I ended up with my legs spread and my butt sticking up in the air.

Turning his head to survey the mat, Sully lifted his eyebrows and twisted his lips to one side. "I'm not sure I can do this."

"Yes, you can, Daddy," Claire said. "You're an aff-leet. You can do anything."

"Don't quit, Daddy," Skyla pleaded. "You have to try."

Sully shot me a *what're you gonna do?* look and blew out a long breath. "I'll try."

I gave him a tense smile of commiseration. “Good luck.”

He first tried drawing his left foot beneath him, but the yellow row was too close to where his left hand rested on the row of green circles, and his thigh muscles were literally too big to allow his leg to fold beneath him like that.

“Okay, I’m gonna have to spin around and face downward, I think,” he said.

“Remember not to stop touching with your other foot and your hand,” Skyla warned, well versed in the official rules of Twister.

“Got it,” Sully said.

He drew another breath then in one swift move, swung his left leg up and over to the nearest yellow dot, spinning on his right toe and right hand so that he now faced the mat. To his credit, he pulled it off.

Unfortunately, his new position put him directly *over* me. And behind me.

Close behind me.

So there we were, both of us with our legs spread wide, Sully’s chest pressed against my back, and his pelvis pressed tightly to my backside.

This *definitely* reminded me of what I’d read.

Claire, who was twisted like a little pretzel and looked entirely comfortable anyway, laughed out loud. “Look, Angelina’s giving Daddy a piggyback ride!”

Suddenly the space between our bodies seemed to lessen. There was a distinctive pressure against my bottom. I gasped and dropped to the mat like I’d been shot.

“Oh no, Angelina. You losed.” Claire gave me a look of ultimate sympathy.

“Yep. That’s too bad,” I blurted, scurrying out from beneath Sully and off the mat. “Okay, who wants to play Operation now?”

SIXTEEN
Distraction

Sully

I didn't stick around for the next game, and *not* because I sucked at Operation—I was the fucking master at extracting that little funny bone without setting off the buzzer.

No, I just needed to escape.

My excuse was that I had to get ready to meet up with Wilder. It was true—I was supposed to meet him at Padraig's—just not quite this early. The baseball game didn't start for a while yet.

But I'd changed clothes then practically run out of the house with a quick kiss for Skyla and Claire and barely a glance at Angelina.

What the hell had I been thinking agreeing to a game of Twister with her? I should have left the instant I saw her in those clingy yoga pants.

Those skin-tight pants might very well have been the straw that broke the camel's back. Or maybe it was that dry-humping position we were in that had done it.

Either way, I was one miserable broke-back camel.

For the past several weeks I'd been falling harder and faster every day. It had started with attraction, of course. I mean, she was absolutely gorgeous. But it had become so much more than that.

I liked Angelina. I admired her.

And I *wanted* her.

No. No, no no. I slammed a hand on the steering wheel, letting out a loud, frustrated noise.

All my fears had come true. I'd become the cliché of the single dad with a crush on the nanny. Only "crush" didn't seem quite the right word in this situation.

If it had been *only* about how she looked in yoga pants—or a bikini—and *holy shit*, how that woman filled out a bikini—it would be one thing. I could handle it. After all, I'd been around lots of beautiful, sexy women and been married to a supermodel.

But Angelina was alluring in a whole different way. Her voice, her gentle nature, her sense of humor, her kindness, her innocence, her unique view of the world. I could go on listing her attributes until the English language ran out of words.

It had gotten to the point all I wanted to do was be with her, bask in her sweetness, and yes, in her mind-scrambling beauty.

But I couldn't do that, or at least I *shouldn't.* Not with how the girls were thriving under her care. I'd never seen them so happy. And especially not after that near-miss on Family Fun Day when I'd experienced the legitimate fear she'd leave us because of my stupid mouth.

I'd been as careful as possible since then. I couldn't mess up again. I had to find a way to get over this... *whatever* it was that kept her on my mind during most of my waking hours and made her the star of all my dreams at night.

Probably should lay off the romance books. I'd started reading them long before meeting Angelina after Anouk had informed me I had "a lot to learn" when it came to romance. I figured, what better way to learn than to read books about what women liked and wanted written *by* women for women to read?

But now I couldn't help but think of Angelina in place of the main female character in every book, no matter how the author might describe the woman on the page.

Anyway, this had to be the best timing for a guys' night out *ever*. A night of talking sports and swapping war stories could only do me good.

Stepping into Padraig's, I saw a passing waitress who told me to sit wherever I wanted. I chose a booth with a good view of the TV screens, ordered a seltzer, and waited for Wilder to arrive.

About fifteen minutes later, the former jock/former SEAL stepped through the pub's front door.

Spotting him, I lifted a hand so Wilder could locate me.

As I watched the tall, jacked security expert make his way to the booth, I noticed several heads turning.

The female ones *kept* turning, following his progress, and I was reminded of Angelina's words. "I remember him."

I was stunned by a rush of competitive adrenaline. Wilder Lowe *wasn't* the kind of guy women overlooked or easily forgot, but it bothered me that Angelina had noticed my friend enough to remember his name *and* what he did for a living.

Of course she was like that with everyone. She paid attention when people spoke. She *listened* instead of just nodding her head, waiting for her turn to talk.

Wilder reached the table, giving me a big smile and a quick back slap-bro hug combo before taking the booth seat opposite mine.

"How's it going? How's the training coming along?"

"Good. Good," I said. "I'm at the point where I need to

be. Just gotta keep my mind on the game, you know? How's business?"

"Great," Wilder said. "Too good, actually. If you ever want to retire and get into the personal security business, you're hired. I've got more requests for bodyguards than I can handle. I'm even taking on some clients myself again until I can cover the gap."

I laughed. "Well, we'll see how this fight goes. I might be *ready* to retire after going twelve with Travis Diggs."

Wilder laughed in commiseration. "He's no joke, that's for sure. I'm sure you saw he's got a warm-up fight tomorrow night?"

"Yeah. Pretty gutsy, scheduling that while he's training for me. He knows I'm gonna watch the tape."

"'Gutsy' is one word. 'Overconfident' is another. Stupid, too. I wouldn't give you *any* advantage if I were him. So how are the girls? Any great escapes lately?"

I chuckled. "Not one. You did a solid job. Though I could probably leave the doors unlocked these days and not worry about it. Their behavior's gotten way better lately."

"Oh yeah? They get used to the new living arrangements?"

"That... and I hired a nanny. She's amazing with them. They're like different kids. They absolutely love her."

Wilder studied me with an amused half-smile. "What do *you* think of her?"

Shrugging, I looked away at a TV screen, making my tone as blasé as possible. "I like her. She's good with them. And she's... nice."

Wilder sat back in his booth seat, folded his arms across his chest, and shook his head, laughing softly. "Oh man... you've got a thing for the nanny."

My eyes lasered to his, my tone suddenly harsh. "I do not. That would not be... smart."

Wilder shook his head, still grinning. "No. But it would

be understandable. I mean, she's there in your house every day, taking care of your kids, making your life easier. Is she young?"

I gave him a grudging nod. "Twenty-three."

Wilder nodded. "Mmmhmm. What's her name?"

There was a long moment when I hesitated, sizing up my friend across the table. "Angelina."

Wilder, who'd been in mid-sip, choked on his beer. "Angelina the hot preschool teacher? Oh, dude—you are in *so* much trouble. That woman is *smokin'*."

I battled a surge of possessive animosity, actually had to suppress a growl.

"I hadn't noticed," I lied through gritted teeth.

"She's also planning to become a nun—did you know that?" Wilder said, clearly not buying the lie.

"Maybe. She *might* become a nun. She's weighing her options right now."

Wilder nodded, his lips twisting in a thoughtful expression. "I see. And do her *options* include being Sullivan Reece's new woman?"

I frowned. "Of course not. She's my kids' nanny. And she's gonna be a nun."

"*Might* be a nun," Wilder corrected. He took another drink. "Say you *did* have a thing for her... would that be so bad? She sounds like the total package. It's obvious you like her. Yeah, it's inconvenient that she's the nanny, but it's not like it would be the first time in history. I mean, it's practically a celebrity rite of passage."

"Yeah, it *would* be that bad," I told him, finally starting to crumble under the strain of interrogation.

Rubbing my forehead, I stared down at the scarred wood tabletop. "No matter how amazing she is, how sweet and funny and smart and yeah, 'smokin',' I can't go there. I don't want to be *that guy*. If I ever made a move... tried to take it to another level, and it didn't work out... my kids could lose their nanny."

"So get another one. Date Angelina and hire someone else."

I shook my head adamantly. "No. There's no one like her. She's the best person to care for my girls, and they deserve the best. I'd be the world's worst father if they lost her because of my selfishness. I'm just gonna... you know, get over it, put her out of my mind... move on."

My tone of voice wasn't convincing even to myself, but what else was there to do?

"Well, I admire your self-control, and it *is* legendary. But it's my personal opinion you can't help who you fall for. It's just one of those things. I mean—"

Wilder stopped mid-sentence and whipped his head around. Someone had turned up the volume on one of the TV monitors where a beautiful young pop star was singing the national anthem.

Her name was Jade. I'd met her at a couple of star-studded parties, and like everyone else, had been hearing her songs on the radio for years.

Staying in his uncomfortable twisted position, Wilder stared at the screen behind him, remaining motionless until the last note ended and the singer's pretty face disappeared from view.

When he turned back around, Wilder's face looked different. Flags of color decorated the crests of his cheeks and the bridge of his nose.

Interesting.

He shook his head. "Sorry man. What was I saying?"

"You can't help who you fall in love with," I supplied in a tongue-in-cheek tone.

I had the sneaking suspicion Wilder's opinion on the matter came from *personal* experience and that experience just might involve Jade. She was originally from Eastport Bay, after all.

"Right." Wilder nodded. "But if you're determined not to go down that road, I do have an idea for you."

"What's that?"

Wilder smiled. "Distraction."

"Distraction?" I could hardly spend any more time training, and how did you distract yourself from someone who lived in your house?

"If you can't have the one you want," Wilder said, "then find someone else to distract yourself with. Works pretty well for me. And I have the perfect person for you."

"Who?" The idea had merit—in theory. But I hadn't found myself even looking at another woman since meeting Angelina.

"Bree Steele."

"The movie star?"

Wilder nodded. "She's in Rhode Island for a couple of months making a film. Her manager hired my firm for security. She's mentioned you, wants to meet you. She thinks you're, quote, 'a stud.'"

The silly term made me smile. The actress was certainly pretty, but we'd never even met, and I didn't particularly care for her films.

Still, maybe Wilder was right. Maybe going out with someone was what I needed to get my mind off the 24-7 Angelina show. It was worth a try anyway.

"Okay sure. So how does this work? You want to give her my number so we can set something up?"

"Absolutely. She's been filming mostly during the day, so maybe you guys can go out tomorrow night."

"Sounds good."

Well, that was overstating it a bit, but it had to be better than spending another night close to Angelina, fighting the urge to lean closer and smell her hair, disciplining myself not to touch her or even let my gaze linger too long.

Who knew? Maybe I'd even like this Bree Steele woman. Stranger things had happened.

Like falling in love with your kids' nanny.

Oh yeah, I needed help. Fast. Maybe Bree would be available for breakfast and lunch too?

SEVENTEEN

Lady in Red

Angelina

I adjusted the straps of the red dress, taking a moment for one last check of the mirror before leaving the bowling alley bathroom.

Yes, the dress was *way* too nice for an outing with the girls and the other nannies and their charges, and yes, it looked completely stupid paired with bowling shoes, but I didn't care.

Sully was out on a date.

With a movie star.

I'd also styled my hair in long, loose curls, applied a spritz of perfume, and even a bit of mascara and lip gloss.

Maybe I shouldn't have been surprised when he told me this morning he wouldn't be at home for dinner. I definitely shouldn't have been surprised when he mentioned who he was taking out.

Of course he would date beautiful, glamorous starlets. Bree Steele probably wasn't even the first.

But I'd been caught off guard anyway. I'd gotten used to having him home every night, to the shared smiles at the girls' cute recitations of their day, to the sound of his big, barrel-chested laugh. I'd come to count on my nightly fix of Sully-time after missing him all day while he trained.

"Are you okay?"

The voice drew me out of my daydream and back to reality where my friend Lorie, another nanny, was watching me with obvious concern.

"Oh, yeah. I'm fine. Did Skyla take her turn?" I re-focused on the group of little girls chattering happily while they rolled hot pink bowling balls back and forth in the return rack.

"She's next," Lorie said. "So… who is he?"

"Who is who?" I looked around, searching for the unidentified male in question. Had Sully walked in without my noticing?

"The guy you're thinking of."

"Oh. No one. I mean, I'm not thinking of a guy."

"Okay," Lorie said, clearly disbelieving. "I was just wondering if maybe it's the guy you have a date with later tonight."

"Me?" The idea seemed ludicrous. "I don't have a date."

"Really? Cause I've never seen you wear makeup. I've *never* seen you this dressed up. And that dress? That's a man magnet if I've ever seen one. So you might as well fess up."

"I promise—I don't have a date."

"But there *is* a guy." It wasn't a question but a statement.

I couldn't keep up the act. Closing my eyes in mortification, I said, "It doesn't matter anyway because he doesn't see me that way."

"How do you know?" Lorie asked.

"He's dating someone else."

"Well, if he ever gets a look at you in that red dress…" She held her hands inches apart then slammed the pinched fingertips together. "Magnets, baby."

She waggled her eyebrows, making me laugh in spite of my misery. "I doubt it. But thanks."

Sully probably wouldn't even *see* the "look" I'd spent so much time creating for him. He'd left the house early this evening while I was still getting ready, and he probably wouldn't be home until very late.

He might not come home tonight at all.

My stomach cramped with a sick, twisting pain. I wasn't sure how I'd be able to handle it if Sully started seeing this woman—or someone else—regularly.

The mental image of another woman spending time at the house with him and the girls, holding his hand, and kissing him, and doing... *romance novel stuff* with him filled me with a sense of outrage so heated I felt like I might spontaneously combust.

Not that I had any right to complain. He wasn't mine, would never *be* mine. He was a single man with incredible good looks, natural charm, tons of money, and unlimited opportunity—naturally he'd want to date.

Movie stars. Models. Successful, famous, *experienced* women who understood everything there was to know about attracting and pleasing a man. I was an idiot for even thinking of him in a romantic way.

When bowling was done, I'd take Skyla and Claire out for frozen yogurt as I'd promised, give them their baths and their bedtime stories, and then I'd march right to my own room.

I'd scrub off the stupid makeup and change into my plain, unsexy pajamas, pull my hair into a ponytail, and go to bed with a book as usual.

One of my *own* books, a historical mystery.

Only after we'd gotten home and the girls were asleep, I *didn't* go to my room.

Instead, I went back downstairs, made myself a cup of hot chocolate I didn't even want, and carried my book to the comfy leather sectional that anchored the family room.

Curling into a corner of it, I flicked on a reading lamp and waited. And waited.

And waited.

The longer the wait stretched, the stronger the feeling grew inside me. It was like nothing I'd ever felt before, an acidic blend of longing and alarm. I turned pages after barely skimming their contents, using so much force I nearly ripped one.

Finally, at fourteen minutes to midnight, the door from the garage opened. My stomach leapt into my throat.

Sully walked into the adjoining kitchen, dropped his keys on the counter, and let out a long, audible sigh.

So either the date had been not so great—or it was amazing.

I wasn't sure why I cared so much which one it was, but I had a suspicion. That feeling I'd never experienced before? I suspected it was jealousy. Which was beyond stupid.

He hadn't seen me yet. I was scrunched down in the couch cushions so only the top of my head and my eyes peeked above them. It was possible I could slip off the couch and tiptoe away, darting up the stairs barefoot before he spotted me here.

But then he turned and saw me. His shoulders rose and fell in a quick startle reaction.

"Oh. Hey. I didn't know you were there. What are you doing up? Everything okay?" He walked toward the living room.

Right. Naturally he would assume the reason I'd waited up for him was to tell him something about one of the girls. My mind scrambled, searching for something, any little tidbit I could share that would serve as a legitimate excuse.

Unfortunately, I wasn't accustomed to lying. I couldn't come up with a thing.

Without me even thinking the words first, they came out of my mouth. And they sounded decidedly surly.

"Did you have a nice time?"

Sully slowed his pace then came to a stop beside the sofa.

His gaze traveled from the top of my unbound hair, down the length of the red dress to my bare, red-tipped toes. Then it meandered back up again, stopping momentarily at the ruffled v-neckline.

By the time his eyes met mine, my heart was doing a convincing impersonation of a trap drum. Goodness, what this man *did* to me.

He still hadn't answered my question, and apparently he wasn't going to. Instead, he said, "You look amazing."

The drum in my chest was now performing an impressive double-stroke roll.

Making a valiant attempt to keep my tone casual, I lifted my shoulders and let them fall. "The girls and I went bowling."

"Bowling, huh? That bowling alley's going to see a major uptick in business if the league guys think the place attracts women like *you*."

There was a full drum corps in my chest now, and my belly somersaulted, simmering with nerves.

"There were several nannies there. All of us are in our early twenties."

"That's *not* what I meant. I'm talking about this." He waved his forefinger up and down then in a wide circle, the gesture encompassing my whole look.

Sully walked around the arm of the sectional, moving like a prowling cat and taking a seat not right next to me but one cushion over. It was close enough for me to smell his cologne, an earthy compound of sandalwood and citrus with a hint of leather.

Though he'd shaved earlier, his beard was coming back in, the shadow of it just under the skin, making my palms itch to reach out and glide over his strong jaw.

And that was when I spotted it—a splotch of red on his ear. Concerned, I leaned toward him, trying to get a better look. "Did you hurt your ear?"

Sully reached up instinctively. "No."

Rubbing the spot, he studied his fingertips. "It's not blood. It's..." His eyes met mine again. "Nothing. It's nothing."

It was lipstick.

My face heated in a flash of embarrassment—and temper. What a little fool I was, waiting up till all hours of the night while Sully was out canoodling with another woman.

In an abrupt motion, I stood and gathered my book and cup.

"It's late. I should get to bed. And you must be tired after..." I shook my head, feeling ridiculous. "...whatever you've been doing. Good night."

I started to walk past him, intending to scoot around the couch and flee upstairs as quickly as my feet would take me.

Sully's hand shot out and engulfed my wrist, stopping me. The paperback dropped to the carpet with a soft plunk.

"Angelina. Look at me."

Swallowing hard, I forced my gaze to connect with his. The light blue eyes held a knowing smile.

"I didn't kiss her. Her lipstick's on my ear because we went to a nightclub. The music was really loud, and she leaned over and spoke next to my ear a few times so I could hear her. Nothing happened between us."

So he *knew*. He could tell I was jealous. He felt sorry for me.

Ugh.

I stiffened and tugged at my manacled wrist, wishing fervently I had just gone to bed, that I'd never put on this stupid red dress in the first place.

"I don't care," I lied. "I mean—it's none of my business.

You don't have to explain anything to me. I don't care what you do."

Sully rose from the couch, keeping his gentle hold on my wrist, towering over me now. We were standing close. I could feel the warmth of his body, and that yummy cologne smell was more intense. More intoxicating. My heart raced so hard I felt dizzy.

"Are you sure?" His voice was a soft tease. "Because it kinda sounds like you do."

He released my arm and brought his hand up to push my hair back from my face. Two fingers lingered on my cheek, caressing it in the barest whisper of a touch.

The gesture was gentle, almost reverential, and it caused a shiver to pass through me, lifting all the downy hairs on my arms and the back of my neck.

Sully whispered, "If I didn't know better, I might think you were a little... jealous?"

All my breath left my lungs in a whoosh. I felt like I'd been punched in the solar plexus. I was a trapped bird, desperate to escape.

On the other hand, I also felt like this was the only place I could possibly want to be—dangerously close to this dangerous man, at the epicenter of his focus.

I shook my head rapidly, training my gaze on his chest, his bicep, anywhere but those probing ice-blue eyes.

"No," I managed to whisper. "I wasn't. I'm not."

Sully's hand opened, sliding into my hair, lifting it and sifting through the length of it.

"I would be," he said quietly. "If I thought you were out with some guy, having a good time, letting him kiss you and run his hands through this gorgeous hair... I'd be *wicked* jealous. Just thinking of it right now is pissing me off. I'd hate it."

Now I lifted my eyes, searching his for signs that he was joking, that he was teasing me.

There were none. He looked deadly serious in fact.

There was heat in his gaze, and his Adam's apple made a slow circuit up and down the thick column of his throat as he swallowed.

"Angelina… I went out with Bree tonight because—"

"Daddy?"

The small voice from behind me made me jump away from Sully and whirl around. There, standing in her pink nightgown and clutching her stuffed dachshund, was his oldest daughter.

"Skyla." I crouched and moved toward the child. "Are you okay, honey? What's the matter?"

Sully went to her as well, picking her up and kissing her sheet-marked cheek. "Did you have a bad dream, baby?"

Skyla shook her head, the messy dark curls bouncing. "No. Claire is coughing really loud and woke me up. She's sick, I think."

I rose and hurried toward the stairs. "Okay, thank you for letting us know, honey. We'll check on her."

Carrying his daughter, Sully followed me up the stairs, both of us moving quickly toward the littlest Reece's room. The problem was obvious before I'd even opened the door—I recognized the loud, harsh cough that strongly resembled the bark of a seal.

I turned back to Sully.

"It's croup. Go start the shower—as hot as it'll go—and shut the bathroom doors to keep in the steam. I'll bring her in."

EIGHTEEN

So Much for Keeping It Professional

Sully

"Is it bad? I mean, is croup dangerous?"

I'd never heard a cough like that in either one of my girls. It was terrifying, especially when I saw how much difficulty Claire had drawing breath in between coughs.

The worst part was the scared look in my baby's eyes, as if she was begging me to make it better, to help her breathe normally again.

"It's not great... but it's common," Angelina said, her voice ultra-calm. "It makes the rounds at the preschool every year. Most kids get over it pretty quickly."

She sat on the edge of the tub in the bathroom that connected my daughters' rooms.

Claire was in her lap, stripped to her Elmo underwear, her tiny body racked with another round of convulsive coughing.

She'd vomited twice already. Angelina told me it wasn't from the virus itself but from the force of the coughing.

She rocked the little girl, rubbing her back, and looked up at me with worried eyes. "The steam doesn't seem to be helping. Want to get Skyla dressed? That way she'll be ready if we need to go to the hospital."

"The hospital?" I could hardly think now over the panic. How did Angelina look and sound so calm?

"We'll give it a few more minutes. But if she doesn't get some relief soon, I don't think we should take chances," she said. "You hear that whistling sound when she breathes in? It's called stridor. Her air passages are swollen and constricted. Steam is supposed to help but..."

"Let's go now." I strode forward and plucked my child from Angelina's lap, cradling her close to my body. "Can you grab some clothes for her and bring Skyla down? I'm going to start the car."

Within minutes, we were on our way to the closest hospital, but Claire's coughing had seemed to subside the minute the night air hit her. Still, I drove like Dale Earnhardt while Angelina sat in the back seat between the girls.

I met her eyes in the rearview mirror. "What's going on? Is she breathing?"

"Yes," she assured me. "It's actually a lot better now. I read this happens sometimes. We probably should have just taken her out into the yard and walked her around a bit." She hesitated. "Do you want to turn around?"

"No. I want to take her to the emergency room—just to be safe. Her airway's gotta be about the size of a sippy cup straw."

"Okay good. Me too." Angelina resumed murmuring reassuring words to Claire while Skyla slept in her booster seat, worn out from the busy day and oblivious to the tension that filled the car.

By the time we reached the hospital, Claire was breathing easily and acting almost normal. Skyla had woken up, and the two girls were using silly voices to talk to each other in the back seat.

Angelina looked much more relaxed now. I also noticed she had on mascara for the first time since I'd met her and the barest trace of lip gloss too.

Was that for me? Or had she just decided to get all dolled up for her bowling date?

Wait—it hadn't been a date-date, right? I wasn't really sure *who* they'd met up with. Just as quickly as it had occurred to me, I dismissed the notion. Angelina would never take my girls along on a personal meetup with a guy—not without mentioning it to me. I didn't think she even went on dates.

Though her official work hours ended at seven-thirty when the girls went to bed, I couldn't think of a night when Angelina hadn't stayed in.

Now that I thought about it, that might be kind of strange —a twenty-three-year-old woman who stayed home every night.

Maybe it was just what she was used to living with her mom. From the minimal information she'd shared about her personal life, I gathered the woman was a little odd—maybe a lot odd.

Angelina noticed me looking at her and gave me an apologetic smile, lifting her narrow shoulders and letting them drop.

"She seems fine now. I guess I overreacted. I'm sorry I scared you. I just... love her so much."

My heart shot up into my throat then fell back into place where it pummeled my sternum. There was a stinging in my nose and behind my eyes. I blinked hard. "It's okay. Believe me, I understand."

For a few seconds neither of us spoke. We just held sweltering eye contact through the mirror.

Finally, Angelina broke the silence. "What do you want to do?"

Kiss you, my mind screamed. Out loud I said, "Let's go

ahead and go in, since we're already here. It wouldn't hurt to have them check her out. I'm not sure I'll be able to sleep otherwise."

I dropped off Angelina and the girls at the entrance so they could check in while I parked the car.

It was only when we were in the waiting room, seated side by side watching the children play on the floor with the provided toys, that I started breathing easier again. Claire really was okay.

I'd been so frightened. And I'd been clueless while Angelina had been a total pro, instantly taking action to try to help my baby. I reached over and squeezed her fingers.

She returned the pressure, giving me a tight-lipped smile, then withdrew her hand to clasp it with her other one in her lap.

Before tonight, I wouldn't have believed it was possible to admire her more, but I'd have been wrong. She *loved* my daughters.

The events of the night had elevated her from mere rock-star status to Wonder Woman levels in my eyes—and that wasn't even counting the incredible near-kiss moment we'd shared right before everything had gone haywire.

We needed to talk about *that* by the way.

I needed to find out if Angelina really had been jealous of my date with Bree or if it had all been wishful thinking on my part.

Because I'd been doing a *lot* of wishing lately where she was concerned. And I'd done a *lot* of thinking tonight.

The whole time I'd been out with the actress, my attention had been fractured. I'd caught myself missing entire minutes of her steady chatter wondering where Angelina was at the time, whether she and the girls were having fun, whether she was missing me as much as I was missing her.

And then I'd had to discipline myself—again—and ask Bree to please repeat what she'd said.

All in all, I hadn't had a *terrible* time with her. I just hadn't had a good one. Not like the evenings I spent with Angelina.

Fuck, if I could have a great time with her sitting on the living room floor playing Chutes and Ladders, what would an actual evening out be like? I was starting to think it was high time to find out.

After seeing a doctor and being advised to give Claire clear liquids, use a humidifier, and make sure she got plenty of rest, my family—plus Angelina—left the hospital and went home. Both girls fell asleep in the car, and I carried them upstairs, one in each arm.

Once they were tucked into their beds, Angelina and I met at the top of the stairs.

"You tired?" I asked.

"No. I'm wired, actually. I don't think I could go to sleep right now if I tried."

Yes. Relief and pleasure washed through me. "Me, too. I could use a drink. But since I don't drink when I'm in training, I could go for some almond milk."

"Yeah, a cup of tea sounds good to me."

We went downstairs together. The silence between us wasn't awkward, but it *was* telling. There was so much to say, I didn't think either of us knew where to start. I decided to take the initiative once we both had our drinks and were seated back in the living room on the sectional.

"Weird day, huh?" I said.

Angelina flared her eyelids and gave a small laugh. "Definitely. Weird *week*. I can't believe family fun day was only a week ago."

"Um, about that... I want to apologize."

"For what?"

"You know, for what I said about your clothes—and your

hair. That wasn't right," I admitted. "And it's not even true. You have to know I think you look great every day. I was just… my feelings were hurt because you didn't like my gift, and I was acting like a baby. I hurt *your* feelings, and I feel terrible about it. It's been bothering me ever since then."

"Sully," she said softly.

Pulling her legs up onto the couch, she wrapped her arms around herself, gazing at me with wide, dark eyes that seemed to almost shimmer in the dim lighting.

She was so fucking beautiful, and it felt wrong that she was sitting so far away. I wanted her right next to me, close enough to touch, close enough to draw those pretty legs over my lap where I could run my hands over that silky looking skin, and sink them into her hair, and—

Whoa boy. Simmer down.

"I did like your gift," she said, her tone sincere and a little sad. "I love all those clothes. I know you were only being generous like you always are. It just… it made me feel kind of funny."

"Why?"

"Well, for one thing, I'm not used to getting gifts—definitely nothing big and overwhelming like that. And, well…"

She seemed reluctant to go on. "And?" I prodded, dying to hear what she was so hesitant to say.

"Well, sometimes it feels like there's something… *happening* between us, and I didn't know if maybe the gift meant something or if it might change things."

She shook her head in tiny rapid jerks. "Never mind. Forget I said that. I mean, you went out on a *date* tonight, and I'm just—"

Throwing her hands up in the air, she made a strangled sound. "I am so stupid. Forget it. Please just forget it."

She shot up off the couch, grabbed her teacup, and scurried to the kitchen, leaving me sitting in dumbfounded silence.

So she *had* been jealous. She'd also been feeling the same tension around me that I'd felt around her these past few weeks.

And apparently, she had no idea how to talk about it.

I was filled with a strange mixture of excitement and sympathy. I'd always suspected from her demeanor that Angelina was inexperienced with men. But now, I wondered if it went further than that.

Slowly, I got up and walked to the kitchen, trying to decide how to approach her without scaring her away.

Angelina stood at the sink, washing the cup. I came up behind her and stopped, leaning back against the kitchen's large center island.

"You're right," I said. "There is something happening—at least on my part. As I was starting to tell you earlier, I only went out with Bree because a friend set us up... but mostly it was because I was trying to distract myself—from *you*."

Angelina turned around to face me, her eyes wide, her breathing shallow. "You were?"

I nodded. "Yep. But it didn't work. It's been getting harder and harder to ignore, this..." I gestured back and forth between us. "...attraction I feel for you. 'Attraction' isn't even the right word. It's a lot stronger than that. I mean, yes, I think you're gorgeous—everything about you is beautiful—your eyes, your skin, your lips, your hair, your body, your voice. Your little toes."

Angelina looked down at them, attempting to hide a deep blush.

"But it's all of you. Your laugh. The things you say, the way you see the world... the way you love my baby girls."

Taking a breath, I continued my true confessions. "But I didn't think I should do anything about it. I mean, you're thinking about being a *nun* for Chrissakes. Also, you work for me. I didn't want to make things awkward for you—especially if you didn't feel the same way. And until tonight when I came home to find you waiting up for me in that sexy red dress, I didn't think there was any chance of that. I thought I was just some old dude creeping on the young nanny."

"You're not that much older than me—only three years."

"Yeah, but as they say, it's not the years but the mileage. I haven't exactly led a chaste life. I mean, lately, yes—I might as well be a monk. But before I got married, I... danced with a lot of girls. You seem, I don't know... untouched by the world. Pure."

Her smile disappeared. "I don't like that word. My mother uses that word."

"Okay, well, innocent then, whatever. I didn't want to put any pressure on you or make any assumptions, especially since you live here."

She nodded. "It *is* complicated." After a moment's pause, she gave me a quizzical look. "You really couldn't tell I was attracted to you, too?"

My soul soared. "You are? I didn't know. I *hoped*, and then I was mad at myself for hoping. But I really had no idea."

"Even when I put on that bikini?"

"All I knew about that bikini was how much I liked you *in* it. Honestly, I thought you wore it to punish me for what I said. Believe me, it was a *very* effective punishment."

Angelina covered her giggle with one hand but then she got serious. "I kind of *did* want to punish you. But more than that, I think I wanted you to see me as a woman—*not* a frumpy old one."

Closing my eyes, I dropped my chin and shook my head. "I wish I'd never said that. Sometimes I can be a real jerk."

"No," Angelina said. "I've never seen that. *I* was the jerk. I'm sorry for what I said about your wife leaving you. I had no right. I don't know the first thing about marriage and having a family."

I took a step closer, stretching out a hand to sweep her hair back from her shoulder and sliding it around to caress the nape of her neck.

"That's not true. You've done more to make this house a home than I could ever do. You've made us feel like a real family—it never really felt that way with Anouk. It was like Skyla and Claire and I were just... in her way, you know? Like we were obstacles preventing her from doing what she *really* wanted to be doing."

I stopped, took a breath then reconnected with her eyes.

"When I was growing up, I didn't really even know what a family was supposed to be like, which is why I think Anouk and I got married in the first place and stayed together as long as we did. I didn't know there was anything better than what we had. Now I do. Because of you."

As I spoke, Angelina's chin tilted up, and her eyelids drifted lower, lower. Unless I was a complete dope—and the point was debatable—she wanted to be kissed. By *me.*

There was no way I was going to turn down an invitation like that—not from this woman who'd so subtly but thoroughly worked her way into my heart.

Not when it was all I'd been fantasizing about for weeks. Well, not *all* I'd fantasized about. In my fantasies it started with kissing and turned into touching, tasting...

So much for keeping it professional.

Lowering my face to hers, I felt her soft breath strike my lips, and it was like a match to gasoline, lighting a fire in my veins from head to toe.

Her lips were even more lush and delicious than I'd imagined them to be. And she was even more sweetly passionate than I could have hoped.

Her hands came up to grip my shoulders then they were sliding up and down my arms in frantic, grabby motions that made me think she'd been wanting to touch me as much as I'd been wanting to touch her.

The busy little hands slid up to my neck and around it, sinking into my hair and gripping as if she was falling, and the strands were the only things keeping her from plunging to the bottom of a ravine.

I barely felt the slight sting. I was too swept up in the sensations rampaging through the rest of me. Heat, joy, desire. Pleasure so acute my skin felt like it was lighting up everywhere she touched it.

"Sully," she whispered, and the sound of her voice was fierce and reckless, like she was so overcome with wanting me she didn't know what to do with herself.

Yes.

I knew that desperate feeling—I was the *personification* of that feeling.

After all these weeks of burning for her, of denying my feelings because they were inappropriate, unrequited, *wrong*, I would finally be allowed to turn my fantasies into reality.

Because they *weren't* unrequited. She wanted me, too. The woman of my dreams wanted me just as ferociously as I wanted her.

Cradling her small face in my hands, I covered it with kisses, lingering on her pillowy soft lips once more before moving to her neck, that sweet, unbelievably pretty neck I'd daydreamed about kissing every time she wore her hair up.

God, I wanted her so badly it literally hurt, wanted *all* of her at once.

As my lips coasted from her neck to her collarbone and my hands twisted in the skirts of her dress, I disciplined myself to slow down. I *would* have all of her—in time. We were inevitable.

For now, I nibbled when I wanted to devour, browsed when I wanted to buy out the whole store. Wrapping an arm around her lower back, I drew her against me, but I kept my kisses gentle and my hands confined to safe territory, stroking her back and gripping her waist.

Only when Angelina was writhing against me and making the most desperate sounds into my mouth did I allow myself to touch her in the way I was craving.

My hand, which had stayed obediently in the vicinity of her waist and back, slid up to curve beneath her breast, and *fuck me* did that feel good.

Angelina seemed to like it, too—a lot. Which only made me more ravenous. Shaking with adrenaline, I pushed one strap from her shoulder while kissing her throat and upper chest.

When I slipped my hand inside the dress, I discovered she wore no bra with it. Her nipple tightened into a perfect bud under my touch, and it took all my strength not to rip the whole dress off then and there.

Angelina shivered and gripped my bicep with one hand, her short nails digging into the skin while her other hand caressed my nape and scalp. She moaned softly, a sound so thick with pleasure and desire I could come just from listening to it.

As it was, my dick was throbbing and rock hard. Her hand on the back of my head exerted the slightest pressure, and I took it as a sign to proceed. I pulled the side of the dress down further, exposing the satiny slope.

"Angel... you are so beautiful," I murmured before dropping my head and pulling the peak into my mouth.

Angelina's legs buckled as she melted against me. I bent one knee, supporting her weight on my thigh. Palming her bottom with one hand, I guided the front of her body back and forth in a slow, deliberate rub against the ridge of my erection while I used my lips and tongue in dragging licks over one breast and then the other.

Tangling both hands in my hair now, Angelina panted and strained against me. The sounds she made were a combination of surprise and delight, and it was just about to send me into a fucking frenzy.

"Oh my God, Angel, you taste so good. I want to taste you everywhere."

At the very limits of my self-control, I dropped to my knees and pushed the bottom of the dress upward, revealing white panties that were the perfect blend of innocent and sexy.

My mouth literally watered. I leaned forward and started to press a kiss to the front of the delicate fabric.

As if some mythical wizard had blasted us with an invisible shockwave, Angelina sprang away from me.

"No," she yelped. "We have to stop. We can't... *I* can't... do that."

And now my heart was pounding for *two* reasons. I tried to untangle my racing thoughts enough to keep up with the abrupt change in her behavior.

"What's wrong?" I looked around, getting to my feet. "Are you worried about the girls? Did you hear one of them?"

She shook her head, still backing away from me with one hand clutching the top of her dress trying to pull it up and the other hand thrown out in front of her. It was shaking.

"No. But we shouldn't do this. You're my employer. I'm your children's nanny."

I chuckled, stepping toward her. "I'm willing to overlook that. You seemed pretty okay with it too a minute ago." I thought for a second. "Was I moving too fast?"

Angelina had backed herself into the kitchen table, causing one of the chair legs to scrape loudly on the floor. She nodded vigorously up and down then side to side, like a little bobblehead doll.

"I don't even know how it happened. One minute we were talking and then suddenly we were kissing, and you're such a good kisser, and I knew better, but I just couldn't help it, and then..."

Her rambling words drifted off to nothingness. She just stared up at me with huge dark eyes. I wanted nothing more than to grab her and kiss her again, to remove whatever doubts she seemed to be struggling with, but some deeper instinct told me that would be a mistake.

My hands raised in a gentling gesture, I stalked slowly toward her. "You're right. That was definitely too fast. I'm sorry. It's been a long time for me, too. But we can go slow. I'm fine with that."

Now Angelina's head swung back and forth on a swivel. "It hasn't been a long time for me."

I stopped in place, dropping my hands to my side. "What do you mean?"

Did she have a *boyfriend* I'd somehow never heard anything about? When would she have even seen the guy?

Jealousy roared to life inside me, converting the driving passion from moments ago into clouds of smoky displeasure.

Whoever the guy was—he was *gone*. I would see to that.

"I mean..." She took a shaky breath. "I mean, it's been *never* for me. I've never been with anyone. Ever. I've never even kissed anyone before tonight."

What? My mind went blank for a second.

How was it possible in this day and age a woman Angelina's age—who looked like *her*—could possibly be a virgin, much less a never-been-kissed virgin?

"You can't be serious. That..." I turned and pointed across the room as if the specter of the two of us in each other's arms was still visible there. "...was your first kiss? In your *life*?"

She nodded. "Yes. I know it must seem weird to you, but I've never dated anyone. I never went to school with boys, so there was no possibility of even a stolen kiss under the stairwell or whatever kids do at co-ed schools."

"Oh. Well."

The raging emotion swirling in my chest subsided a bit, and tenderness seeped in to fill the vacuum.

"Wow. I don't think I've ever been anyone's first *anything*, much less their first kiss."

I shook my head, trying to wrap my mind around it. "If I'd known, I would have done a better job of it or something."

Angelina, who seemed to have settled a bit now that I understood, gave me a shy smile. "I don't know how it could have been any better."

And just like that, all the hard-charging energy was back, filling me with the desire to reach out and pull her into my arms again. But I didn't.

"I'm glad you liked it, but just wait. I promise you... it gets better than that." At the bashful turn of her head, I added, "I'm glad I was your first kiss, Angel."

"Glad" was such an inadequate word. "Ecstatic" would have been a better choice.

For a moment her eyes lingered on mine, then her gaze dropped to my lips before landing on the floor.

"It can't happen again."

NINETEEN
Kind of Simple

Angelina

Sully did a literal double take before his gaze locked onto mine, searing into me like a blue laser.

"You must be joking." He gestured with his hands, the way he did when he was worked up over something. "You can't possibly think things can just go back to normal after *that*. I mean, I've never felt anything like that in my life."

Neither had I, obviously. And I was pretty sure it wasn't a *good* thing I felt it now.

Before we'd kissed—and done all the rest—it was still possible to lie to myself, to tell myself everything was okay, it was normal, that I could handle the situation.

Which was that this arrangement was temporary.

In a few weeks, it would end. The girls would go back to their mother in New York, Sully would leave for his title fight. I would either move into the monastery to begin my postulancy or I'd find another job and another way of life.

Two months ago, it had seemed like a good plan, a way to give myself time to decide what I really wanted in life.

But I'd changed since then. I was turning into a person I almost didn't recognize.

And if I let Sully kiss me again, if I let things keep moving down the path they were on, I'd *have* no more choice in the matter.

I would want to stay with him forever. I'd never be able to leave when the time came.

Already I felt a physical pain in my stomach when I thought about living apart from him. I could not—could *not* —allow myself to fall in love with him. Which meant no more kissing and *definitely* no more of the other stuff we'd done tonight.

"I'm not joking, Sully. It can't happen again."

"Why?" His tone was ragged, tinged with desperation. "This is *right*. Don't you *feel* it? I could swear you felt it too."

He started moving toward me again, his hands outstretched as if prepared to pull me against him so he could kiss me again and prove his point.

I couldn't back away any farther without crawling across the kitchen table, so I held out my hand, palm-up like a stop sign.

"No. Don't come any closer. I don't..." My throat tried to close up to prevent the lie from escaping. "I don't want you to touch me again. I mean, I *do*, but I don't."

My chest tightened. I pushed my hair behind my ears, swallowing repeatedly. "It's confusing. I'm confused, and I don't like feeling this way."

Sully looked like it was killing him, but he did stop. He gave me a nod of understanding and pushed his hands into his pockets. His tone was soothing, like one I'd use with one of the girls when she was upset.

"It doesn't have to be confusing. I mean, it's kind of simple really. I like you—like, really, really like you. I think you like me, too."

"I do." I almost laughed at the ridiculous understatement. "But it's not simple. You're my boss, and this is only temporary, and in a few weeks it'll be over. And I can't be casual about this."

"It doesn't have to be temporary, either. And I *don't* feel casual about it. I feel—"

"No," I interrupted in a panicky voice. "Don't say anymore. We've already stepped so far over the line I don't know if I can even stay and keep working here."

That shut him up. He looked scared. "You're thinking of leaving?"

"I don't want to. But..." My mind cast about for the right words. "It wouldn't be good for the girls—for us to be involved. I can't let myself be distracted, and you're... very distracting."

Now he was smiling.

"I'm not complimenting you," I clarified. "That's *not* a good thing. If I'm not going into religious service—which I'll probably still do—I'll be doing childcare professionally in some capacity. And this... this is *not* professional behavior. There's probably even some sort of code against it."

"I'm not going to report you to the Board of Nanny and Preschool Teacher Ethics, if that's what you're worried about," he teased.

"Sully, I'm serious. Please take this seriously."

His expression sobered. "Okay, I'm taking you seriously. Just tell me one thing."

"What?"

"Are you sure this isn't about the fact that was your first kiss, and you're a virgin, and you might be a *little* bit scared because you're experiencing sexual desire for the first time?"

"No," I blurted then modulated my tone. "I don't know. Maybe."

The sound of the words "sexual desire" coming out of his

sexy mouth had my mind even more scrambled than it was before, and the place between my legs squeezed in frustrated tension.

"I just know that I can't handle this right now. There's too much up in the air in my life, and I'm pretty sure I shouldn't be making major life decisions under the influence of... of..."

"Lust?" Sully supplied helpfully.

I closed my eyes, mortified and ashamed and still a little turned on in spite of myself. When I managed speech again, my tone was calm and even and filled with determination.

"If it happens again... if we can't... control ourselves... I won't be able to stay. I'll have to move out and quit my job."

Sully's brows pulled together. "I don't want that."

"Me either. So I think we should just... keep it... professional. Do you think you can do that?"

For a long moment, he just stared at me, biting his lower lip, barely breathing as far as I could tell.

Then he blew out a long exhale. "If that's what you really want."

"It is," I insisted.

"So I'm your boss, and you're my employee, and that's it, right?"

"That's it." Why did I feel a twinge of disappointment that he was agreeing so easily? And *why* did this whole conversation make me feel so hollow inside? I was a *mess*.

Another lingering look, another long exhale on Sully's part. Then he nodded. "Well, then, I guess I'll see you in the morning... Miss Rappaport."

"Goodnight... Mr. Reece," I breathed as I watched him turn and go up the stairs, leaving me in the kitchen alone.

So. Alone.

Damn.

I inhaled sharply, covering my lips with my fingertips, though the swear hadn't actually crossed them.

My mouth felt tender, a little swollen, and aching to be kissed again. I guessed *it* wasn't confused.

The reality of kissing Sully and touching his body, of feeling him touch me had been *so* much better than what the book had described. It was going to be hard to forget. I mean, you couldn't *unfeel* something.

Dropping into a chair at the kitchen table, I rested my face in my palms. How was I going to manage these last few weeks living under his roof… when all I dreamed about was being underneath *him*?

I'd *have* to manage it… somehow.

We would go back to being employer and employee, and at the end of the summer we'd go our separate ways. Then I'd move on to my new life—whatever and wherever it was—with my heart intact.

* * *

After collecting and washing the remaining dishes, I started a load of laundry then went upstairs to go to bed.

On the way to my room, I passed the home theater and heard noise coming from inside. Peeking in the open door, I saw the outline of Sully's neck and head as he watched something on the giant screen.

It was a sports program—boxing. If I wasn't mistaken, one of the fighters on the screen was the guy who was challenging Sully for the World Heavyweight title next month, Travis Diggs. He must have had a fight tonight, or maybe it was a recording of an old fight Sully was watching to prepare.

Seeing the man strike his opponent, the power behind his punches and the rage in his fierce eyes and expression, I shuddered. I didn't want Sully to get into the ring with him.

But it wasn't my decision to make, and not that many

minutes ago I'd just ensured I would have no influence on his decisions now or in the future.

He wouldn't care about my opinion, and in a matter of weeks he wouldn't know about or care about my decisions either.

Sullivan Reece wasn't mine to worry about and protect—no matter how much I might wish otherwise.

TWENTY

New Source of Willpower

Sully

My body still vibrating, my hands still tingling with the thrill of having touched her at last, I put as much distance between myself and Angelina Rappaport as possible.

I'd called her Angel tonight for the first time—the first time out loud anyway—and that was what she'd felt like in my hands, soft and sweet and too good to be true.

As it turned out, those moments of exquisite closeness *had* been. I felt like a fallen angel myself, cast from Heaven straight to Hell where I would be cursed to burn for her forever with no relief.

What had happened? What had I done wrong?

I didn't think I'd pushed that hard or that far. Certainly I hadn't done nearly half the things I'd been fantasizing about.

And she'd definitely been right there with me for at least a few minutes. But I'd blown it by moving too fast. I'd scared her. And then she'd scared me right back by threatening to leave.

I was more than scared actually. I was terrified of her

leaving me—and the girls of course. My first thought *should* have been for them.

That proved how hard I'd fallen for this woman in spite of all my vows to play it cool, keep it professional, and use my famous self-control.

Ha! If my trainer and sparring partners could only see me now, a knotted mess of unrequited longing.

Well, I'd have to tap into some new source of willpower because there was no way I would risk running off the best thing that had ever happened to my daughters. And to me. We all needed her too much to let her get away.

Angelina was like a dessert that was too beautiful to eat. Delicious, but to have it, you'd have to destroy it.

Even if I never got to kiss her and touch her like that again, I had to have her in my life in some capacity. I'd take whatever I could get—and probably a whole helluva lot of cold showers.

Grabbing the remote, I turned on the big screen and the DVR, hitting play on the fight I'd recorded earlier tonight. I hadn't even heard what the outcome was thanks to my date with Bree then being at the hospital with Claire then alone with Angelina and *thoroughly* distracted.

No. No re-living that scene. Put it out of your mind. Time to concentrate on work.

I steered my mind back to the fight, which was beginning now on the screen in front of me. The only thing I knew about it was that it must have been epic because I'd gotten a text from the promoter asking if I'd watched and asking me to call once I'd seen it.

My trainer, Tony, had also texted, and there'd been a missed call from him. His text had read:

-Did you see? Are you okay?

What the hell? I would respond once I'd watched the recorded footage. I assumed Diggs had won the match and probably in spectacular fashion. A first-round knockout maybe?

I settled in to watch, following the action closely. As I always did when preparing to face a challenger, I made mental notes about the other boxer's form and habits, about the unconscious signals he gave that telegraphed his next move.

Though I'd faced many fighters—some of them more experienced than this twenty-year old phenom—I'd never seen anyone quite so innately powerful—or so vicious.

The fight didn't end in the first round but went to the fifth, when Diggs had apparently had enough of toying with his opponent, Roy Gray.

He delivered a crisp right uppercut to Gray's jaw, followed by a hard left to the side of his head. Gray dropped to the mat, unconscious on impact.

Medical personnel rushed into the ring, moved the man onto a stretcher, and rushed him away as Diggs stood looking coldly on.

A shudder worked its way through my body as I listened to the analysts talk about the hit and give updates on Gray's condition. They announced he'd suffered a seizure before reaching the hospital and had been taken in for emergency brain surgery.

I switched channels to a live sports broadcast for more updated information. I had to wait through some baseball highlights first, but the topic switched to the fight and the latest information on Gray.

The sports anchors said he was currently in intensive care in extremely critical condition—and in a coma. From their word choice and tone, it was clear he wasn't expected to survive.

Switching off the TV, I sat in the dark home theater. It wasn't news to me that Travis Diggs was dangerous. I'd never underestimated the young contender, knowing he'd be the best fighter I'd faced in a long time.

The truth was any fight on this level could be a man's last. When punches were being thrown with an impact of a thousand pounds of pressure per square inch, and a title fight was the equivalent of being in a car crash—each and every round —there was considerable risk.

We all knew it. It was something you accepted then put out of your mind, telling yourself it wouldn't be *this* time, *this* fight, convincing yourself you could be invincible one more time.

But tonight's events were a reminder of how quickly things could change.

Roy Gray had been at the top of his game, young, healthy, and confident about stepping into the ring with Diggs. He hadn't expected this outcome, just like I never expected to lose.

I'd never been afraid to fight before. It had been a way of life for me since I was thirteen years old and had wandered into Tony's Gym one night when my mom was out with yet another new guy.

Bored and sick of the cold, lonely apartment, I'd gone out for a walk on the streets of Worcester. The gym door had been open, and I'd stepped inside, attracted by the noise and lights.

Tony had welcomed me and told me to come back anytime. The chance meeting had set my life on a whole new course.

But things were different now. I had a *lot* to lose. I couldn't allow myself to end up like Gray and leave my little girls alone with Anouk as their only parent.

Which meant I had to focus more and train harder for this fight than I ever had in my life. I could not allow anything or anyone to distract me—not even Angelina.

It was for the best anyway. If she'd didn't want me, it would be stupid of me to keep on wanting her so much.

Well you said you needed a new source of willpower. Here it was on a silver platter.

I would put a clamp on my feelings for Angelina and redirect all that pent-up frustration and desire toward preparing for what could very well be a fight for my life.

TWENTY-ONE

A Night Out

Sully

For the next few weeks, Angelina and I barely saw each other. I got up earlier and made my own breakfast, getting down to the gym and training all day without taking a break.

I encouraged her to go out with friends in the evenings after she'd prepared dinner for the girls, telling her I'd handle their bedtime routine alone.

On the nights she stayed home, I went up to the theater alone and studied footage of old fights, looking for any advantage I could use—and preserving my focus and peace of mind.

For her part, Angelina went back to wearing her frumpy old lady clothes and to pulling her hair back into that severe bun-thing. It annoyed the shit out of me, but I disciplined myself to channel even that irritation into my prep and training, doing my best to save every scrap of emotion for the ring.

Even when she got a call that her mom had been taken to the hospital, I obeyed her wishes, kept my distance, and let her go alone though everything in me wanted to be with her and comfort and support her during what had to be a difficult time.

All in all, I thought I'd done a pretty good job of turning things around, of mastering my longing for her. Until the night of her birthday.

The last thing I needed was a distraction—the title match was only four days away, and it was actually my last night at home before leaving for New York where the fight would take place at the Barclays Center.

But I just couldn't let the occasion pass without doing something special for her.

No one else would, and besides, she deserved it. She deserved every good thing anyone could give her or do for her. She'd changed the girls' lives, changed *my* life—even if she didn't want to be a permanent part of it.

This morning I'd made sure Skyla and Claire made cards for her and gave her flowers and sent them all off to spend the day visiting art museums, which I knew Angelina loved. When they got home, I took over, encouraging her to take a bath and relax while I gave the girls their dinner and put them to bed.

Once they'd dropped off to sleep, I searched for Angelina. She was in the kitchen rummaging through the refrigerator.

"Hey," I said from the entry to the room.

She whirled around. "Hi. Did you... need something? Are you hungry? I was just about to heat up some leftovers if you want me to fix you something too."

"Actually, I was hoping we could talk."

"Sully..." Her tone was a warning.

I cut her off before she could go further and turn me down. "About the girls... since I'm taking them back to their mom tomorrow. I want to be able to, like, give her a full update on how they're doing, what all they learned this summer and stuff."

Angelina dried her hands on a kitchen towel, barely meeting my eyes. "Of course. Where? The living room?"

"I was thinking we could sit outside. It's a nice night. I've been cooped up in the house all day."

"What if one of the girls gets up and needs something?"

I pulled a baby monitor from my pocket and waggled it. "Got it covered."

"Okay, fine," she agreed.

My stomach twisted with nerves. This was the moment of truth. For days I'd been making private phone calls setting it up so she wouldn't suspect anything. The final preparations had been made after dark. Hopefully everything was ready.

"Hold on—I have to send a text real quick," I said.

I took out my phone and brought up the thread of communication with the party planner who'd helped me, tapping in the message she'd been waiting for.

-Coming out now.

Then I nodded to Angelina and went to the back door, opening it for her. As soon as she stepped onto the dark terrace, the event coordinator did her thing. The lights went on, revealing my surprise.

Toward the back of the yard, past the pool and overlooking the ocean, sat a newly delivered gazebo. It was the wooden kind, octagon-shaped and strung with fairy lights all around.

In the center of it a cloth-draped table had been set with dinnerware for two, wine glasses, flowers, and candles. A waiter from a local catering service stood off to the side holding a covered platter, ready to serve Angelina.

She stared at the scene in front of her, lifting both hands to cover her mouth and nose, then she turned to me wide-eyed.

"What is this?"

I shrugged. "I thought we could eat while we talked. You did ask if I was hungry."

With a hand on her lower back, I urged her to walk with

me down the terrace steps and across the yard. Angelina stayed quiet and looked like she was sleep-walking—she might have been in shock.

When we reached the table, I pulled her chair out for her then took the one opposite her, opening the wine bottle and pouring some into each of our glasses. Then I lifted mine and tipped it toward her, smiling even though it felt like my heart was tearing in half.

This wasn't just a birthday celebration—it was a farewell.

"To the birthday girl. May this year be her best ever... whatever it may hold."

Angelina's eyes filled with tears. She lifted her glass and clinked the rim against mine.

"Thank you, Sully," she whispered. Her voice sounded thick and raspy like she might be struggling not to cry. "I... I'm so shocked, I don't know what to say."

"You don't have to say anything. Just enjoy your birthday dinner."

She took a sip from her glass and set it down beside her plate. The waiter took that as his cue to begin serving. Removing the lid from his platter, he delivered two plates of appetizers to the table followed by a main course of seafood scampi with a mixed green salad.

As Angelina began to eat, she started looking and acting more like herself. She took another sip of chardonnay.

"This is my first time having wine," she told me.

"I know. That's why I ordered this one—the caterer said it was a nice 'starter wine.'"

"Sounds like the bottle should have training wheels on it or something." She laughed. "It's also my first time eating out for my birthday."

"You're kidding."

She shook her head. "No. My mom didn't believe in being 'frivolous,' and she definitely didn't believe in going out. I actually started cooking my own birthday dinners after about age ten."

"Well that sucks—pardon my language, but it does. No Chuck E. Cheese? No princess parties?"

"Not a one." Angelina gave me a sad smile, then her face brightened. "This is wonderful, though. The food's delicious."

"Well, you know, I would have taken you out to someplace fancy like the Cliffhouse or something, but I thought you'd probably tell me no."

She laughed. "You'd have been right. But you found a way around it, Mr. Sneaky. I guess if you can't bring Muhammad to the mountain, you bring dinner to the backyard, right?"

Looking down at herself and the casual sundress and flip flops she was wearing, she added, "I sort of feel like I should be more dressed up or something, though. I just threw this on after my bath."

"*You*—look perfect," I said honestly.

Angelina dropped her face, apparently trying to hide a blush that was still obvious. Once again, she looked like she was fighting back tears. "When did you have time to do all this? I mean, they built a gazebo in one day?"

"It's a pre-built one actually. They just had to deliver it, which they did while you were out with the girls, and then the catering company and the decorators came and did their part tonight. All I did was lift my 'big fat wallet,' as you like to say. No muscle necessary." I grinned at her. "It's really not a big deal."

"It *is*." She blinked, looked away, took another breath, and went on. "It is a big deal. I can't believe you went to all this trouble for me. It really is the best birthday present I can imagine."

"Oh this isn't your present."

She blinked again. "It's not?"

I shook my head, twisting my lips to the side trying to contain the huge smile that wanted to come out. "No."

Picking up my phone, I sent another text then set the phone down again.

"*This* is your present."

TWENTY-TWO

Lucky the First Time

Sully

The beginning notes of a classical composition reached us through the darkness, coming from the direction of the pool house.

Then the strings of lights around them turned on, and the two violinists, the cellist, and the viola player were revealed.

Angelina squealed and clapped. "Oh my God a real string quartet! I've only seen them on YouTube." After listening for a few seconds, she said, "Is that Brahms' opus number sixty-seven in B flat major?"

I laughed out loud. "If you say so, Angel. All I know is it's Brahms. I told them that's what you like so they'd better play it all night."

She turned back to face me, her face flushed and those tears finally winning the battle and streaming down her cheeks.

"Sully... I'm overwhelmed. This is just... *wow*. No one has ever done something this thoughtful for me before. And no one has *ever* known me well enough to know exactly what I'd like. Thank you."

Reaching across the table, I swiped my thumb under her eye. "You're welcome, Angel. Happy birthday."

And now *I* was about to cry. I switched the subject.

"So how's your mom doing? We never talked about it after you went to visit her in the hospital."

Her mood changed instantly. "She's home now—I think. I only saw her for a few minutes, and it didn't go well. She didn't even want her doctor to tell me what was wrong with her since I'm 'no longer a family member,' but they said they were going to discharge her in a day or two. She only let me in so she could say what she wanted to say... then she took me off the approved visitor list."

My jaw unhinged. "What? Aren't you like, her *only* family member?"

"Not now. I'm disowned."

"So, was that what she wanted to say to you? That she took you out of the will or something?"

Angelina's expression shuttered. "I don't really want to talk about her anymore, if that's okay."

"No problem." I wasn't sure what I'd been thinking even bringing it up on what should have been a happy night. If Angelina was going to leave, I wanted her to do it with only the best memories.

"You know what Skyla said to me tonight at bedtime?" I asked, trying to bring some lightness back into the conversation.

"What?"

"She burrowed into my chest and said, 'I just want to cuddle with you, Daddy. I don't want to do anything but cuddle you right now.' God, I'm gonna miss having them here every day."

Angelina's hand went to her chest, resting over her heart. "They are just so sweet. Claire said to me today, 'I love you and

Daddy better than anything. I love you more than any of my toys—even the downstairs toys—even the pool toys.'"

I laughed and raised my eyebrows. "Wow. That's pretty big."

"I thought so." Her smile matched mine.

Of course I knew better than to say it out loud, but I thought it was pretty significant that Claire had included Angelina in that declaration. Inside my head the words were screaming at an almost deafening pitch—

Can't you see *it? Don't you* know *you're supposed to stay?*

But then, the girls weren't staying. So that meant Angelina couldn't really *be* their live-in nanny anymore. They were due to go back to Anouk's place in New York and start school there next week. I was taking them with me when I left tomorrow.

Honestly, I didn't know how it was all supposed to work, but to me it seemed obvious none of this had been an accident. It felt like Angelina was *meant* to be part of our little family.

She'd agreed to stay here in the house and keep an eye on it until my return from New York. Once it was just the two of us and she was no longer in my employment, we could have a whole *new* kind of discussion.

I assumed she was still trying to decide whether to begin the postulancy thing or look for new employment and new housing, and I desperately wanted to weigh in on that and make sure she understood all of her options.

In fact, I was dying to ask her about her plans *tonight*. But she hadn't brought it up, and I didn't want to upset her any further on her birthday. This night was supposed to be about *her*—not what I wanted and needed.

So, we listened to the quartet play and finished our meals while chatting about safe subjects like the activities she'd shared with Skyla and Claire this summer, plans for their upcoming school year in Manhattan, and the title fight.

"Are you going three days ahead of time to sort of settle into the environment?" she asked.

"Basically. I'll stay with my trainer and the rest of my team in a friend's empty apartment. It's near the venue and the location of the press conference and pre-fight weigh-in."

Silently I added, *And far from* you.

I'd need a few days of distance from Angelina to get my head in the right place for the fight. I loved being around her, but I was also aware she made me... soft.

Not in a bad way for everyday life—God knew I had plenty of rough edges that needed softening—but before a bout against arguably the toughest fighter alive today?

No, I couldn't afford any softness.

"Plus, I thought it would be good for the girls to have a few days to settle back into their old rooms and old routines before school starts, to readjust to how Anouk does things."

Angelina nodded thoughtfully. "Change can be hard on little ones. I know they've been very happy here with you."

"And with *you*."

She looked away and picked up her nearly empty wine glass, finishing its contents. I didn't refill it because I knew she wasn't used to drinking—she'd already had two glasses.

Much more and I'd have to carry her back to the house and tuck her into bed.

On second thought...

I was saved from making a *very* bad decision by the waiter, who returned with a miniature birthday cake ablaze with candles. We both sang the birthday song to Angelina before she fanned out the flames and closed her eyes to make a wish.

When she opened them, she studied the cake. It was decorated with white buttercream frosting and real flowers.

"Edible flowers," she whispered. "This is beautiful. There's no way I could eat all this, though."

"You? That's *my* piece," I joked. "Nah, actually I'm staying off sugar until after the fight. I told them to make it four servings, though, in case you want to share it with Skyla and Claire in the morning—and have a piece for breakfast yourself."

"You really are the best man I've ever known," she said in a soft voice that brushed over me and raised goosebumps on my neck and arms.

Or "duck balls" as Claire would call them.

The combination of that voice, the look in her eyes, and her utter gorgeousness was causing a reaction below the belt as well.

Which was pointless. Not only was there *no* chance of having sex with Angelina tonight, but every trainer I'd ever had in my life preached the "no sex in training" gospel.

Definitely not in the week before a fight.

So even if pigs flew and the pool froze over here in August and she *begged* me to make love to her... I couldn't.

So you can just stand the fuck down, big guy.

I deflected her sweet comment with a joke. "I'd say I'm flattered, but I'm pretty sure I'm the *only* man you've ever known."

Angelina laughed. "True. True."

Her eyes closed for a long blink before she opened them and absolutely paralyzed me with an intense look. "I guess I got lucky the first time."

Wait a minute—*was* that... flirting?

Was she trying to tell me something? Had she changed her mind about us?

Or maybe she was tipsier than I realized. I tried to read her eyes, but she turned away and focused on the string quartet.

After a few minutes, another sound caught my notice—a light patter. And then it grew heavier. It was raining. *Shit.*

The musicians stood and hurried into the pool house, where I assumed they'd left their instrument cases. The catering staff ran for cover as well, joining us under the gazebo.

Angelina looked up at me. "Was there a storm in the forecast?"

"I don't know. I didn't think so. Maybe it'll pass quickly."

No such luck. The drops hitting the surface of the pool and the roof over our heads steadily grew in size and speed until it was a full-on gusher.

The waiter, who huddled close to the table now, stared at his phone. "The radar shows a pretty big system moving up from Connecticut. There's a lot of red and yellow coming this way."

Uh oh. Angelina put into words what I was thinking. "Claire's afraid of big storms."

"I know." I grimaced. "If she hears thunder, she'll get up and come looking for us."

"Looks like we're making a run for it then," she said.

I nodded, turning to the waiter. "We've gotta get back to the house. You guys are welcome to hang out in the pool house until it's over—or as long as you want. The bar in there's fully stocked."

"Really? Thanks man—I mean, Mr. Reece."

I smiled at him and slipped several folded bills into his hand. "Thanks for the great service. Have a good night."

Then I offered my hand to Angelina. "Ready?"

She wince-smiled and nodded, and we stepped out of the gazebo onto the wet lawn, breaking into a run and sprinting up the grassy incline to the house.

TWENTY-THREE

Knockout

Angelina

Sully and I burst through the back door into the kitchen, dripping and laughing.

"I think my *bones* are wet," I said. "I could barely even see where we were going out there." Belatedly I added, "Oh, I hope we don't mess up the floors."

"It's just a little water. And the cleaners are scheduled to come tomorrow," Sully said.

I nodded. "Still, we should go to the laundry room and not drip through the whole house."

We crossed the kitchen toward the adjoining laundry room where we could put our wet clothes right into the washer.

Thankfully there had been no thunder and lightning—yet—and the baby monitor was still quiet. Only the gentle shush of the girls' white noise sound machines could be heard.

Hopefully neither of them would wake—or at least not until we'd had a chance to dry off and change.

Once inside the laundry room, Sully began stripping off his wet garments, completely free of body shame the way so many athletes seemed to be—not that he had anything to be ashamed of.

On the contrary, he was in better shape than he'd been when I'd first met him, and that was saying something. When he pulled his sopping shirt over his head, I experienced a head-rush that caused me to wobble a bit on my feet.

Muscle upon muscle rippled beneath the wet, satiny skin. His arms, chest, and shoulders were just massive, and unless I'd forgotten how to count, his abdomen now featured an *eight*-pack.

He smelled *phenomenal.*

Standing so close to him in the tight quarters of the laundry room, I had the craziest urge to lean forward and lick the large vertical tattoo that covered his right ribs.

It spelled "family," and the Y ended at just the top of one of the v-lines that disappeared beneath the waistband of his boxer briefs.

Sully plucked a clean folded towel from the top of the dryer and started rubbing himself with it.

"You okay?" he asked, his voice a soft rumble in the quiet space. "You're just standing there."

I shook my head and blinked rapidly, trying to fight off the mesmerizing pull I felt toward his body. "Yeah. Yeah sure. I'm just... a little cold."

"You should get out of that wet dress." Grabbing another towel, he draped it over my shoulders. "Here, I'll turn around, and you can take it off and wrap yourself in that. Can't have you getting chilled."

The truth was, I was having the opposite problem. In spite of being rain-drenched, I felt hot all over like I was running a fever, and the cause was no mystery.

It was being close to him again.

During the past few weeks, Sully had done precisely as I'd asked, pulling away and returning to an impersonal, professional, employer-employee relationship. He hadn't touched me or even gotten within a few feet of me.

It had nearly driven me crazy.

I'd thought it was torture having him so close by and tempting all the time, but once he'd essentially removed himself from my daily life, I understood the true meaning of the word "torture."

And now tonight, with the whole surprise birthday dinner, and the string quartet, the sweet things he'd said, and the way he'd looked at me... well, I was questioning *everything*.

I'd told Sully we could never kiss again, never have a repeat of that intimate—and much replayed—scene in the kitchen. But this was our last night together—and I craved his nearness so much I could barely stand to be in my own skin.

I felt lightheaded, oversensitive, and very confused.

Oblivious to all of it, Sully turned his back to me. That did *nothing* to help my addled state. His back was as beautifully sculpted as the front, and it took all my strength to look away and quickly undress, replacing my sodden sundress with the bath sheet.

"Okay," I wheezed. "I'm decent."

Sully turned back around. His eyes dropped to my face then dropped further to the top edge of my towel where a little more cleavage than I'd intended was exposed.

I literally heard the air rush out of his lungs.

"You're..." He swallowed hard, his Adam's apple traveling the length of his throat. "... a lot more than decent. You are absolutely stunning. Forgive me for saying it. I know you don't like it, but my God, Angelina. You're a knockout."

For a few moments I stood there, staring into his eyes, struggling for breath, struggling with my own battered conscience.

Then I whispered, "I don't mind you saying it. I like it."

Was I really doing this? It was pretty obvious Sully was a

dry pile of kindling right now and I was striking matches like a pyromaniac. But I couldn't seem to stop myself.

At some point during the evening, I had taken leave of my senses and become a creature of impulse, of instinct, and every instinct I possessed was driving me toward *him*.

"You... look good, too," I said in what might have been the understatement of the century. "I mean, you look like a superhero or something. Like a Greek god. Seeing you like this, it's hard to believe you're a real person."

I placed my hands on his abdomen, finally allowing myself to explore the fascinating terrain I'd ruled strictly off-limits even while fantasizing about it daily.

A tremor went through Sully's body. Heat radiated from his skin, and he began breathing like he was in the middle of a punishing workout.

"What are you doing?" he muttered in a voice that sounded like tumbled gravel.

"Touching you. Feeling you. I've wanted to do this for a long time."

Now that I'd started, I couldn't stop myself. Barely able to believe my own shocking behavior, I ran my hands up his sides to his hard chest then over the defined trapezius muscles he'd honed through hours upon hours of weightlifting.

Sully clenched his teeth, his breath whistling through them as if he was in pain. He didn't touch me but kept his hands clenched at his sides.

"I thought you said—" His sentence broke off, replace by gasping breaths. "I thought you said it could never happen again."

We both knew what he meant by *it*. Instead of being shamed by my own hypocrisy, I pressed myself against his body, memorizing the feel of him, craving every bit of closeness I could steal in these last few hours we had together.

"I know what I said. But you're leaving tomorrow, and the

summer is ending, and so is my job. This is my last chance to have… *you*.”

His eyelids flared in surprise, and if I was reading his expression right, with excitement as well.

“So then…” He licked his lips. “It would be okay with you… if I… kissed you?”

In contrast to his usual bravado, he seemed unsure, conflicted. But I could also tell he was highly aroused—unless he’d tucked one of the pool noodles into his boxers when I wasn’t looking.

I didn’t answer his question in words but slid my hands from his shoulders to behind his neck and tugged his head down to mine. I was dizzy with desire.

When his lips met mine, they were hot, and wet, and drugging. They were everything I’d been missing since that first night he’d kissed me and spun my world off its axis.

At first our mouths were the only point of contact, but then Sully clamped his arms around me and dragged me against him. He kissed me again and again, his hands moving over me greedily.

“You feel so good, Angel,” he murmured against my lips. “I’ve been dreaming of this, wanting this, every day and every night. I didn’t think it would ever happen.”

“I’ve been thinking of it, too,” I confessed. “You feel amazing. Even better than I imagined.”

The enticing pressure between us grew—thicker, harder, and I slid one hand between our bodies, wanting to touch him —*there*.

Shaping my fingers over the outline of the rearing length, I stroked up and down, relishing in a newfound sense of power. This enormous man was completely in my thrall, trembling under my touch, gripping my shoulders as if he might fall down without their uncertain support.

For one exquisite moment, Sully froze. I wasn’t sure if he

was waging some sort of internal battle, but then suddenly it was as if some kind of physical restraints had been removed.

"Fuck it," he said on a harsh exhale then he gripped my hips and lifted me, setting me onto the top of the dryer.

After that, it was no-holds-barred groping and kissing and fondling and tasting, and all I could say was the hero in that salacious novel I'd read had nothing on Sullivan Reece.

The way he used his hands and mouth was driving me wild. I couldn't breathe, I couldn't think. I couldn't have stopped if the lives of everyone I'd ever met had been riding on it.

Somehow without my realizing it the towel that had been wrapped around my chest had slipped to my waist, and Sully was holding both my breasts, fondling them, murmuring against my cheek, my neck, my ear about how good I felt, how much he wanted me, how beautiful he found me and how much pleasure he wanted to give me.

And then he stopped talking and set about fulfilling all those promises. He slid an arm behind my back, tightening his hold until my chest arched upward. He used his other hand to cup my breast, plumping it for his mouth.

Sealing his lips around the taut nipple, he licked and sucked and pulled rhythmically in a searing velvet assault that had me squirming, mindless, seeking something I didn't have words for.

The noises I made didn't even seem to come from me. I'd never felt so desperately empty in my life, and my hips rocked forward in a blind search for contact with his body—any part of him.

I needed to feel him with my whole self, hold him as close to me as possible. I wanted to stretch out beside him and take his full weight on top of me, to memorize every contour of his incredible body.

"Sully," I whimpered. "Let's go upstairs."

TWENTY-FOUR

One Perfect Night

Angelina

He answered me with a groan. "Angel. We can't. Not tonight."

"Why not?" I whined in a tone that would have made the four and five-year-olds in my care seem mature.

"Training. The fight. It's only a few days away. I'm not supposed to fu—" He stopped himself. "I'm supposed to be celibate until the fight."

"Why?"

"It's a rule my trainers have always had. And I need every possible advantage if I'm going to win against someone like Travis Diggs... so I can come home to Skyla and Claire and..." He hesitated, adding, "...all the people I love."

My brain sort of understood, but my body did *not* get it. I was too worked up, pushed far beyond reason and in a physical state I'd never experienced before in my life. I writhed against him, desperate, shameless.

"But I want you. I *need* you. I'm aching. *Here*." Sliding my own hand between my legs, I showed Sully exactly where I wanted him.

A low growl preceded his response. "Angel, you are *killing* me."

Renewing his erotic assault, he took my mouth in a lewd, hungry kiss. One of his hands fondled my breast, caressing it and teasing the sensitive tip with his thumb. The other hand headed for an even more sensitive place.

"Oh God, you're so wet," he gasped.

For a few seconds his hand moved over my panties, rubbing and stroking tenderly and setting off fireworks in my body. Then his fingers slipped beneath the cotton panel.

The fireworks became lightning bolts.

I was overcome by what he was doing to me, the sensations coursing through my body, all centered on that white hot spot of pleasure. As his tongue plunged into my mouth in rhythmic strokes, his fingertips rubbed circles over the soft folds. It was impossible to stay quiet—or still.

Though I'd never experienced anything like this before, my body seemed to know what to do. It compelled me to rock into his hand as the maddening strokes and swirls continued.

"Yes, Angel," Sully murmured against my damp cheek then moved his tormenting lips to my neck. "You're so beautiful. You feel amazing, and I can't wait to hear you come for the first time."

He didn't have to wait long. He thrust a strong finger inside me, maintaining the maddening, measured stroking on the front of my body as he caressed my inner walls.

My breaths became loud and fast, interspersed with whimpers of his name and the word *please* over and over. My entire body was tight, my bottom lifting off the dryer and toward him, rising with the steadily building pleasure.

Sully slid his finger deeper and moved his mouth to my breast. The minute his tongue swirled over the stiff nipple, the swelling pleasure burst. I couldn't move, paralyzed by the stunning sensation.

What I could do apparently was scream. Sully moved quickly to muffle my wails with his mouth, kissing me and kissing me until the shattering spasms subsided and I slumped forward, resting against his chest, boneless and heavy and in absolute awe at what I'd just experienced.

At the experience *he'd* given me.

My hands clung to his biceps as I kissed his chest then rested my forehead in the juncture of his neck and shoulder.

"I'm sure I shouldn't have done that." I said through ragged breaths. "I can't believe I did. I can't believe I begged you like that. I don't know what happened to me."

"I do. We're a done deal, Angel. You want me as much as I want you. It's that simple." He rubbed his hands over my back and stroked them down my hair.

"You're right." I nodded rapidly against his neck. "I do. I do want you. Let me touch you now."

I sat up and reached for him. "I want to feel you without these on."

Running my hand down the front of his stretchy underwear, I gripped the alluring shape beneath it, fascinated by its pulsing heat—and rather intimidating size.

When I started tugging at the waistband and slipping my hand inside, Sully stepped back with a pained laugh.

"I can't. Not tonight." He pressed his palms on both sides of his head and squeezed. "Believe me, I want to—more than anything. But I'll be back in a week—after the fight. Then we'll have all the time in the world. We can do this the right way."

That's when all the glowy, good feelings evaporated, and a hollow ache moved in to take their place.

Wincing, I put my hand over my knotted belly and pulled my hair over my shoulders to cover my chest. "I won't be here when you get back."

Sully's head jerked back. "What are you talking about? A

few minutes ago you said you wanted to make love with me—unless you wanted to go upstairs and do a puzzle. I thought that meant you wanted to be with me."

"No. I mean, yes, that's what I want—to be with you—that way," I said. "So much. But just for tonight. This is our one chance. I want it so I can keep the memory with me and have it always... after I go into religious service."

"What?" Sully literally staggered backward. His face was a portrait of disbelief and displeasure. "No. You can't mean that."

I slid from the dryer to the floor, coming to stand in front of him and looking up at him. From this angle he seemed like a giant. I did my best to make eye contact, to make him understand.

"I do. The girls don't need me anymore. I made a promise... and I've decided I'm going to keep it."

"A promise that was coerced out of you when you were a little girl. You're just scared. This is all new, and it's probably overwhelming, but you don't have to be scared, Angel. I'm going to take care of you. Everything's going to work out."

"It's not because I'm scared. It's just something I have to do."

"And what about me?" The hurt in his eyes made my chest feel like it was cracking in half. "You *have* to leave me—after all we've shared? After tonight?"

A hard lump formed in my throat, radiating pain and nearly choking my speech.

"You'll be fine," I managed to say. "Like you said, you've 'danced with a lot of girls.' There will be someone else. Lots of someone elses, I'm sure."

"Is that what this is about? You think I can't be faithful? Angel, I haven't even thought of another woman since I met you."

"That's not true. You went out with that actress."

"And thought about you every fucking minute I was with her. I couldn't wait to drop her off and get home to you. No one is like you—no one ever will be. I don't want anyone else —ever."

"Sully," I let out a pained exhale, my chest aching. "Why are you doing this? You knew this was a possibility all along. I told you about my plans. I'm doing God's will."

He snorted, clearly not convinced. "Have you ever considered that maybe God worked things out so that we'd meet? So that you'd come into our lives when you did? Maybe God's plan all along was for you to stay with me and Skyla and Claire."

"Skyla and Claire are leaving tomorrow. Besides, I don't really have a choice. I *have* to do this. It's a matter of life and death."

Now Sully's eyes narrowed in suspicion. "What happened when you saw your mom? What did she say to you?"

Though I'd never intended to tell him, I felt like I owed him the truth. I took a deep breath before answering.

"She said... she said she was sick because of me, because I broke my word to God. And I know it's true because she warned me it would happen, and then it did."

Sully slapped the wall beside him. "That's bullshit. She's manipulating you just like she manipulated you your whole life."

The charge made me mad. I wasn't sure if that's because it was false—or true. "And what are *you* trying to do right now?"

"Me? I'm looking out for you," he said. "I want you to have what *you* want—not what someone else *tells* you to want. That's what someone who loves you does. They put your welfare above their own. And I love you, Angel. I've fallen in love with you."

I'd promised myself I wouldn't cry tonight—or tomorrow

when I said goodbye to Sully and this little family I'd grown to love.

But I couldn't stop the tears. They flowed freely as I reached out and stroked his cheek then ran my hand down his chest.

"I don't want to argue with you. Can't we just have this one perfect night together? If you'd go upstairs with me and lie down with me just this once and love me like that, it would be enough to last me my whole life."

Instead of being moved by my impassioned plea, Sully looked even angrier.

"Hell no. I'm not going to take your virginity in a one-night stand and then wave goodbye. And once won't be *nearly* enough for me. I've wanted you every day since you moved in, and that's never going to change."

Grabbing me roughly he pulled me against him, pressing my cheek to his sternum. "When I make love to you, Angel, it'll be the first of thousands of times—hundreds of thousands if I have my way."

I wasn't sure about his math, but the sentiment behind it was clear—he wanted forever.

And I couldn't give it to him.

I pulled out of his embrace and shook my head sadly. "I'm sorry."

Swallowing back a sob, I said, "I'll start packing my things tonight. Tomorrow after you and the girls leave... I will, too."

"No," he grunted. Then, softening his tone a fraction, he said, "No—just stay here until you leave for the monastery. I don't want you to have to go crawling back to that evil bitch who raised you and listen to her 'I told you so's.' I won't come back until you're gone."

TWENTY-FIVE

Tourniquet

Sully

It was a good thing we were leaving this morning. I didn't think I could stand being in this house for one minute after Angelina left.

Hell, I might never come back to it, just put it on the market a move on. Every room of it held her memory, and if I couldn't have her, I didn't want to live with her ghost.

She knelt in the foyer, hugging Skyla and Claire as if she'd never see them again. She probably wouldn't.

A hollow ache filled my chest and stomach. For a fleeting moment, I allowed myself to wish things were different, that I was just a regular guy with a normal job, that I'd met her in a normal way.

I cut the unproductive thought off at the root. Wishing didn't make things come true, it only made you miserable.

"You girls are going to have the *best* school year in New York," Angelina said, wearing a wobbly smile. "I just know it. And you're going to make so many new friends and have so many adventures in Manhattan."

"I don't want to go to New York," Claire whined as she clung to Angelina's neck.

"Me either," Skyla said, sounding less whiny and angrier. "I want to stay *here* and have adventures here—with *you*. My heart can't be happy without you."

I know how you feel kiddo.

Carefully peeling Claire from her body, Angelina rose to standing. Her face was red, and she was swallowing repeatedly, clearly fending off sobs.

I felt my own throat go sore as if I'd swallowed a large, spiky ball.

"You'll come back to Eastport Bay soon to visit your daddy," she said with forced brightness. "And you'll have lots more wonderful times here with Daddy in your home."

The silent implication—that *she* wouldn't be there—screamed in my mind. I was no fortune teller, but it wasn't hard to predict the place wouldn't feel nearly so much like a home without her.

Don't think about it. Do what has to be done.

I stepped forward, picking up the girls' suitcases. "Okay, everyone in the car. Do you have everything you want with you for the ride?"

Instead of answering me, both girls started crying. Angelina took each of their hands and led the way out of the house, opening the car's back door and fastening my daughters securely into their booster seats where she gave them each one last hug and kiss.

Up to this point, I had avoided meeting her gaze. I'd stormed out of the laundry room last night and hadn't emerged from my suite until about ten minutes ago. But after shutting the car door, I allowed myself to turn and look down directly into Angelina's beautiful brown eyes.

They shimmered with unshed tears, and the armor I'd spent the night forging around my heart cracked a little.

She swallowed again. "Thank you. For everything... giving me a place to stay, for being so generous... especially for allowing me to be a part of Skyla's and Claire's lives. They're amazing little girls. And you're a good father—never doubt it."

My conscience shouted at me. If I were actually a good father, I'd never take my daughters away from this good woman's influence and leave them with their aloof, disinterested mother. Maybe if the girls were with me full time, Angelina would have stayed.

Out of obligation of course. To *them*.

I would have settled for it.

At least it would have given me more time to break through her resistance and show her what a mistake she was making.

But what could I do? Anouk *was* their mother, the girls were going back to her, and Angelina's mind was made up. She was determined to leave me, and there wasn't a damn thing I could do about it.

"Thank *you*," I said, my voice coming out like a handful of gravel.

Some of the emotion I'd successfully repressed as we loaded the car and got the girls ready to go was beginning to leak out around the edges of my self-restraint.

"You've been... good for them."

And that was about all I could say without losing total control and turning this into a sonnet about how much she'd changed *all* of our lives then dropping to my knees and begging her to stay.

She nodded, her lips pressed tightly together. "Good luck on Friday," she whispered. "I'll be praying for you."

Then she turned and went back into the house.

I watched until the door closed behind her, walked around to the driver's side of my car, and climbed inside.

Then I cinched the emotional tourniquet back in place and drove away from the greatest source of happiness I'd ever known.

TWENTY-SIX

Fight Night

Angelina

The empty house felt like a ghost town as I wandered through it, finding and gathering a few little items the girls had left behind—some small toys under the table in the family room, a load of forgotten laundry in the dryer, a hair bow in the pantry, of all places.

I'd box them up and send them to New York tomorrow.

The goodbyes this morning had nearly been the death of me. Those sweet little faces, their eyes red and puffy with uninhibited tears, would haunt me forever.

Somehow in the past three months I had come to think of Skyla and Claire as *mine.* I knew I could never replace their mother and I'd never want to, but they didn't feel like *just* my job either.

Parting with Sully had been far less emotional on the surface, but deep down it had cut even deeper.

As he'd stared down at me with those fathomless blue eyes, I'd had to resist the nearly overpowering urge to cling to him and kiss him goodbye.

What is wrong with me?

I'd gotten exactly what I'd initially sought from this summer job—time to think about what I wanted for the rest of my life.

The problem was what I wanted had become abundantly clear—I wanted *him*—a life with him and his daughters. But that wasn't possible.

I had a week left until I was scheduled to report to the monastery. It seemed like I should *do* something with that time. Through my generous salary, Sully had provided the means for me to take a trip, to have a once-in-a-lifetime adventure before I settled down and began the new life I'd chosen.

But I couldn't think of a single thing I wanted to do. Nothing that didn't involve him anyway.

Just the thought of getting on a plane alone or taking the train somewhere left me feeling exhausted. Besides, the fight was in three days, and I was so consumed with worry over Sully's safety I wouldn't be able to enjoy myself.

All I could really manage to do in the interim was hole up in the house with Sully's collection of romance novels and lose myself in the stories. At least when I was reading them, I wasn't actively worrying or wallowing in my own confusion.

Plus, I learned *a lot*. Some of it made me blush and squirm.

All of it made me long for Sully.

Finally, Friday night rolled around. I hadn't intended to watch the bout, knowing how awful it would be to see him in pain, but I was unable to keep myself away from it.

I went to a nearby sports pub that was showing the match and found a seat at the bar, ordering some food and a steady stream of overpriced seltzer waters with lime in order to keep it.

My stomach was a sack of raw nerves as the fight began. The plate of food sat in front of me untouched.

Since coming to live with the Reece family, I had seen

some clips of boxing matches and even a few boxing movies, which naturally, Sully loved.

This fight was nothing like those.

Maybe it was the fact that it was live that amplified the brutality. Most likely it was the fact that *he* was the one in the ring being struck repeatedly.

The blows were so powerful I wasn't sure how either fighter remained standing after the first ones were traded. But it went on and on, round after round, with Sully giving as good as he got.

By the eleventh round, both men were bloodied and swollen and looked thoroughly exhausted.

I didn't know how much more I could take. I felt like hitting the people seated around me when they oohed and aahed and cheered at a particularly nasty blow.

How could they be *enjoying* this?

Sully's handsome face, which had earned him plenty of cruel taunts from Travis Diggs leading up to the match, was nearly unrecognizable with one eye swollen almost shut and turning shades of blue and purple.

One side of his chest was discolored as well. He was protecting his left side, and Diggs got in a jab there whenever possible, causing Sully to wince and stagger.

By the twelfth round, the fight was nothing short of a horror show. As the crowd around me grew rowdier and more demonstrative, I desperately wanted to leave the bar. But I couldn't bring myself to look away.

It was like a horrific crash on the side of the road—you didn't *want* to see the mangled mess but could hardly keep your eyes from straying there.

Both boxers seemed to be having a hard time staying on their feet, but neither would give in. They hung on each other in between jabs, sweating profusely, breathing heavily, two battered titans locked in an epic battle for survival.

Toward the end of the round, each of them seemed to get a final surge of energy.

Sully rallied with a hard left and right combination to Diggs' face. I hoped it would be enough to knock the guy out or at least take the last of the fight out of him, but Diggs volleyed with a series of rapid punches to Sully's left rib cage.

He cried out so loudly the television mics picked up the sound. His ribs had to be broken. Tears sprang to my eyes for the hundredth time tonight. I felt like I'd been punched myself —I literally couldn't take anymore.

Sliding off my barstool, I started to leave when the final bell rang, signaling the end of the fight.

"It's going to be a split decision," the guy next to me said to his friend.

The bartender nodded in agreement, adding, "I love the guy, but I think Sully lost it this time. You never know with a judge's decision though. If it's close, they'll usually call it in favor of the champ."

The bartender was right. After a few minutes of conferring, the official winner of the fight was announced. It was Sully.

He was clearly too tired to celebrate, but he stood in the center of the ring while the referee raised his right glove high.

And then Sully collapsed.

TWENTY-SEVEN
In Sickness or Health

Angelina

Racing back to the mansion, I turned on the TV in the family room, frantic for new information.

Calling Sully's phone was useless of course. My own phone rang, and I was about to let it go to voicemail when I saw Cinda's name on the screen.

I swiped the screen, hoping my friend had gotten a report on Sully's condition somehow. Her husband *was* a prince, and they had billions of dollars, so it was possible.

"Hi. Have you heard anything?" I said, my voice sounding breathless.

Cinda was considerably more composed but still sounded worried. "No. I was hoping you had. Alex and I were watching. It was awful."

"I know. It's horrible. I kept thinking I couldn't stand one more minute but then I couldn't stop watching. I had to find out what happened. Oh Cinda, what if..."

My words were cut off by a sharp, unexpected sob, which was followed by several more.

Cinda made soothing noises into the phone, murmuring

platitudes about how it was all going to be okay. When I calmed down, Cinda's consoling tone became a knowing one.

"You're in love with him."

"No." I sniffled, grabbing a tissue from the bathroom. "No, I'm just worried about the girls. If anything happens to him, they'll be devastated. They love him so much."

"And so do you. It's okay to admit it. This is me here."

"I *can't* love him," I argued. "I'm going to be a nun."

"Are you?" Cinda asked. "Still?"

Another sob broke free. "I don't know. No, I don't think so. I don't know how I can. Oh Cinda, what am I going to do?"

"Only you can answer that one, but I *do* know love when I see it, and I can tell you... it's worth it—all of it. Okay, well I'll let you go, but will you promise to call if you get some news?"

I promised and hung up, running back to the TV and turning up the volume. After an agonizing wait, I finally learned Sully had been taken to Mount Sinai Hospital where he'd been diagnosed with a concussion, a cracked orbital bone, four broken ribs, and a ruptured kidney.

The announcers began talking about the other fighter's condition, but I turned the TV off and began gathering my things in preparation for a trip to New York.

It was only when I'd made it to the garage, packed bag in hand, that it occurred to me—I wouldn't be allowed in to see him at the hospital.

I wasn't family. I wasn't even his children's nanny anymore. I was no one special in his life.

On top of that, I wasn't even sure he'd *want* me there, considering how I'd rejected him on our last night together.

All I could do was wait, like the rest of America, for reports about his condition on TV. No, actually, there was one more thing I could do. Pray.

Though I'd been taught God wasn't into making bargains,

I was desperate enough to try it anyway. I'd offer Him anything He wanted if He'd just let Sully be healed and whole again.

If He'd let him live.

No matter what was required of me, I'd do it. Sully was worth it.

* * *

Two days later, I awoke early, startled by my ring tone.

Who would be calling me at six a.m.?

I didn't recognize the number, but it was a New York area code.

My heart leapt. *Maybe it's Sully.*

He could be calling from a hospital phone. Or maybe he'd instructed his doctor to let me know how he was doing.

All I'd been able to glean from TV was that he was still in the hospital and had asked for privacy. I was frantic for an update on his condition—anything to let me know whether my prayers had been heard.

I scrambled to answer the call. "Hello?"

A lilting female voice responded. "Is this the nanny?"

What? What a strange impersonal way of asking. It had to be a doctor or nurse though, and I was too eager to take offense.

"Yes. This is Angelina Rappaport. Do you have news about Sully?"

"Sully?" There was a bit of snark in the woman's heavily accented tone. "That's rather casual for an employee. This is Anouk Reece. I'm calling to inform you that *Sullivan* is on his way to Eastport Bay by private ambulance. He'll be there in about four hours. And I'm putting the girls on a plane as unaccompanied minors. They'll need to be picked up in two hours. Can you arrange for this?"

My head was spinning. Sully was on his way home. And apparently so were Skyla and Claire.

"You're sending the girls here?" I asked, just to be sure I was clear on the situation. "I thought they were starting school tomorrow."

Anouk's tone morphed from snark to irritation. "They don't *like* it here. I don't know what you did, but their behavior is worse than ever. Besides, I have to go to Bali tomorrow. Pregnancy ruined my career for a few years, but I'm finally getting bookings again, and I have to take them. With my work picking up, there's no way I can watch the children."

I was in shock. Once they'd gotten past the first difficult week, the girls had been a delight to be around. And I'd thought the split custody arrangement was a done deal.

But Anouk seemed to be saying she was forfeiting her time with them, giving Sully full custody of their daughters.

"Can *he* take care of them?" I asked in confusion. Maybe his condition wasn't as bad as the media reports had made it sound. "I thought he was very badly injured."

Anouk let out a huff of irritation. "He said *you* would handle it. Was he wrong? I'll text and tell him to call the service and get another nanny. I don't have time for this. He'll have to work it out."

"No. He wasn't wrong," I rushed to answer. "Of course I'll handle it. I'll pick them up and be here to meet the ambulance. Don't worry about a thing."

Anouk didn't sound particularly *worried*, but the last thing I wanted was for Sully to be trying to make phone calls to a nanny placement agency from the back of an ambulance, and that was definitely where this conversation was headed if I didn't comply with Anouk's demands.

"Good," the woman snapped. "Here's their flight information..."

Four hours later, I stood in the driveway of Sully's home

with Skyla and Claire, watching the EMT's unload him on a stretcher.

My insides vibrated with excitement and also a bit of fear. On one hand, it felt like I was getting my "family" back. The reunion with the girls at the airport had been joyful.

On the other, I had no idea what to expect from Sully.

Would he ask me to stay here and take care of his daughters a while longer, or would he want me to vacate the house as planned and make other arrangements for their care?

As the attendants wheeled him closer, it became apparent he was in no condition to make any decisions *or* any phone calls. I stifled a gasp at his broken appearance.

Sully looked as if he was wearing a purple eye mask, both eyes horribly swollen and ringed with dark bruises. A butterfly bandage held his left eyebrow together. His right jaw was also discolored and swollen.

He wore no shirt, only a wrap around his ribcage, and on the left side of his chest near his shoulder there was a grapefruit-sized bruise so dark it nearly hid his tattoo.

My heart squeezed hard, seeing him so hurt. Cinda had been absolutely right—I *was* in love with him.

All I wanted was to take care of Sully, make him better, to give him anything and everything he needed and be there in whatever capacity he needed for as long as he wanted me to.

Worries about my own future were superseded by a determination to make sure the girls were comforted and cared for—and that Sully was restored to full health.

There was a possibility he would never be the same again physically, and that would be okay too. It wouldn't change the way I felt about him.

I wanted him... in sickness or in health.

I wanted him just the way he was—forever.

TWENTY-EIGHT

Always a Choice

Sully

Everything hurt.

I lay in bed, aching from head to toe. In the past I'd compared the twelve rounds of a boxing match to being in twelve car accidents.

The fight with Travis Diggs had been more like being run over by twelve Mac trucks. I was actually a little surprised I'd survived it.

My body was a full buffet of pain, the variety of it dazzling. Some of it was dull like a series of throbbing headaches under my skin. Some was sharp, especially around my cracked ribs.

I probably should have still been in the hospital—my doctor hadn't wanted me to leave so soon.

All I'd wanted was to be home. To be away from all the questions and prying eyes and well-meaning words of encouragement.

To be alone with my pain. My failure.

Now I wondered if I'd made a mistake insisting on recovering at home. The only thing worse than being poked and prodded by the hospital staff was being cared for by Angelina.

"Hi. You awake?"

The soft, feminine voice came from my bedroom doorway, triggering an involuntary surge of pleasure and longing. Angelina slipped into the room like a beautiful ghost, tiptoeing silently to my bedside.

My response was a grunted, "*Now* I am."

I knew I was a horrible patient. Grouchy when I should have been grateful, complaining when I should have kept my mouth shut. I couldn't seem to help myself.

I hated lying in bed, doing nothing all day, hated being so *helpless.* I hadn't been this needy since I was a child.

But that wasn't the worst part.

The worst part was having Angelina so near all the time. Her gentle touch when she helped me shift positions, the delicious smell of her hair and skin, the sweet sound of her voice as she inquired about my comfort and whether I needed anything.

Though she must have had her hands full with the girls and I knew she was only here out of "saintly" obligation, she came any time I called. Nothing was too much to ask. She was as kind and caring as a literal angel—and just as untouchable.

But that didn't stop me from wanting to. I craved her. I wanted her warmth and sweetness close by all the time.

All the mental effort I'd put into trying to break my addiction to her had been useless. I was right back where I'd been the night before I left—yearning, lovesick... pathetic.

The power she had over me was fucking terrifying, frankly, and I was growing more and more desperate to break the spell.

It would have helped if she rose to the bait of my rudeness and snapped back at me, but it seemed the more cantankerous and demanding I was, the more irritatingly patient she became.

"It's time for your pain meds." Angelina shook two pills into her hand and offered them to me with a cold bottle of water.

I snatched the bottle with a resentful scowl, the rough movement causing a fresh burst of pain in my side.

"Careful. You're going to re-injure your ribs," she warned.

"And *you're* going to turn me into a junkie."

Angelina rewarded my snarling tone with a sweet smile. "I'm giving you exactly what your doctor prescribed at the exact intervals he prescribed. If you don't take them, you won't be able to sleep, and you need sleep to heal."

Grumbling, I washed down the pills with a swallow of water. Angelina nodded in satisfaction and turned to go.

Wait—she was leaving already? A sudden tide of stifling heat rose from my chest to my neck. Before she reached the bedroom door, I said, "Wait."

Angelina turned back to face me. "Yes? Is there something you need?"

"More water."

She gave me a quizzical glance. "The bottle I gave you is still half-full."

Frowning, I looked at it. "It's too warm."

"I took it out of the refrigerator just before coming up."

"Well, something's wrong with the refrigerator then," I replied in a testy tone. "Have it checked."

"I'll be sure to do that. And I'll be right back with some ice."

She left the room and returned within a few minutes, a glass full of ice in hand along with a fresh bottle of thoroughly chilled water. Opening the bottle, she poured it over the ice and offered me the glass.

Though I wasn't thirsty, I took a sip.

"Cold enough for you?"

"It'll do," I muttered.

Angelina gave me a beatific smile, almost visibly biting her tongue. "Anything else I can do?"

I looked around the room, searching, then lifted a hand to point at the dark drapes that blocked the natural light from the floor-to-ceiling ocean-facing windows. Even that slight movement made my ribs ache and my head dizzy with pain.

"There's a crack in the curtains. I can't sleep with all that light coming in."

She gave the curtains a confused look. "They're completely closed."

"They must not be. There's a ray of light coming in, and it's right in my eyes."

Out of sheer goodness, Angelina crossed the room to the windows and tugged the already closed panels more tightly together, causing them to overlap.

"Better?" She turned back to me, looking at me over one shoulder.

That was when I noticed she was wearing her hair loose. The long sweep of it was like a golden river cascading down her back. The curling ends danced at hip level, drawing my eyes where I'd been trying to keep them from going, to the curves of her waist and hips and ass.

My fingertips dug into the sheet and blankets, gripping the linens until my hands shook.

Hopefully Angelina couldn't detect the reaction from where she stood in the dark room. I couldn't let her see how she affected me—not after she'd told me she didn't want me.

"Yes. You can go now," I gritted out.

Without further comment, she slipped from the room, and I let out a long breath.

I could *not* afford to mess up again—not when the girls and I were so dependent on her. If I lost control of myself and got out of line again, Angelina would leave for sure.

The only thing more powerful than my desire to have her was my desire to *keep* her.

I tried telling myself it was all about the girls. They were here permanently now—and I was thrilled about it. After seeing them with Anouk in New York, I knew living with their mother wasn't the best thing for them.

What had I been thinking at the beginning of the summer when I'd suggested Anouk move into the house in Eastport Bay with us? Thank God she'd said no.

When I was honest with myself, I had to admit there was much more to my determination to keep Angelina at a distance than my fear of losing Skyla and Claire's nanny.

I wanted to keep her too, and I was terrified of scaring her off again.

* * *

Over the next several weeks, I slowly healed. I was able to get up for small stretches of time during the day now and go to the bathroom alone—thank God.

Wilder Lowe had earned friend-for-life status, stopping by every morning during the first week to help me in and out of the shower. There was no way tiny Angelina would have been able to support my tall, heavy frame, and there was even less chance I'd ask her to touch me when I was undressed.

My willpower was considerable, but I wasn't superhuman.

She remained the perfect nurse, continuing her gentle ministrations with patience and tenderness. Meanwhile, I was nearing a breaking point. I was either going to strangle her or kiss her.

Of course either would drive her away, so I contented myself with merely imagining both scenarios. The kissing one was my more frequent fantasy by far.

Angelina had also enrolled the girls in school—Claire in

the preschool where she used to work and Skyla in kindergarten at the nearby public elementary.

Each day when the girls returned home, they ran into my room to show me what they'd worked on at school. My bedroom walls had become a gallery of colorful crayon drawings and finger paintings—a beautiful view that cheered me despite the lingering gloom from the disastrous title fight.

I couldn't move past it. The fight promoter Frank Balletto had called this afternoon just after my daughters' visit, informing me that Travis Diggs was demanding a rematch.

Angelina came back into the room during the call. She'd left to fix the girls a snack and settle them in the home theater to watch a princess movie.

Clearly piecing my end of the conversation together, she questioned me when I hung up. "Why would they ask you to fight him again? You won."

"I didn't *win*," I spat, sounding harsher than I'd intended. "It was a judge's decision, and pretty much everyone agrees it only tipped my way because I was the defending champ. I was a disgrace."

Angelina looked horrified. "You're not going to *do* it, are you?"

I gave her an *Isn't it obvious?* look. "I still have to defend the title when there's a legitimate challenger. Considering the fact Diggs almost killed me, I'd say he's pretty fucking legitimate."

"Considering the fact he almost *killed* you, I'd say you're crazy to even think about getting into the ring with him again."

Her tone was more forceful than I'd ever heard it, and a crease marked the space between her delicate little eyebrows.

"What about Skyla and Claire? What if you don't make it next time?"

"Thanks for the vote of confidence." I smirked.

"This has nothing to do with confidence. I watched the fight. You were *not* a disgrace—you fought hard and stayed with him for twelve full rounds. But Sully, you have people counting on you... people who love you and want you to be around for many years to come."

She seemed unaccountably emotional. Angelina really did care about my daughters. "Is it really worth dying for?" she asked.

Sighing, I shrugged, finally able to execute body language without severe pain. "It's not like I have a choice."

"Of course you have a choice." Angelina drew close to the bed where I was propped against the headboard with the covers bunched around my waist.

As she sat on the edge of the mattress, a long lock of golden hair fell over the front of one shoulder. My fingers twitched with the effort of restraint, longing to reach out and touch the silky curl, to tug on it and force her to lean closer.

Her ever-present honey fragrance had my senses in a state of vibrating awareness. Unable to help myself, I stared at her face, hungrily taking in the big brown eyes, the creamy skin, the heart-shaped lips that tempted me like chocolate-dipped strawberries.

She wore a skirt and a soft-looking wrap sweater with a v-shaped neckline that basically forced me to look at her chest. Which, by the way, looked absolutely amazing.

Angelina was apparently unaware she was in imminent danger of being pounced upon like a gazelle being attacked by a starving lion. She returned my gaze with wide, innocent eyes.

"There's always a choice," she said. "And every choice requires considering all your options."

It was hard to keep my voice sounding normal and not like the growl of the predator I felt like.

"And what are my options?"

She licked her lips, making self-control that much more

difficult. "Well, you should know... it's not just the girls who would be devastated if something happened to you."

"It's not?" My heart kicked into a gallop, spurred on by a fusion of surprise and excitement. The beating was so loud in the quiet bedroom I was worried she might hear it.

"No."

She shook her head slowly and obeyed my unspoken command to move closer. "There are other people who need you, who... *want* you to be here."

Angelina's breathing was light and fast. The only other time I'd heard her breathe like that was that night in the laundry room when I had my lips on her skin and drove her wild with my hands.

Remember that night, I cautioned myself even as my own breathing picked up pace. *Remember the decision she made—how she chose to leave.*

Her fingers trembled as she stretched out a hand and placed it on my bare chest, stroking the spot where a large bruise was still healing.

"This looks much better," she said softly.

All I could do was nod, struck dumb by a shock of sheer pleasure. Though her touch was light, it affected me like a bolt of lightning, sending a surge of energy through my entire body and making all my nerve endings hum with an agony of hunger.

I am so fucked.

I was completely enthralled by this woman. This sweet, innocent, very young woman who didn't mean anything by the physical contact and probably had no idea what she was doing to me.

All my instincts demanded I reach out and take her, pull her to me and kiss her senseless. It would be a repeat of the mistake I'd made our last night together, compounded by a factor of infinity.

She was going to leave as soon as I was fully healed, and I didn't want to risk doing anything to speed up that eventuality.

Don't do it. Don't mess things up.

Staring into my eyes with vulnerable sincerity, she whispered, "I wouldn't be able to stand it if I lost you."

And the battle was over.

I covered her hand with my own, pressing her soft, cool fingers into my blazing skin. Beneath it, my heart felt like it was going to explode. My breath caught in my throat as I tried to speak.

"Angel... I would never leave you. And I wish you didn't want to leave me."

She gasped and leaned toward me. Before I could react or even think, her lips were on mine, and my body and mind were on a rollercoaster ride with no safety bars.

TWENTY-NINE

Possession

Angelina

The past few weeks with Sully, witnessing his struggle with unthinkable pain and his determination to grow stronger every day, watching him stoically endure the daily indignities and forced intimacy of being taken care of by another person, only solidified what I realized the night of the fight.

I was in love with Sullivan Reece.

I'd seen his constant grouchiness for what it was—the frustration of a powerful man over being hurt and helpless. And in the past few days, I'd come to understand he was struggling with something else—his desire for me.

The first few weeks following the fight, he gave no indication he was still interested in me as anything more than just a caretaker for his children.

Those searing life-changing moments of intimacy we'd shared had begun to seem like a fluke born sheerly of male-female proximity and an exceedingly high testosterone level. I vowed to keep my feelings to myself, to do my best to take care of him and Skyla and Claire until he was healed and told me it was time to go.

But now I could see it—my feelings for him were not unrequited. Perhaps he was no longer in love with me the way I was with him, but he *was* interested.

Today, I'd simply run out of willpower and selflessness.

Sully was clearly on the mend. When I'd learned he was considering risking his life in the ring again, I'd been unable to hold back any longer. I *had* to let him know how I felt.

And when he'd pressed my hand to his heart and called me Angel, I'd had no choice but to kiss him.

But now I wasn't feeling so sure of myself. While I abandoned all propriety and restraint and pressed ardent, desperate kisses against his lips, he stayed still, as cold and immovable as a marble statue.

I'd been hoping he would wrap his arms around me, sink his big hands into the hair he seemed so fascinated with, and return my kisses with the same kind of fervent need I felt charging through my own body.

But he wasn't responding to me at all.

Was I too late? Had he met another woman in New York before the fight?

No women had called the house or come by to see him, but he did have a cell phone. Perhaps he'd been speaking to someone, perhaps he *had* moved on.

Perhaps the longing looks he'd been giving me lately were just a product of my imagination? Maybe God really was punishing me for reneging on the promise I'd made so long ago.

Mortified, I began to pull away.

As if a dam had burst, Sully was suddenly in motion. He was everywhere, all around me, wrapping his strong arms around my back and waist and pulling me tightly against his chest.

Yes.

He dragged me forward until I was in his lap, and his lips

captured mine. He kissed me with voracious hunger, mesmerizing me with his mouth.

It was *more* than kissing. It was a possession.

With every hot, silky caress, Sully claimed me, put his brand on me, and I was flooded with heat and joy and love so acute I thought I might not be able to endure it.

He broke the contact—I might not have had the strength to ever stop—and stared into my eyes. His large hands still clasped my face, holding me with a touch so possessive I felt faint.

"I hope that was okay."

I nodded rapidly, though my thoughts were still scrambled along with every hormone I possessed.

"More than okay. I *don't* want to leave you, Sully."

His expression grew fierce. "Good. Because this is *right*, you and me. No one can tell me any different, and I don't want you to doubt it, either. This was meant to be. Don't feel bad about kissing me—or guilty or weird, or whatever other crazy thought is going through your head right now. I know you're my kids' nanny, and I'm your boss, and yes there's a monastery in New Jersey missing a junior nun, but there are obstacles and complications in every relationship. We'll figure it out. I *want* you. I guess I've made that abundantly clear."

He chuckled and gave me a self-deprecating look that bordered on an apology. "But more than that, I love you. I'm in love with you Angelina."

Tears swarmed my eyes. "I love you too. I've been in love with you for a long time—weeks."

Sully beamed. "I've got you beat, Angel. I think it was the first day for me."

I laughed, a gush of joy filling my soul. "Always so competitive."

"You got that right," Sully said. "And I'm claiming my prize right now. I don't want you to ever kiss anyone else. I want to be your first and only. And I don't want you to go into the monastery or get another nanny job. I don't want you to leave us *ever.*"

"I don't want to leave you. I want to be with you always, Sully. And I want to be with the girls and see them grow up."

Sully's mouth descended to mine again, beginning a new round of kisses that left me breathless and squirming and filled with so much happiness I felt like I'd float up to the high coffered ceilings if he wasn't holding me so securely to him.

Abruptly he stopped the kiss and lifted his head.

"The kids are just down the hall." He sounded like it had just occurred to him.

I struggled to gather enough breath to respond. "Yes. The kids. They *are* watching a movie—a long one."

He smiled. "Do you think you'll be able to keep the decibel level down?"

I slapped at his shoulder. "That was *your* fault. You have to promise not to make me lose my mind this time."

Sully shook his head and kissed me before rolling off the bed and crossing the room to lock the bedroom door.

"I can't promise you that, Angel."

Click.

THIRTY

Death and Taxes

Sully

It was a literal dream come true, Angelina waiting for me in my bed with her hair streaming down around her in golden waves and that look on her beautiful face.

I was nervous. I wanted to make this perfect for her, but I'd heard the first time wasn't always that great for a woman. The last thing I wanted was to hurt her or give her any sort of negative feelings about sex.

The trick would be to make sure she was completely ready for me, absolutely begging for it—and to maintain a sense of humor in case it didn't go a hundred percent according to plan.

I went back to the bed, undressing and sliding into it then pulling Angelina into my arms, encouraging her to stretch out next to me so I could just hold her against my body and let her get used to that.

She felt incredible, slim and strong and soft all at the same time. One of her legs was thrown over my thigh, her skirt riding up, and I was already getting excited, feeling the warmth of her sweet center pressed against me.

"So, should we pull up some You Tube videos?" I joked, remembering how she said that was the way she learned to do anything she had no experience with.

"That won't be necessary," she assured me. "I read the novels from your closet."

I did a double-take, embarrassed she'd found my secret stash. A romance novel collection wasn't exactly in the manly man handbook. "You did?"

She nodded, smiling.

Oh well, if we were going to make a life together, I guessed it was better we didn't start with any secrets. "How many of them did you read?"

"All of them?" She ran her fingers over my chest and stroked them down my abdomen, tracing the delineations of the muscle cut.

"I had a lot of time to kill while you were gone, and then I sort of got addicted and just kept going. I know how things work now," she informed me in a pert, overly confident tone.

"Is that so?"

I smiled and slipped a hand into the neckline of the cashmere wrap sweater, engulfing her breast in my hand and rubbing over the nipple in a slow, luxurious circle.

Her head dropped back on my arm, and she moaned.

"Yes," she whispered. "You can't do anything that would surprise me."

A low chuckle. "Well now that sounds like a challenge."

Rolling onto my knees, I hovered above her, spreading her beneath me and working at the fastenings of the sweater and bra as I kissed and stroked her, telling her all the ways I wanted to please her, pleasure her, satisfy her every need and desire.

Angelina kept trying to touch me, and I had to grab her hands and press them above her head each time.

"Angel," I whispered. "I appreciate the enthusiasm, but it's been a *long* time for me. If you want this to last more than a few seconds, you're going to have to keep your sweet little hands to yourself until I give you the all-clear."

"I don't care," she protested. "I want to touch you, too. I want to taste you."

A full body shudder went through me, and I had to discipline myself not to give into the temptation. Of course I wanted those soft little hands on me, that beautiful mouth wrapped around my cock—*of course* I did.

But we had a lifetime for that—at least I hoped we did. Tonight was all about *her* and her pleasure. I could barely even remember my first time—there was certainly nothing special and beautiful about it.

I wanted hers to be unforgettable.

Once I had her clothes off and my beautiful girl naked beneath me, her gorgeous hair spread over my pillows and sheets like a nest of spun gold, I set about kissing her from head to toe.

Angelina was incredibly responsive, sighing and squirming and moaning at the attention of my hands and mouth.

I worked my way down her body, kissing and licking her silky stomach, her hipbones, her thighs. When my mouth ventured to the soft curls between her legs, she protested, bringing her hand down to cover herself.

"Not there," she said in a mortified tone of voice.

"Oh yes, sweetheart," I countered, gripping her wrist and pinning it to the bed. "*Definitely* there. Trust me, Angel. I'm not going to do anything to hurt you. You're going to like it. Just let me show you. Let me..."

Shaking with desire, I nuzzled into the heat and softness, my tongue sliding over the layered flesh, seeking and finding the aroused peak of her pleasure. She stopped resisting and sank her fingers into my hair, pushing herself into my mouth as I licked steadily into the silky wetness.

I sensed the growing tension in her body and worked hard

to master the rapidly building urgency in mine.

As I devoured her, Angelina clamped her knees around my head, arching and groaning, her fingers twisting in my hair and her hips pulsing in sync with my steadily teasing rhythm.

She was close. I could feel it, and I resisted the urge to speed up, to change the disciplined pace. When she came, it was a thing of absolute beauty. She thrust herself against my face, cried out, and held a high arch, frozen in a sort of suspended animation before collapsing to the bed.

After a few seconds, Angelina tugged me upwards. "I want you inside me," she whispered. "I'm so ready."

As if there was even a chance of me saying no, she wrapped her hand around my dick and ensured it was a certainty.

Sunrise. Sunset. Death. Taxes. And making love to Angelina. There was *no way* this wasn't going to happen.

I slid the head of my cock against her, gauging the wetness, and determined that no, virgin or not, lubricant would not be necessary today. This woman *was* ready for me.

I was so far beyond ready for her I was actually afraid of embarrassing myself.

The good news was, if that happened, she literally wouldn't know any better. The bad news was I really, *really* wanted it to last.

We were already ahead of the game—one orgasm beyond the odds, but I was a gambler today. I wanted to go for the big prize—making her come again, this time with me inside her so I could feel her sweet body throbbing and squeezing around me for the very first time.

I positioned myself over her and, whispering against her temple and her ear, nudged against the tight entrance to her body.

"Just relax sweetheart. It might be a little uncomfortable this first time."

Completely undaunted, she raised her knees and dropped

them open, spreading herself to me.

I had to close my eyes for a second and do some deep breathing. Then, feeling the hot, wet clench of her intimate flesh on my tip, I literally couldn't hold back any longer. I drove forward, pushing inside and filling her.

For a moment, I was worried. She went stiff and cried out as I thrust through the barrier of her virginity. But she stroked my back, kissing my neck and encouraging me.

"Don't stop. I'm okay. Don't stop."

I began again, rooting deep. The feeling was impossible to describe—the enveloping warmth, the intense connection, the juxtaposition of slickness and friction. The knowledge that I was the first man to ever discover her like this.

I felt like a fucking astronaut or something.

Grinding my teeth together and groaning between them, I pumped harder, paying attention to her every sound and facial expression. At one point I sensed I'd hit a sweet angle and did it again and then again.

Angelina arched her back and rose to meet me, undulating her hips in a way that threatened to end this whole thing when it had barely begun.

"Angel, hold on. I need a minute. I'm not going to be able to—"

My warnings were cut off by her rising cries, and I realized she was right on the verge.

Well okay then, let's do this thing.

I dropped my head to her shoulder and began a steady drive, pinning her with my weight, pleasuring her with the building friction between us.

All the while I prayed I could hold on long enough to get her there. As for me, I could have come the second I slid inside her, but I was determined to be not only her first but her last. I kept up a measured pace, feeling her tense around me, her hands frantically grappling over my back and her wild panting and broken gasps filling my ear and pushing me closer and closer to the tipping point.

"Come for me, Angel," I breathed against her neck. "You feel so good. You feel like heaven around my cock. Nothing has ever felt as good as fucking you."

For a second, I panicked. I just said "fucking you" to a virgin. Maybe I should have said, "making love," but then I realized I'd worried for nothing.

Her breath caught, and her whole body stiffened beneath me then shuddered. And then she was making the sweetest, most erotic noises I'd ever heard in my life. I seriously wished I was recording them because I would absolutely listen to this on repeat in my earbuds all day every day.

Once she came, there was absolutely zero chance I was going to last any longer. I followed her, thrusting deep one last time then collapsing on top of her, my forehead dropping to rest against hers and our rapid breaths mingling.

In the aftermath, I held her close to me, literally unable to stop kissing her. I pressed my lips to her face and neck and shoulders and chest.

"That was absolutely the best I've ever had," I said. "Just so you know, there's no way I'm letting you leave now. Not ever."

"Silly man—I already told you I didn't want to leave. What did you think I was doing sticking around here while you invented non-existent cracks between the curtains and demanded the world's coldest ice water?"

I chuckled, ashamed of my antics but not sorry for them. They'd worked, hadn't they? "I just wanted to keep you nearby, and the only way I knew to do it was to be a complete pain in the ass."

"Well, I recommend a new strategy," she said. "Just keep doing what you did tonight. You have just created an addict. I couldn't leave even if I wanted to."

THIRTY-ONE

Moving In

Angelina

"Then it's settled?" Sully asked. "You'll stay?"

"I'm not sure how I feel about living in your house and taking a paycheck from you if we're in a relationship, but I'm *definitely* not going to become a nun now, if that's what you're asking."

He laughed out loud. "There's one answered prayer. We'll work on the rest."

Sully stared at me as if I were his favorite sight in the world, and my heart glowed.

"I feel like celebrating," he said. "Have you ever been down to the wine cellar?"

"I know where it is, but I haven't really paid much attention to what's in the bottles because I don't really drink. Did you want me to get something for you?"

He nodded. Placing a hand on each side of my waist, he slid me from his lap to the floor.

"There are a bunch of bottles of Dom Perignon down there and some Cristal too. Take your pick. Teetotaler or not, we're going to have at least one toast. If you don't mind getting that and putting it on some ice to chill, I have an errand to run."

He got out of bed and headed for his enormous walk-in closet.

"An errand?" I asked with concern. "Are you sure you're strong enough for that? You haven't left the house since you got home from New York."

He turned around and gave me a brilliant smile. "I feel strong enough to *lift* the house. With one hand."

At my threatening glare, he laughed. "I'll take the elevator down to the garage and walk slow. That sound okay, Nurse Angelina?"

Marginally comforted, I turned and walked to the bedroom door, giving him a flirtatious glance back over my shoulder. "See that you *do*, or I'll have to force you back into the bed and strap you down."

"Oooh. I can't wait."

Feeling as if I floated down the staircase instead of walking, I retrieved a bottle of champagne from the basement wine cellar and carried it into the kitchen where I plunged it into an ice bucket before launching a search for champagne flutes.

I was on the top step of the stepladder, reaching into a high cabinet when the security alarm went off.

The girls.

They must have finished their movie and started playing. It had been a long time since they'd tried to leave the house without permission, but maybe their time in New York had undone some of the good habits I'd instilled in them.

I checked the home map readout on the electronic security panel in the kitchen. A tiny red light blinked in the location of the front door. Calling their names, I walked quickly to the grand foyer to stop the girls from leaving.

"Skyla... Claire... you know you're not supposed to open the door without asking first."

When I stepped into the foyer, I stopped short at the sight of not two mischievous little imps but *three* people standing together just inside the front door.

Skyla. Claire. And their mother.

I recognized Anouk instantly from her pictures. No one had told me she was coming to visit the girls. Maybe it was a surprise?

"Mommy's here," Claire announced.

"That's why we opened the door, Angelina," Skyla said reasonably. "It's okay to let Mommy in, isn't it?"

Anouk Reece set a hand atop each of her daughters' heads and curved her lips into the least friendly smile I had ever seen. She stared straight at me as she answered for me.

"Of course it's okay, darlings," she purred. "I live here."

All the breath left my body. The shock was so great I couldn't even compose myself enough to come up with a standard greeting.

All I could manage was a weak, "What?"

Anouk's cold smile grew even more feral. "I live here. This *is* my family's house, after all."

Only then did I notice the suitcases clustered around Anouk's feet. Glancing out the open door I saw several more sitting on the front porch.

"You're... moving in?"

A black hole formed in my chest, its dizzying force swallowing my heart and lungs. It was making a play for all the strength I had in my body, weakening my knees.

"Are you going to live with us now, Mommy?" Claire asked, tugging on the hem of her mother's designer dress.

Anouk gripped her daughter's tiny wrist, breaking her grip. "You mustn't pull on this darling," she snapped. "It's a Stella McCartney couture."

Resuming eye contact with me, the woman said, "I spent time with Sullivan when he was in the hospital in

New York. I'm surprised he didn't mention it." Her tone turned lethal. "He's *my* husband, after all. He needed me. He still does."

She stroked her mini-me daughter's heads, her multiple rings and long, expertly manicured fingernails snagging their wild curls. "So do my sweet girls."

Skyla squirmed away and took off for the stairs. "I'll go tell Daddy you're here." Naturally she assumed her father was home.

"Me, too," Claire echoed and followed her sister, leaving Anouk and me alone in the cavernous marble entryway.

"We won't be needing your services any longer," Anouk informed me quietly. "Since I'll be here full-time from now on."

My brain fought the discordance between what had happened twenty minutes earlier and what was happening now. Nothing was making sense.

What about the things Sully had said to me? We had made love. What about that?

I glanced toward the door to the garage, but there was no sign of his return.

Finding my voice, I asked, "What about your career? You said it was taking off again. You said you didn't have time to take care of Skyla and Claire. That's why you sent them here."

"I sent them *here* because they're *happy* here in Eastport Bay," the woman purred. "And I'm sure I will be too. You wouldn't understand, but the life of a model isn't easy. You hear me say I'm flying to Bali, and you think I'm going off to have a party. It's hard work, and the industry is full of vultures and liars and users who only want you until you get your first wrinkle. Add stretchmarks to that, and they're done with you. I've had enough of it. I'm *tired.* I'm ready to settle down now."

In all of that, I hadn't heard a word about Anouk's feelings for Sully—apart from his usefulness as an ATM. Did she even love him anymore? Had she ever?

"Was Sully expecting you?" I asked, utterly confused.

Why hadn't he told me his ex-wife would be moving in? How had he imagined it would work with all of us living together?

Anouk raised one perfect eyebrow. "Of course. He *invited* me to move in. He said he and the girls needed me, that he wanted us all to live in the same house again. Didn't he tell you?"

A rock-hard ball of ice formed in my throat as the pressure built behind my eyelids. *Oh no*—I was going to cry, right there in front of this hateful woman.

"He... didn't mention it."

Anouk's red lips contracted in a pretty pout worthy of a lipstick ad. Her brows drew together, and she tilted her head in a sympathetic posture. Her tone, however, held nothing but glee.

"Oh dear. You have a crush on him, don't you?" She giggled. "Poor baby. He mentioned how naïve and ignorant you are. Imagine... developing a *thing* for your boss... while taking care of his children every day?"

She made a little tut-tut noise before the pout morphed into an expression that was far more threatening. "I wouldn't mention *that* when applying for new nanny jobs. The other wives might not be as understanding as I am, and Eastport Bay is a very small town compared to New York. You might find yourself out of work as well as homeless."

Anouk's smile returned. "Now run along and pack your things. Go quietly and I'll write you a nice, bland reference letter with no mention of your attempts to seduce my husband while he was injured and on pain medication."

When I stared at her open-mouthed, she added, "Hurry now, before my good will runs out."

THIRTY-TWO
Dismissed

Sully

My errand took longer than I'd expected. As it turned out, finding the perfect ring for the woman of your dreams wasn't easy.

I'd never ring-shopped before—Anouk had picked out her own and told me what to buy. But I wanted Angelina to have just the right one.

If I let her choose her own, she'd probably pick one with a tiny chip of diamond you'd need a magnifying glass to see. That wasn't going to cut it.

There was no diamond big enough and beautiful enough to express the enormity of my love for her, but I was determined to give it my best shot.

When none of the jewelry stores in Eastport Bay had what I was looking for, I drove to the next town then the next.

By the time I finally returned to the mansion, velvet box in hand, it was after eight p.m. Hopefully Angelina hadn't worried about me being gone so long. She hadn't called or texted though, so I assumed everything was okay.

The house was quiet, which was to be expected—the girls were always in bed by this time.

My heart skipped a beat, anticipating Angelina's reaction when I dropped to one knee and presented her with the tiny box.

Would she cry? Probably. I'd kiss away the happy tears and any others that occurred for the rest of our lives.

I checked the living room, the kitchen, even the laundry room for her. Where was she?

Maybe she'd gone up to take a bath as she loved to do most evenings. Maybe I'd join her. That thought got my pulse humming and had my cock straining my zipper.

Reaching the tall central staircase, I spotted something. It was small and red, lying on a stair about halfway up. Thinking it must be one of the girl's toys, I climbed toward it and bent to pick it up.

It was a rose petal. What was that doing here? A few steps up there was another one. And then another and another.

I followed the trail of petals to the top of the stairs and down the wide hallway. It led to my bedroom.

With each step the butterflies in my stomach increased their frenzied flapping. I was shocked by Angelina's very clear and very tempting invitation—she'd gone from virgin to advanced-level temptress in record time. *Thank you, romance novels.*

But of course I was fucking thrilled. She was the most desirable woman I'd ever known. I was deeply in love with her and eager to show it every chance I got. In fact, I planned to make it my new mission in life to ensure Angelina would never even think about another man.

Pushing open the bedroom door, I announced, "I'm home, Angel."

All the warm feelings rushing through my body iced over in a flash freeze.

There in the middle of my bed, with the bed sheet barely covering her bare chest, was Anouk. She was smiling like she'd not only eaten the canary but had picked the bones clean and licked her fingers afterward.

"You've never called me Angel before," she purred. "I like it."

"*What* are you doing here?" I roared, then remembering my daughters were sleeping and Angelina was somewhere in the house, I stepped into the room and closed the door.

Moderating my volume, I demanded, "Get out of my bed."

"Why?" she pouted. "Did you want to fuck me somewhere else?"

"No. I don't. Why are you even here? What are you doing in Eastport Bay? I thought you were in Bali and then going to Paris."

I glanced nervously over my shoulder at the bedroom door. Angelina could walk in here any minute. As far as I was concerned, it was her bedroom now, too, and after what we'd shared earlier today, she'd certainly expect to come in without a knock.

I didn't even want to think of what would happen if she were to walk in on *this* sleazy scene.

When I looked back in Anouk's direction, she'd gotten out of the bed, but the situation was no better. She was completely nude, strutting toward me in a brazen display of toned flesh she clearly expected me to admire.

"I missed you." Reaching me, she stretched her arms up, as if intending to wrap them around my neck and press herself to me.

I took a step back. "Put some clothes on. There are other people in this house you know."

"The girls are asleep." She gave me a challenging grin. "Oh

—you mean the *babysitter*. I dismissed her. I'm sure she's long gone by now. Where were you by the way?"

"Dismissed?" My voice was at a roar again, but I couldn't help it. "What does that mean? You gave her the night off?"

"Is that not the right word?" Anouk asked. English was her second language, and sometimes she was uncertain of her vocabulary. "Let me clarify. I relieved her of her duties... fired her, let her go."

I let out a frustrated sound, and my hands came up to clench in my overgrown hair. Better my scalp than my ex-wife's neck.

"You had no right to do that. God only knows what she's thinking right now. Where did she go?"

Anouk gave a delicate shrug. "How should I know? And why are you so upset? Oh dear, you two weren't 'fooling around' were you?"

She made air quotes when asking, obviously assuming the answer was yes.

"No—we weren't," I lied for Angelina's sake. Besides what we'd done today couldn't be classified as fooling around. It had been damn near a religious experience.

"Not that it's any of your business. She's not the kind of woman you 'fool around' with. Speaking of that, what happened to Pierre—he *was* your latest fling, right?"

Another shrug. "It didn't work out. Neither did Vittorio, the jerk."

"Ah, well, I'm sure it's just a temporary slump. Go back to New York, Anouk. You'll find someone new in no time."

"I can't go back to New York." She pouted. "I sold my apartment—I needed the money."

Ah, mystery solved. So *that* was why she was here.

Though my alimony payments to her were substantial, Anouk had never been what you'd call "thrifty." She regularly blew through it and her own earnings and called asking for more whenever she was between wealthy boyfriends.

Now that she'd given me full custody of our daughters, there were no more child support checks.

Letting out a long sigh, I rubbed the back of my tense neck with one hand.

Annoying though she might be, I couldn't let the mother of my children be homeless. I'd help her find a new place to live, help her get back on her feet again, and *then* send her packing. For now, I had a more urgent matter to deal with.

I spun and headed for the door. "Get your clothes on," I said over my shoulder in a weary tone. "And keep an ear out in case one of the girls wakes up."

Anouk followed me, stopping in the open doorway. "Where are you going?"

"To find her."

THIRTY-THREE
One and Only

Sully

I checked Angelina's bedroom suite, just in case. It was empty, her closet and drawers cleaned out.

What a nightmare.

My head spinning with anxiety, I dialed her number. A ring tone sent me running to the attached bathroom where Angelina's phone sat on the counter.

Oh shit. She really had left me.

No wonder. I could imagine the things Anouk must have said to her. Angelina must be so confused and hurt. I shook my head to clear the mounting fear. This was no time for panic—I had to think clearly.

Where would she go?

I dialed the Wessexes' number. Cinda answered. "Hi Sully. Everything okay?"

"Is Angelina there?" I asked, not even bothering to answer her question.

There was a beat of silence before she responded. "No. I haven't heard from her. We're getting ready to fly to Aubernesse in the morning." Her tone sharpened with concern. "Is she missing? Did she go out for a walk alone or something?"

"No. Nothing like that. Look, I don't have time to explain, but there was a misunderstanding between her and my ex-wife, and she left. Where would she go besides your house?"

"Well, as you know, her mom lives right down the street, but they're estranged. Did you check the area hotels?"

"No, but I'll do that next. If you hear from her, please let me know, okay?"

I raced downstairs to check the garage, though I'd pulled in and parked only a short time before. Was it possible one of the cars was gone, and in my excitement I just hadn't noticed?

Flinging open the door to the garage, I found all my cars present and accounted for, which meant Angelina had left on foot—unless she'd taken a cab or something. *How* was I going to find her?

Before the panic could set in again, I decided to start calling the hotels within walking distance. Of course there were a ton of bed and breakfasts throughout the area as well, but I had to start somewhere.

None of them had a guest registered under Angelina's name. She could be using a fake one for all I knew. The fact was, if she didn't want to talk to me, it was going to be damned near impossible to find her.

In a flash of inspiration, I dialed Wilder's number. If anyone could find her, it would be a security expert.

"Hey buddy. What's up?" my friend asked. A woman's laugh in the background told me Wilder wasn't alone.

"Hey man. Sorry to bother you. I've got a problem."

"What's going on? The girls okay?"

"Yeah, they're great. It's Angelina—she's disappeared."

Wilder's tone shifted from friendly curiosity to all-business. "When was the last time you saw her?"

"This afternoon. It's not a kidnapping or anything. She left... after my ex showed up."

"Ooohhh," Wilder said with understanding. "So I'm guessing you went ahead and made your move then?"

"Yeah, and everything was going great. But now things are all messed up. I've got to find her, Wild. I've already checked with Cinda Wessex and a bunch of hotels, but she could be anywhere. She's got some friends who are nannies. She could be staying with one of them, maybe. She could have gone to the airport and gotten on a plane for all I know."

"Okay, calm down. We'll find her," Wilder assured. "Let's start with some questions. First... does she have any family in the area?"

* * *

Wilder got back to me in under an hour. "I found her."

"You did?" My pulse pinballed through my veins. "How? Where?"

"You're not gonna believe this—she's about two houses down the street. She went to her mom's house."

My head jerked back in shock. "Wow. I didn't think they were even on speaking terms."

Angelina must have really been devastated to go home to her mother. "Thank you—really—I owe you one. And I'm sorry I bothered you. You must think I'm an idiot."

"Nah—just a man in love. It'll make you do some stupid shit, that's for sure. Let me know how it goes. And Sully?"

"Yeah?"

"Good luck."

After making sure Anouk would remain in the house with the girls, I walked down the street to the corner home where Angelina had grown up.

The mansion was very old and in poor condition despite

its size and the grandeur of its design. The stone exterior walls had stood up well to the wind and the waterfront humidity, but the paint on the window frames was chipped and worn to the point of being non-existent, and the heavy wooden front door was warped and cracked. Vines crept up to nearly the roofline in some spots.

The place almost looked uninhabited except for one low light in a first-floor window and one behind a high tower window made of stained glass.

Was Angelina up there? My heartbeat was louder than the ancient brass door knocker as I waited for someone to respond.

After the second knock, the drapes on one of the lower windows parted then quickly closed again. Well, *somebody* was home, and I wasn't leaving until they answered the door.

I kept knocking until finally I heard the slide of a deadbolt. The big old door creaked open to reveal a woman.

"Mrs. Rappaport?"

"It's *Miss,*" she corrected with a hiss.

"Miss Rappaport, hello. I'm Sullivan Reece. I live down the street. Your daughter's been working for me for the past—"

"I know who you are," she snapped. "My daughter doesn't want to see you. Ever again."

She started to close the door, but I grabbed the edge of it, stopping its motion. "If I could just speak to Angelina for a minute. You see, there's been a terrible misunderstanding."

"The only one who doesn't understand is *you*, Mr. Reece. Angelina has seen the error of her ways and repented. She's pledged her life to God and will stay on the straight and narrow path from now on."

With effort, I gentled my voice. "I would never try to interfere with her relationship with God, Mrs., uh *Miss* Rappaport. My intentions are completely honorable. I want to marry her. I want to take care of her and treat her with the utmost respect. I love your daughter."

She laughed, a dry, unpleasant sound. It reminded me of a fairytale witch's cackle. "You men and your promises of *love*. I fell for it once, but Angelina has been taught better. And thanks to *you* she's learned the most convincing lesson of all. Go home, Mr. Reece, and leave my daughter in peace. You're not welcome here."

Understanding I'd get nowhere with this woman, I stepped back and let her close the door, but I was far from defeated.

I highly doubted Angelina was feeling any peace—not if she loved me even half as much as I loved her. I'd have bet just about anything she was in the same kind of turmoil I was.

Because she *did* love me. And when you loved someone as much as I loved *her*, you didn't fold the tent at the first sign of difficulty. I was no stranger to prolonged battles. If I had to climb that stone tower with one hand tied behind my back, I'd find a way to speak with Angelina tonight.

I walked to the sidewalk, but instead of following it back to my house, I stood watching the Rappaport mansion until the first-floor light blinked out. Then I navigated the overgrown grass and shrubbery to get to the rear of the mansion and the tower where Angelina had told me her room was located.

The structure had to be at least forty-five feet tall. Ancient and covered in ivy vines, it looked like something out of a medieval tale. There was a single square window near the top, larger than the small round stained glass one in the front. The light was still on, casting a square of golden color on the dark lawn far below.

Apart from that one high window, there were no openings—no door, no outer staircase, no windows lower down. It was a veritable fortress against lovesick suitors.

I had to laugh at myself. I was definitely no Prince Charming. But I'd read the stories to my daughters over and over again at bedtime. Who knew they'd serve as an instruction manual one day?

Picking up a handful of pea gravel from an untended flower bed, I tossed one of the tiny pebbles at the window. It plinked against the windowpane.

Nice. First try.

I waited expectantly, but there was no response. So I tossed another couple of stones at the glass, hoping I'd gauged the speed correctly and didn't break it.

Finally, a figure appeared in the window. It was Angelina. She looked ethereal in a white nightgown, her hair braided to one side and hanging in a thick rope over her shoulder.

She pushed the casement windows open and peered into the darkness.

"Angelina," I whisper-shouted. "Down here."

She leaned out and looked down, and a long spill of golden hair fell through the opening. My heart swelled with love and determination. There was no doubt this was the one and only woman for me—I just had to convince *her* of that.

If I could have reached it, I would have grabbed onto that golden rope and climbed up to her then and there.

THIRTY-FOUR

Far From Okay

Angelina

My heart pounded, vibrating the front of my floaty, high-necked gown.

Far below my bedroom window, a shadowy form stood on the lawn looking up at me. There was only one person it could be—the last person I wanted to see.

"Sully? Is that you?" I called into the night.

"It's me. Are you okay?"

What was he *doing* here? From what I'd seen of Anouk, I doubted the woman would take kindly to her husband tossing pebbles at another woman's window like some kind of romantic novel hero.

And this was no fable—it was real life. Whatever Sully and I had shared, it was over. Now I just wanted to be left alone to lick my wounds and resume the safe, predictable life I'd left behind three months ago.

Mother was all too happy to help in that regard. She'd been positively gleeful to see her prodigal daughter return, administering the *I told you so's* in a surprisingly mild dose and offering the commiseration that only another member of the

Broken Hearts Club could give.

I actually understood my mother a little better now after experiencing what she'd always tried to protect me from. I wouldn't wish this pain on my worst enemy.

My hope was that things could go back to "normal." Just as I'd walked away from Mother's plan, I planned to slip neatly back into it now.

The numbness and boredom of my former life would be a welcome refuge from the devastating pain that had clobbered my heart at Anouk's revelation that Sully had invited her to be part of his life again.

But now Sully was *here*—asking if I was okay.

I was *far* from okay. Just seeing his face in the dim moonlight and hearing his voice brought on a fresh torrent of longing, not to mention worry over what would happen if Mother looked out the window and saw him there.

"You shouldn't be here," I scolded him, leaning down so he could hear my suppressed tone. "Didn't my mother tell you I don't want to talk to you?"

"Yes, but I had to see you. I couldn't believe you were gone when I got home. I need to explain about Anouk."

"There's no need to explain. She's your wife."

"My *ex*-wife," he corrected. "I don't know what she said to you, but there hasn't been anything between us except custody-sharing for years."

"She *told* me you invited her to move back in with you."

"What? She lied." There was a pause before he said, "Wait—yes, I did. But that was months ago, at the beginning of the summer. I was desperate. That was before I'd even met you. Everything's different now."

"Not everything. She's still Skyla and Claire's mother. It's right that she lives with them—with you. I'm not going to interfere with someone's marriage."

Sully let out an exasperated noise. "There *is* no marriage except the one I want to have with you."

There was a rustling of clothing down below. Sully was digging in the pocket of his light jacket. "Would you *please* come down? There's something I want to ask you, and I'd rather not do it from forty feet away."

My heart thudded faster. "No," I yelped, drawing back until I was barely visible in the window.

"Go away, Sully. Please. I think I hear Mother coming. We must have wakened her."

When he didn't budge, I leaned out the window again, pleading. "This isn't going to work. I made a mistake taking the job at your house."

"This isn't about some job. This is about *you* and *me*."

Extending an arm high over his head, he held something up to me. I squinted to see it better.

"I left the house today because I wanted to get this for you," Sully said.

The moon came out from behind a bank of clouds, and a large gemstone of some kind sparkled in its cool, magical light

A ring. He was holding a ring.

My heartrate took off for the stars then crashed and burned. This morning I'd have been thrilled to have Sully offer me a ring. But now... it was too late.

"You shouldn't have done that," I told him.

"*Of course* I should have. I love you Angelina. You love me too."

I shook my head, unable to force out the words that would deny the greatest truth of my life.

"You should be giving that ring to Anouk," I said instead. "She's Claire and Skyla's real mom, and if she's ready to be there for them—for you—I'm not going to stand in the way. I *won't* break up a family."

Sully let out a desperate sounding laugh. "I'm not gonna

be with Anouk, okay? I don't love her, and I don't think she *ever* loved me. I'm not even attracted to her anymore. She'll be leaving in a few days."

Hope and wretched love tugged at me like an invisible lasso. If I wasn't careful, it would drag me down onto the stones below, and I'd be crushed all over again.

An exterior light switched on downstairs, illuminating the back yard. Mother was definitely awake.

She'd be none too pleased at the Romeo and Juliet scene playing out on her lawn—especially after what I'd told her today. She had decided Sullivan Reece was every bit as bad as the man who'd jilted her as a young woman—maybe worse.

"Sully... you have to go—please," I pleaded. "Before my mom freaks out."

Sully laughed. "I'm not scared of your mom—even if she does kind of look like a wicked witch."

"You should be. She'll call the police. She'll have you charged with trespassing. You don't want an arrest record—think of the girls. Our arrangement was only ever supposed to be temporary, Sully. The summer's over. Go home before you wind up in jail."

Sully's arms lifted and fell to his sides with a frustrated slap. "What are *you* gonna do? Stay up there in that ivory tower of yours alone forever, a perfect little martyr? I guess *that'll* make your mom happy."

"I won't be alone," I said. "I'll be with my new sisters."

It took Sully a few seconds to put it together. "*No.* Don't tell me you're planning to go to that monastery."

"I'm leaving tomorrow."

It hadn't been a hard decision to make actually. I knew I'd never want a husband and family apart from Sully and his daughters. If I couldn't have him, I didn't want anyone.

And though it wouldn't match my ideal vision of the perfect family, the other nuns in my order *would* be a sort of family. I looked forward to beginning a new life far away from Eastport Bay—and far from temptation.

When I'd come home this afternoon, weeping and inconsolable, my mother had made the phone call, delighted to help me escape the "evils of man." The religious order had accepted my excuse for reporting late for discernment, commending me for sacrificing myself to help a family in need over the summer.

"Think about what you're doing, Angelina," Sully pleaded. "You *can't* become a nun. For one thing, you're in love with a man—me. For another, you have way too much passion to bottle it up under a habit and spend your life unmarried and alone. You told me earlier today that I have options. The same goes for you. I'm giving you another one right now—stay here and marry me. Be my wife."

A sob scrambled up my throat, and I had to suppress it to speak. "Sully, it's too late. It's done. This is over."

"No, *this* is crazy," he said, the volume of his voice rising with emotion. "Can you please just come down and talk to me? I need to see your eyes when you tell me it's over. I need to feel you in my arms when you say it's too late."

The sob defeated my efforts to control it. "I can't. Please... just go home and get on with your life."

"You *are* my life."

He looked around, stuffed the ring back into his jacket pocket. "You know what? If you won't come to me..."

Striding forward, he stretched one hand up and grabbed onto a gnarled vine, pulling himself onto the tower wall.

"What are you doing?" I gasped. "You're not planning to climb all the way up here?"

"Well, I'm not gonna stop halfway, Angel," he said, grunting with effort—and what looked like some rib pain—as he grabbed another vine and hoisted himself higher.

"You'll hurt yourself," I protested, filled with concern. "You're not fully healed yet."

Sully continued to climb. The fool really did intend to scale the tower.

"I can live with a little pain. What I can't do... is live without you. If it's not you, it's gonna be no one."

My heart melted along with my resistance. My hands came up to cover my mouth as the tears flowed.

Sullivan Reece, you absolutely devastate me.

Aloud I said, "Wait. Stop. I'll come down."

THIRTY-FIVE

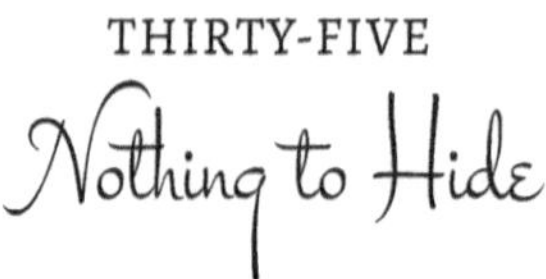

Sully

Angelina disappeared from the window above, and I rested, hanging onto the vines about ten feet off the ground.

Honestly, I was relieved she'd changed her mind about coming downstairs to talk to me. This was the most cardio I'd done in weeks, and though my bruised hands had mostly healed, their full strength hadn't yet returned.

Overhead I heard noise—it sounded like her bedroom doorknob rattling. *Good.* She'd be down in a minute. Releasing my grip, I dropped to the ground and rubbed my sore ribcage.

But seconds later she poked her head through the window opening again. "I can't get out. Mother's locked me in my room."

"What? That's crazy. Does she *do* that kind of thing?"

Angelina scrunched her face in dismay. "Afraid so. I don't want you to climb up though. It's too high. You might fall. I'll try to sneak away in the morning and come see you."

"No. Uh-uh. No way."

I moved toward the tower again, restarting the climb. No

way was I taking the chance that her mother might somehow persuade her to change her mind again. And from what I'd seen, the woman wasn't above forcing Angelina into the car in the morning or having someone else do it.

Nope—I had to have my woman in my arms *tonight.*

Vine by vine, I scaled the tower's outer wall. If I hadn't been injured, the climb wouldn't have been that difficult for me. Even now, it would just be a little slower than it would have been if I'd been at full strength. She was worth every bit of effort I could muster.

A siren wailed in the distance. *Getting shot by a cop, however,* would *be a problem.* I picked up my pace, stretching higher, climbing faster.

"Be careful," Angelina begged, leaning even farther out the window to watch my progress.

I glanced up at her. "*You* be careful. I'm fine. Nothing to worry about."

More sirens sang out, much closer this time. Judging from the sound, they might actually be just in front of the house now.

"Hurry Sully," Angelina said. "I'll hide you in my room."

A couple minutes later, I reached the large window, gripping the frame and dragging myself the final bit of distance until I could swing a leg up and hook it over the sill. Pulling my body through the opening, I collapsed to my knees on the floor of Angelina's bedroom, breathing hard from exertion.

"Are you okay?" she asked, sounding more worried than necessary.

I tipped my head back, smiling up at her. "Just dandy."

She kissed me quickly then pulled on my right arm and shoulder. "Hurry. We've got to find a place for you to hide. Maybe you could get under the bed?"

I took one glance at the low bedframe. "Um... that's not going to be happening."

There was a clatter of footsteps on the stairs leading to Angelina's tower room. She looked at me wide-eyed. "She really did it. The police are here. What about the closet?"

Grabbing my hand, she dragged me toward her tiny closet, but I stopped her.

"It's going to be okay. Trust me."

Instinctively I knew hiding would be the *wrong* thing to do. Besides, I had nothing *to* hide. I wasn't a teenage boy sneaking into my high school girlfriend's room, and Angelina wasn't a little girl. She was a grown woman who should never have been locked in a tower in the first place—not tonight. Not ever.

Loud banging on her door preceded an authoritative shout. "This is the Eastport Bay Police. Are you all right in there, Miss Rappaport?"

"I'm fine," she assured them. "Everything's fine. Although I seem to be locked in."

In a lower tone someone asked, "Why is it locked from the *outside*?"

A woman's voice answered, but I couldn't tell what she was saying.

"Are you alone Angelina? Is someone with you?" the officer demanded.

"Just my boyfriend," she said. Her voice sounded high and nervous. I couldn't blame her, but I knew it would alarm the police officers—they'd be coming in any minute now, and probably with force.

A loud, metallic scrape signaled the turn of a rusty iron lock. Angelina's gaze swung to me—it was frantic. I used our joined hands to pull her toward me.

"Come here, Angel. Don't be afraid. I know what to do."

Then I tipped her chin up and kissed her. As I'd expected, Angelina responded to me immediately, going up on her tiptoes and wrapping her arms around my neck. She pressed the front of her body against mine and kissed me back with just as much love and passion as I felt for her.

It was unlikely anyone would mistake her enthusiastic participation in the kiss, but just in case, I dropped my hands from her body and clasped them behind my back as the police burst through the door.

Angelina remained plastered to me, holding on as if she were the aggressor and had no intention of letting me escape her clutches.

Finally breaking the kiss, she turned toward the two uniformed men, who stood gaping with their guns drawn. One of them was middle aged with close cropped salt and pepper hair. His partner was younger, in his late twenties, very thin with sandy brown hair and a mustache to match.

"What's going on? Why are you here?" she asked them.

"Wait—*this* is the 'little girl' you called us about?" the older patrolmen asked Angelina's mother, who hung back in the hallway.

Almost at the same time, the younger officer said, "Is that... Sullivan Reece, the boxer?"

"Hello officers," I said in a friendly tone. "Is there a problem?"

Angelina wrapped her arms around my waist and laid her head on my chest.

The confused looking policemen holstered their weapons. "So... you're okay, ma'am? There's no intruder?"

Angelina smiled. "No, of course not. I told you I was in here with my boyfriend."

Pulling out the ring box again, I corrected, "Not *boyfriend*, Angel—fiancé—if you'll have me, that is."

I gave the officers a grin. "She hasn't said yes or no yet... women love to keep a guy in suspense."

"How old *are* you, ma'am?" the gray-haired officer asked.

"I'm twenty-four. Plenty old enough to know what I

want. And what I want..." She turned to me, "is you. Yes, I *will* marry you Sullivan Reece. I love you with all my heart."

As we kissed, the officers spoke in low voices with Angelina's mother, who sounded none too happy.

"I want him arrested. He's obviously corrupted my daughter," she protested then followed them down the stairs, demanding their badge numbers and threatening their jobs.

Angelina and I went downstairs as well and walked the men to the front door. As the young officer got my autograph, the older one pulled Angelina aside.

"If you need help dealing with your mother's mental problems, Butler Hospital is very good. We could take her in for a psych evaluation tonight, if you'd like."

Angelina smiled and thanked him, shooting a glance at her mother who glowered at them from an antique settee in the nearby parlor.

"No—not this time. I think she meant well. But I'll be sure to let you know if we see any signs of instability in the future. Thank you again officers. Have a good night."

THIRTY-SIX

Let Down Your Hair

Angelina-- October

New England had served up a perfect Autumn Saturday.

Sixty-eight degrees, blue skies, and not a hint of humidity—and thank goodness for that last part. My elaborate updo would never have survived otherwise. It had taken the stylist literally hours to create.

The ceremony had been stunning, with both the bride and groom crying through our vows and one hell of a kiss to punctuate them.

Now we and our guests were enjoying a reception at one of the Village by the Sea's most glamorous venues, a fifty-thousand-square-foot mansion modeled after the Louis XIII hunting lodge at Versailles.

Its French Gothic ballroom featured an enormous fireplace with a surround crafted to resemble a fairytale castle, and the banquet hall had ten crystal chandeliers and a rose marble mosaic floor.

One of my favorite features of the home was its large central courtyard, and that was where I stood now with two of my fellow teachers from the preschool and one of my nanny friends.

"I can't believe how many celebrities are here," my friend Lorie said.

"I can't believe *I'm* here," Katy, one of the teachers said. "I mean, this morning I was scrubbing Play Doh out of the story time rug, and now I'm looking at Adele sharing a plate of salt cod beignets with Mike Tyson. I feel like I'm gonna get arrested for trespassing and thrown out at any minute."

"I was *really* hoping that hot security guy would frisk me when I came in," said Stef, the other nanny. "But he was just standing back and supervising. He's beautiful enough to need his own bodyguard."

"He's single," I offered. "And one of Sully's best friends. His name's Wilder. I could introduce you to him later if you want."

Steph nodded vigorously while Lorie grabbed my arm. "Oh my God—is that *Prince Alexander*?"

"That's him," I confirmed. "And that's his wife Cinda—can you believe she just had twins? They're our neighbors. They flew in especially for our wedding from Aubernesse."

"You really are living a fairy tale," Katy said. "I'm happy for you. And we're so excited you're coming back to the preschool next year. We've missed you there."

I beamed. "I've missed being there. I can't wait to work with the kids again."

The teacher hired to replace me had recently announced her pregnancy and that she intended to stay home with her new baby starting in January. I had eagerly accepted an offer to teach there part-time while working toward an early childhood education degree.

Like my friends, I could hardly believe this was my life now.

I looked around the beautiful courtyard, where myriad

strings of fairy lights cast a magical glow on the collection of actors, models, and professional athletes Sully knew and the regular folks who'd filled my side of the aisle.

The person I *most* wanted to see though was headed my way. Sully reached me and swept me up in a full-body hug so strong I had no further fears about his full recovery from the title fight.

"Hey there Champ," I said as he gently set me down again.

"I prefer the title Champ Emeritus," Sully joked. "But my favorite title is 'Husband.'"

My tone lowering and adopting a seductive note, I said, "Hey there… husband."

Sully made a low growly noise and pulled me close, nuzzling my face with his. "I can't believe you're really mine."

"Till death do us part," I said.

"You won't have to worry about that for a long, long time," he assured me.

After I'd accepted his proposal, Sully had announced his decision to voluntarily relinquish his title and retire from boxing.

He said his longstanding goal of forty wins meant nothing compared to the life he now had with me and his kids, and he didn't want to risk losing it.

After a lifetime of striving, he seemed completely at ease with his choice.

He would still be flying out occasionally to do color commentary on TV for boxing matches. His first one, in fact, would be in December, a title fight for the vacant championship between Travis Diggs and another fighter.

As for my own life-altering decision, I had zero regrets about passing up a life in the monastery in favor of life with this wonderful man and the little girls I'd come to love so dearly.

"And I won't have to worry about anything else happening

to this handsome face," I said, sliding my hands up his tuxedo front and cupping his strong jaws in my fingers.

Sully looked down at me like I was more tempting than the frosting on our fabulous five-tiered wedding cake, which was decorated to resemble a vine-covered tower.

He'd instructed the cake designer to add a little surprise—a figurine of a bride with long blonde hair leaning out of the tower's high window and a groom figure at the bottom, beginning to climb.

"You're my real-life angel, you know that?" he said to me. "I thought you looked like one the first time I saw you, but that's nothing compared to the goodness and light that's inside of you."

After pausing for a long kiss, he added, "You're more beautiful than every actress and model and pop princess here."

"Speaking of that..." I sneaked a glance at a late-arriving guest. "... is that... *Jade*?"

Sully turned to look at the gorgeous brunette who lit up the already glamorous courtyard in a formfitting silver gown that flashed iridescent sparkles as she moved through the crowd.

"Yeah. I wasn't sure if she was going to make it. She had a concert last night in San Francisco, and the fog was really thick there this morning."

I fought off a new wave of disbelief. "You *know* Jade? I love her music."

He smiled. "I know. That's why I asked her to come sing a song at our reception."

At my delighted squeal, his smile widened. "We've met a few times at parties, and she's from Eastport Bay, but I wasn't sure she'd actually come. She has a house here on Atlantic Avenue, but I understand she doesn't come home much, what with touring and all. Want to meet her?"

"I'm not sure. I don't know what I'd say to a famous singer."

"You figured out what to say to a famous boxer just fine."

"*Former* boxer," I corrected with a smile and a quick kiss. "Yes, I want to meet her, but if I start blubbering and speaking gibberish, make some excuse to pick me up and carry me away."

"I don't need an excuse to do *that*—it's what I want to do all the time." He let out a dramatic sigh. "I guess it'll have to wait till the end of the reception though."

A few minutes later I stood face-to-face with the ten-time Grammy winner. The singer-songwriter was as stunning as she was talented with shining waves of chestnut brown hair and the most spectacular green eyes.

Their color was reminiscent of the translucent green mineral popular in jewelry making and Asian carvings and feng shui charms, which now that I thought about it, must have been where the singer's stage name had come from.

As we talked, I found Jade's kindness matched her rare beauty.

"Congratulations. Beautiful reception, and you look amazing," she said to me. Turning to Sully she added, "I'm so happy for you. I don't really watch a lot of boxing, but I watched your last fight. It was brutal. Looks like you've fully recovered though. You've never looked happier. Married life agrees with you already."

"I've got a whole new lease on life," Sully said, squeezing me to his side. "We appreciate you coming. I'll bet you don't get a lot of time in Eastport Bay these days."

"Hardly any. I'm really hoping to take a break though at the end of my current tour. The final date is in Boston, and then I'm planning to just chill for a while and stay here in Eastport Bay."

"Sounds good. I'm loving it here. Such a nice break from New York," he said.

"Where are you from?" Jade asked me.

"Oh. I grew up here in Eastport Bay."

"I'm surprised we haven't met. You look like you're about my age. What are you—twenty-five?"

"Twenty-four, but I went to a really small girls' school, and I didn't get out much, so I didn't know many people my age in town," I explained.

"You wouldn't know it by this crowd." Jade laughed. "It's a who's who of Eastport Bay and Manhattan too."

I rolled my eyes, and my laughter joined Jade's. "Sully wanted a big wedding."

He grinned. "I want the whole world to see what a stunning and amazing wife I scored."

"Well *I* can see how happy you are, that's for sure," Jade said. "And I'm happy for you both. It's nice to attend a wedding where I know there's at least a chance of it lasting."

Sully looked up as his friend and best man Wilder Lowe entered the reception area. "Wilder's back from his perimeter check. We can get started with the toasts soon."

Jade started coughing, as if her champagne had gone down the wrong pipe. I stepped toward her, placing a hand on her back. "Are you okay?"

"Yeah. Thanks." Jade nodded rapidly then coughed again, her eyes watering and turning an even more vivid shade of green. She held up her glass. "This stuff tastes great, but I don't recommend trying to breathe it."

Setting the champagne flute on a nearby high-top table, she gave us both an apologetic smile. "I see an old friend, and I want to say hi to him before he slips away. Congratulations again. Thanks for inviting me."

"I'm so glad you could make it. It was nice to meet you," I said. "I can't wait to hear your song."

"Thanks for coming," Sully said again as he watched the diminutive singer heading in Wilder's direction. A wry grin twisted his lips. "I knew it."

"Knew what?" I asked.

"Nothing. Just something Wilder and I were talking about one night at Padraig's."

Skyla and Claire entered the courtyard, running toward their father and me in their poofy white flower girl dresses.

"Hi Daddy! Hi Angelina! We went up on the roof and looked at the lights on the bridge," Skyla said.

"I like *these* lights," Claire said, looking up at the strings of light spanning the courtyard as she turned in a circle.

Sully swept both girls up into his arms and greeted Anouk, who followed them. She'd brought a date to the wedding—her new boyfriend, a famous art gallery owner from New York. She was living there once again and seemed fairly happy.

"Our offer still stands to keep the girls while you're on your honeymoon," she said. "You can't possibly want them tagging along with you all over Europe."

"Nah, that's okay. Thanks anyway," Sully said.

"Two months is too long to be away from them," I explained. "But we will leave them for a couple of weeks with the Wessexes in Aubernesse while we explore Italy and France on our own. That'll give us some alone time. Thank you so much for keeping them tonight."

We made conversation with Anouk and her boyfriend for a few more minutes until the band at one end of the courtyard announced they were going to take a short break and invited Jade up on stage.

She sang a love song she'd written especially for us. She said it was called *Let Down Your Hair.*

It was one of the most beautiful songs I'd ever heard, and Sully and I slow-danced to it, gazing into each other's eyes.

As the song ended, Sully bent down to whisper in my ear,

"I can't wait to pull out all those hairpins and let down *your* hair. Too bad we have to hang around until midnight."

"That's a different fairy tale, Champ," I whispered back. "As far as I'm concerned, we can leave right now."

Without missing a beat, Sully grabbed my hand and pulled me from the dance floor, raising his other hand and saying, "Thanks for coming everybody. Good night."

Laughing as I quick-stepped to keep up with his digging stride, I blew kisses at my friends and guests. "Thank you. I love you all."

When we reached the waiting limousine and climbed into the back, I scolded my new husband gently. "I *was* kind of joking there. All our guests are going to stay for several more hours, you know."

"Exactly. That's why we're leaving. I can't wait any more. I've waited too long for this night already."

"Not *so* long—we've only known each other for five months."

"That's not what I mean, Angel. I've waited my whole life for you."

A remark that sweet deserved a kiss, and I gave him a very thorough one. When our lips parted, I said, "You *look* like a tough guy but really, you've got a soft, squishy heart of gold. I waited a long time for you, too. Did you know I used to watch you run on the Bluff Walk?"

His head jerked back, and he gave me a crinkly-eyed smile. "You did? Before we met?"

"Yep. I sat up in my tower window dreaming of a different life, one I never thought I'd have, and you ran by. I started looking for you every day."

"That's so weird. I used to look up at that tower every time I ran by, wondering if a princess lived in it. As it turns out, I was right."

I laughed. "I'm no princess... but I *was* in need of rescue.

It's a good thing a handsome prince found me in my lonely tower."

Sully grinned and pulled me tighter into his embrace. "And how does this fairy tale end?"

"Don't you know? You *do* have two little girls who are extra-fond of bedtime stories."

"I might have some idea. Tell me anyway."

I smiled, knowing *this* was the beginning of the life story I truly wanted.

"They lived happily ever after, silly. Now kiss your wife and make all her dreams come true."

Wilder Lowe

Until Sully handed me the guest list, it hadn't occurred to me that *she* might attend the wedding.

Yes, Jade, aka Jessica Bailey, was a celebrity, and this *was* a star-studded event. And yes, she was from Eastport Bay. But she hadn't been back to town for a long, long time—not as far as I knew anyway.

At least her brother, my friend Hap Bailey, hadn't mentioned anything about his sister being home recently.

Not that Hap would even think to bring it up to me. He had no idea his best friend had such an *interest* in his baby sister's comings and goings.

And that was how it was going to stay.

Whenever Hap made the occasional mention of his pride over Jessica's music industry success, I simply nodded and replied with a bland remark of congratulations. Whenever he worried over her latest celebrity romance, I nodded and kept my mouth shut.

I didn't ask any questions about her.

I *certainly* didn't comment on how much she'd grown up.

And I never—ever—mentioned what had happened between us one night years ago.

When I'd spotted "Jade's" name on the elite guest list, my heart had stuttered and stopped before resuming the work of circulating my blood.

On the outside, I'd simply nodded to Sully and launched the appropriate protocol for protecting a high-profile guest of her caliber.

As head of the security for the wedding, I was responsible for the safety of all the guests. *This* one however, might give me a nervous breakdown. All throughout the ceremony, my eyes had drifted to her empty reserved seat in the third row of chairs.

Instead of paying careful attention to the minister's words, I'd wondered whether her plane had encountered storms on its way from California or whether there had been some holdup with her ground transportation on this end.

As soon as the happy couple had kissed, I'd slipped out of the on-site chapel and made some calls, confirming her plane had taken off late and landed in Rhode Island safely. I'd kept an eye out for her arrival ever since, making excuses to stay outside—checking in with the guards, walking the perimeter of the property, and inspecting the blackout screens and thick artificial hedges that had been erected as privacy barriers against the paparazzi and curious locals.

Now it was almost time for the toasts, and I had no choice but to make my way back to the mansion's central courtyard. Reaching it, I pulled a folded sheet of paper from my tuxedo jacket pocket and went over the lines I'd written once more.

A door opened from the mansion into the central courtyard. Alert as always to any change in the environment around me, I homed in on the doorway.

It filled with the outline of dark hair flowing down to smooth, slender shoulders, feminine hips, and long legs sheathed in a slinky silver gown so eye-catching it seemed every head at the reception turned in her direction.

The dress moved like liquid silver over Jade's curves as she entered the courtyard, exchanging hugs with those she knew well and less touchy-feely greetings with those she'd just met.

All the while, I watched. In fact, I couldn't have looked away if I tried. It had been twelve years since I'd seen her in person, not since I was a senior in high school, and she was a sophomore, still a little girl for all practical purposes. I could hardly believe the difference in her.

In the past, I would have put her beauty in the category of "adorable" or merely "pretty." I'd seen her on television since then, but the cameras hadn't done her justice.

Jessica Bailey had turned into a certified bombshell.

Unfortunately, it felt like I was the one who was about to explode. What was I going to say to her? Should I own up to having bought all her albums or keep that to myself?

After a while it seemed like it was going to be a non-issue. She didn't approach me or even wave from across the room. Only once did she meet my gaze, her much-celebrated green eyes flashing my way then flickering away again.

Does she not remember me?

My belly sank in disappointment. I didn't often feel at a disadvantage with a woman. I hadn't met one I cared enough about to actually *worry* about whether she was out of my league.

But this one... she was in a league all her own.

Suddenly, I wasn't sure it was such a great idea to talk to Jessica tonight. With the way she looked, I wasn't certain I'd be as successful at disguising my attraction to her as I had been in high school.

Back then, I'd had my bad-boy persona to hide behind.

Now I felt naked, exposed in a way I'd never allow one of my bodyguard clients to be.

She took the decision out of my hands when she broke away from a conversation with the bride and groom and headed directly for me.

Nerves jumped in my fingers and under my skin. Heat crept from my chest up my neck and into my cheeks. I focused on keeping my face and voice devoid of emotion as she drew close.

"Hi Wilder."

"Good evening, Jade."

She gave me a wrinkle-nosed grin. "Don't call me that. It's too weird for you to call me by my stage name."

"Very well. How was your trip from California…*Jessica*?"

Ugh. Why did my voice sound like that when I said her name? Like I was lingering over it, savoring each syllable? She must have noticed it too because her breathing changed.

This was *not* starting well—I had to turn it around.

"My firm monitored all the guests' arrivals," I added in a sterner tone. "Your plane was forty-seven minutes late. Did you encounter severe weather?"

"Aren't we all business?" Her glossy red lips formed a teasing curve. "What happened to the 'Wild-man?'"

Inwardly I cringed at my old high school nickname. "He grew up. That was a long time and many miles ago."

"I hear you on that one," Jessica said, suddenly seeming weary. "We're both probably completely different people at this point."

She bit her lip for a second then said, "We should catch up —maybe breakfast tomorrow before I fly out again? Or a drink later tonight."

That would be a no and a fuck *no.*

I'd learned my lesson about being alone with her. I could sum it up in one word.

Don't.

"I'm in charge of security tonight—no drinking. And I have to keep circulating to keep an eye on things. Tomorrow morning I'll be busy getting guests to the airport and supervising the decoy vehicles for those who are driving."

She raised a brow, looking less than pleased at my abrupt rejection of her friendly overture. Then her mouth formed a tight, sarcastic smile.

"Okay then. Well, it was *delightful* to see you as always, Wilder."

"Yeah. You too. Have fun at the party."

I turned to walk away, intending to find somewhere to be alone with the pit in my stomach, but Jessica snagged the sleeve of my tuxedo jacket.

"Hey—before you go... I'm supposed to sing a song I wrote for Sully and Angelina, but I'm not sure how I'm going to get up on stage in this dress."

She looked down at her skintight silver gown and sky-high heels, forcing my eyes to go there as well.

"Want to give me a hand?"

A hand. My heart. Whatever you want.

I'd always had difficulty refusing her, and it was no easier now, twelve years later. In fact, in the intervening time it seemed her power over me had only increased.

"Uh, sure. Let me go find some movable stairs or a box or something."

"There's no time."

Jessica pointed at the stage where the band that had been playing was leaving. "Just give me a boost, okay?"

Suddenly, I was catapulted back in time to our childhood days when Jessica's pleas for a hand-up into her brother's treehouse or a push on the backyard swing set had produced nothing but annoyance... and then to years later when her request for help with blocking a theatrical scene had led to a forbidden kiss.

The band's lead singer, who still stood on the stage in the spotlight, cupped a hand over his eyes to block the glare and held the mic close to his mouth.

"Jade... you here yet?"

She raised a hand. "Right here." Then in a low voice meant only for me, she said, "That's our cue," and strode toward the stage with a big wave to the assembled guests.

Left with no other choice, I followed. Reaching the stage, I hopped onto it then turned to reach down for Jessica. She placed her hands in mine, and I pulled her up in one swift, powerful move.

The momentum brought the fronts of our bodies into contact for a moment, and I steadied her with my hands on her waist as she rocked on her stilettos.

"You good?" I asked automatically before letting go. I'd barely exerted myself lifting her, but I sounded out of breath anyway.

Without taking a step backward to break contact, Jessica looked up at me. Those big, spectacular green eyes were as mesmerizing as ever.

"You bet I am. Thanks, Wild-man."

Then she stepped away from me and into the spotlight, leaving me shaking—and grateful she was getting on a plane for the West Coast tomorrow.

* * *

Thank you so much for reading **The Baby-whisperer and the Brute.** I hope you loved it! If you did, I would be so grateful for a review on the retailer where you purchased it. Reviews are so important to help authors grow and help other readers find great books!

The Eastport Bay Billionaires series continues with another standalone, Wilder and Jessica's story, **The Bombshell and the Bodyguard.** Here's a bit about the story:

Meet the Bombshell...

Jessica Bailey, aka Jade, has kissed a lot of frogs. She's not proud of it, and it's earned her some unflattering tabloid headlines... *Jade Leaves Another One Jaded.* But hey, at least she's gotten a string of hit songs out of the experiences. And she's learned a lot from her highly public and lightning-fast relationships—namely what she *doesn't* want in a man.

So when her older brother's bad-boy best friend Wilder Lowe strolls back into her life, looking even more handsome, more dangerous, and *less* interested than ever, she puts on her blinders and does her best to forget about her lifelong crush on him.

Problem is, this time she can't just walk away—her billion-dollar pop career has attracted its share of stalkers—the latest is the scariest one yet—and Wilder is her new bodyguard.

Meet the Bodyguard...

Wilder Lowe isn't in the habit of turning down billionaires as potential clients. He didn't build his own immensely successful security business by being stupid. But when his best friend asks him to act as a bodyguard for his younger and very-much-forbidden little sister—you better believe Wilder plans to turn down the detail.

As a former Navy combat diver, a Frogman, he knows a nuclear depth bomb when he sees one.

But then there's a call in the middle of the night, and when Wilder hears that frightened, all-too-familiar voice, the plea from the one girl he could never say no to, he's lost. He'll do anything and everything it takes to keep Jessica safe.

Even if that means whisking her away to a private island.

. . .

Make sure you never miss one of my new releases by signing up for my Tru Tales mailing list! All my VIP list members get sneak peeks, bonus epilogues, funny Tru stories, and a free novella set in the Eastport Bay universe. Here's where to sign up: https://trutaylor.com/tru-tales/

Next in Series

THE BOMBSHELL AND THE BODYGUARD

The Bombshell and the Bodyguard is the next standalone in the Eastport Bay Billionaires series. It's a best friend's little sister, celebrity/bodyguard forbidden love story filled with heart, heat, and billionaire romance fun! It's available now in ebook and print and soon to come in audio.

Free book

Want a free Eastport Bay story? **The Sleepless Billionaire** is a hot, funny novella set in the world of the Eastport Bay Billionaires. My VIP mailing list members get it for free! Here's where to sign up: https://trutaylor.com/tru-tales/

Also by Tru Taylor

Bookworm and the Beast- A Beauty and the Beast story

Bargain with the Bachelor- A Snow White story

The Baby and the Blueblood- A Cinderella story

The Baby-whisperer and the Brute- A Rapunzel story

The Bombshell and the Bodyguard- A Frog Prince story

Scarlett and the Big Bad Billionaire— A Red Riding Hood and the Big Bad Wolf story

The Grumpy Billionaire- A Sleeping Beauty story (Reid's story)

The Merry Billionaire— A holiday novella (Hap's story)

The Sleepless Billionaire- (Tuck's story) Free when you join my VIP list!

About the Author

Award-winning author Tru Taylor writes small town romance that's hot and sunny (and a little bit funny.)

She runs on Coke Zero and dark chocolate, lives for lunches with her girlfriends, and drives to the town beach several times a week to watch the sun set over the water.

She loves LOVE and will attempt to turn any show or movie she's watching into a romance whether it is one or not. Star Wars? A romance. Lord of the Rings? Clearly a romance. The Expendables? Okay, well not even Tru can redeem that one.

When she's not writing, Tru enjoys watching movies and reading books with happy endings, spending time with Mr. Tru and her two kids, and sneaking Hershey's Kisses from the top shelf of the freezer throughout the day. (Top shelf because... two kids. Enough said.)

Tru is the author of the Eastport Bay small town rom com

series and loves living in a small New England town where she's surrounded every day by the beautiful coastal setting you see brought to life in her books.

Want fun email from Tru? Her VIP mailing list members get true stories of small town romantic comedy, excerpts, sneak peeks, giveaways, and a free novella set in the world of Eastport Bay! Here's where to sign up: https://trutaylor.-com/tru-tales/

Copyright © 2021 by Tru Taylor

All rights reserved.

No part of this book may be reproduced in any form or by any electronic or mechanical means, including information storage and retrieval systems, without written permission from the author, except for the use of brief quotations in a book review. All trademarks are the property of their respective companies.

The Baby-whisperer and the Brute is a work of fiction. Characters, names, places, brands, media, and incidents are either products of the author's imagination or have been used fictitiously and should not be construed as real. Any resemblance to actual persons, living or dead, events, or locales is entirely coincidental.

This book is licensed for your personal enjoyment and may not be re-sold or given away to other people. The scanning, uploading, and distribution of this book via the Internet or via any other means without the permission of the publisher is illegal and punishable by law. Please purchase only authorized electronic editions and do not participate in or encourage electronic piracy of copyrighted materials. Thank you for respecting the hard work of this author.

Oxford South Press October 2021

Editor: Judy Roth

Cover by: Emily Cover Design

www.ingramcontent.com/pod-product-compliance
Lightning Source LLC
Chambersburg PA
CBHW050821190726
48286CB00007B/1947

* 9 7 8 1 9 4 6 1 6 6 2 6 5 *